THRONE
OF BLOOD
FIRE FAE BOOK THREE
SOPHIE DAVIS

Throne of Blood
Sophie Davis

Cover design Jamie Dalton at Magnetra's Designs

Interior design by Breakout Designs

FOR EDITH—
FOR ALL THE JOY YOU
BRING TO OUR
HEARTS.

THRONE OF BLOOD

FIRE FAE · BOOK THREE

TABLE OF CONTENTS

PROLOGUE

TWENTY-FIVE MONTHS, six days. That was the amount of time I'd been living in this hellhole disguised as a tropical paradise. That was how long it had been since the vampires stole me from my family. At first, I'd marked the passage of each day with a small line that I carved into the metal bedpost in my room at the commune, the communal living facility that newly transplanted fae and shifters called home. Once I moved into the tiny one-bedroom apartment in the building where a lot of my fellow fighters lived, I recorded the passage of time with a hashmark on the inside of my closet door. I would need to find a new spot once I relocated to the swanky condo I was in the process of purchasing.

Fighting in an arena for the entertainment of wealthy casters was not where I thought my life would go, but this forced career path was extremely lucrative. At just shy of eighteen, I had more money in my account than I knew what do with.

Like most days, I woke long before sunrise. It was a fight day. And not just any fight day, either. They called it a showcase, a two-day spectacle that put the best fighters our kingdom had to offer on display for visiting royals. The event would culminate with the Sugarcane Ball, a snooty affair where my attendance was mandatory.

I climbed out of bed and trudged to the tiny alcove kitchen to make coffee, then I headed to the shower while it brewed. The voice of my trainer Botto played in my head, reminding me of the importance of rest before a big fight. Even if my adrenaline hadn't been on overdrive, the constant nightmares that manifested from my darkest thoughts every time I closed my eyes made prolonged sleep impossible. He also frowned on caffeine, another piece of advice that went in one of my ears and out the other.

The sky outside my window began to lighten as I sipped my coffee and dried my damp hair. Inky blackness gave way to deep violet, followed by golden pinks and oranges, before finally turning the bright blue that I'd become accustomed to. With a resigned sigh, I dressed in stretchy shorts and a matching tank top, laced my sneakers, and headed downstairs to catch the shuttle bus to the arena.

"Morning, sunshine," called a perky blond shifter as I exited the elevator.

"Hey, Cala." I waved and walked over to join my best friend. "What are you doing up?" I asked around a yawn.

Cala was a decent fighter, but she hadn't been selected for the showcase as far as I knew.

She grinned and pushed the lobby doors open, gesturing me through with a dramatic flourish. "Supporting you. And, you know, if someone dies in battle, I get to take their place."

My brow furrowed. "Seriously?"

She laughed. "I don't know. I was told I'm an alternate. To me that sounds like being the second in a duel. The second only fights if the first dies."

"Hmmm."

Several other fighters I knew were already outside our apartment building. Cala made small talk, while I stood quietly off to the side. The hardest part of being a fighter for me was the mental aspect. I had to be in the right headspace. So, I typically kept to myself on fight days, focusing only on all the weakness I could exploit in my opponent.

This afternoon, I was due to face my toughest challenge yet. His name was Tanner Woods, a dimensional fae with god-like status in the Hawaiian Kingdom. Neither Tanner nor I had ever lost, which was the reason Botto had argued against this matchup. Of course, it was also why the powers that be wanted us to fight. I didn't know Tanner, not really. I knew of him, though. And that was enough to make me queasy. Losing was one thing, though I was in no hurry to experience it, but Cala was right that fighters died not infrequently in the arena. I really didn't want her to have to step in and be my second.

The ride over to the arena was quiet. Several of the other fighters on the shuttle had headphones in, listening to music to get them in the right mood. I stared out the window and tried not to dwell on the shitty string of events that had led me to a point in my life where I might need a second.

Normally on fight days, we were treated to a wonderful spread of eggs, breakfast meats, pastries, and a smoothie bar in one of the arena's conference rooms. On special occasions, like today, the dishes were more lavish, since the breakfast doubled as a meet and greet for the visiting royals. Thanks to the strict diet Botto imposed to keep me in peak physical condition, I skipped the solid foods in favor of a banana-mango-pineapple smoothie with all sorts of vitamin and nutrient supplements.

Cala wasn't as regimented. Her trainer tried to keep her on a nutrition plan, but my best friend was a big fan of bacon and all things fried. She loaded two plates with sweet and savory options from the buffet line, and then the two of us found a corner table far away from where princes and princesses were shaking hands with our fellow fighters and the trainers in the room.

"Mind if I join you guys?"

I looked up into the smiling face of good-looking male fae. His auburn hair was still wet from a recent shower and his hazel eyes had the pompous expression of so many of the top male fighters. But that wasn't why I shook my head no. There was no way I was having breakfast with my opponent.

"What do you want, Tanner?" Cala asked in a bored voice.

"You know who I am, that's great," he replied, sliding into the chair beside me, despite all the signs I was giving off that clearly said he wasn't welcome. Like me, Tanner only had a smoothie.

"Of course we know who you are." Cala rolled her eyes and shoved a piece of sausage in her mouth. She took her time chewing and swallowing, chasing the food with a gulp of pineapple juice before adding, "What we don't know is why you're sitting here?"

He turned to me and held out his hand. "Hi. Tanner. You're Brie, right?"

I glared at his outstretched hand. "Yeah. So?"

Tanner let his hand fall. "We're fighting today. Thought it might be nice if I introduced myself."

"Why?" I asked flatly.

He blinked as if surprised at my less than friendly attitude. "I don't know. I mean, just because we're opponents doesn't mean we can't be friends, right? Obviously you two are friends."

Cala snorted. "Right. That's different. Brie and I aren't really rivals, you know? Our matchups are pretty one-sided. Plus, us girl fighters have to stick together."

Tanner shrugged and sipped his smoothie. "Most of my fights are one-sided, too."

"If you're suggesting you think our fight will be one-sided, then you should have done your homework better," I snapped.

"Huh? What? No. That's not—I'm sorry. I wasn't saying that." He looked around the room at our fellow fighters mixing and mingling with royal casters from all over the world. Then, Tanner leaned closer as if to tell me a secret. I leaned back, unsure why this guy was even here. "Look, all I'm saying, is we all should stick together. All fighters. If we take rivalry too seriously, the casters win. They want us at each other throats. Makes for better entertainment. Let's not give them the satisfaction."

A lot of fighters felt this way. And after a few drinks, it wasn't uncommon to hear this sort of fae-shifter-unity talk. But that talk was dangerous. Particularly with so many caster ears around, not to mention the fact I didn't know Tanner. He could've been a rat, ready to race off and turn me in for rebellious thoughts or something.

I stood. Cala followed suit, even though she still had a stack of pancakes and a pile of hash browns on one plate and a half-eaten omelet and one piece of sausage on the other. My voice was cold when I looked down at Tanner and said, "Excuse me. I need to prepare for my next win. Enjoy your breakfast. It'll be the last thing you taste before the bitter bite of defeat."

With that parting remark, I spun on my heel and stomped off to find Botto.

The rest of the day went just like every other fight day. I passed the time listening to Botto reiterate the same facts and stats about my opponent that he'd been spouting off for weeks. There was a lot of stretching, some light jogging to warm up my muscles, and a few sparring rounds to get me fired up.

The day took a decided turn about thirty minutes before my scheduled match with Tanner.

I was sitting alone in the locker room when Cala barged in, looking both frazzled and excited.

"What's up?" I asked uneasily.

"I'm fighting," she said as she stripped off her silk tank top and shimmied out of her cute black shorts.

"Really? I thought Tanner and I had the last fight of the day."

She paused to give me a pointed look. Admittedly, it took me an embarrassingly long time for realization to dawn.

"Wait. Why? What happened?"

"I don't know." She shook her head and slipped on a baggy t-shirt from her locker. "It sounds like maybe he got hurt in practice at some point today. All I know for sure is that you and I are going at it." Cala reached behind her back and tied the shirt in a knot, exposing her taut stomach. She barked out a laugh and rolled her eyes. "And I know that I'm about to get my ass kicked."

At the risk of sounding as though I was bragging, I knew she was right. Cala and I were a lopsided matchup. She was a good fighter. But I was undefeated.

"I'll go easy on you," I teased.

Cala's expression turned hard. "Don't you dare hold back. I'm no charity case."

The two of us sparred often, but this would be the first time we fought in the arena.

"If you're sure?" I cocked an eyebrow.

Cala's lips parted in a mischievous grin. "Oh, I'm sure. I want you to show those royal assholes what you're made of."

An hour later, I was crowned the winner, and my best friend was receiving tonics to heal her injuries. We left the arena together, our arms linked—a small act of defiance to show our allegiance.

"Let's hit up Hideout," Cala said as we reentered the locker room. She was still limping a little and the bruise around her right eye didn't seem to be going anywhere fast, despite the blue ointment smeared all over her skin.

"Are you sure you're okay? Do you want to see the medics again before we go home?" I asked.

Cala waved off the suggestion. "I'm fine. My body can take a beating. This," she touched her eye gingerly, "will be gone in a few hours. If not, I can just shift. I heal faster in my jaguar form." She swapped her torn, sweaty t-shirt for an oversized hoodie, and then turned to face me. "There is one thing you can do for me."

"Name it," I said, eager to help ease the pain I'd inflicted on my best friend.

"You can pick up the tab at Hideout."

I laughed. "Deal."

We took the shuttle back to our apartment building and both retreated to our separate abodes to shower and change into nighttime attire. Fashion was not my thing, so Cala did come over to select my clothing for the evening. Her taste was a little more ambitious than mine. Eventually we agreed on dark jeans, red wedge heels that Cala brought from her own closet, and a sheer black top—also an item from my friend's wardrobe.

"Are you sure this looks okay? I mean, it's see-through," I said pointedly.

"Only in certain light," Cala replied as she bent over my bathroom counter to look in the mirror while she applied another layer of plum lip gloss. "Hideout is always dark. Besides, you have a great body. Why not show off all that hard work you do?"

We took a cab to Hideout, a primarily fae and shifter nightclub that our fellow fighters cherished. As usual, there was a long line of patrons waiting to get in when we arrived. I felt only a modicum of guilt when Cala and I made a beeline for the bouncers.

Falcon, another fighter, was working the door. He grinned when he saw us.

"Good fight today, girls," he said by way of greeting. His lips quirked into a smirk. "Good to see you up and moving, Cala. Brie really did a number on you."

She rolled her eyes. "Yeah, let's not rehash the fight. It wasn't one of my finer performances. In my own defense, I wasn't supposed to fight today. I was just an alternate."

"Oh, right." Falcon's gave shifted to me. "You were supposed to faceoff with Tanner." He shook his head. "It's too bad. I would've loved to see that fight."

"Maybe next time. If he doesn't get injured again," I told him.

Falcon tilted his head to one side and scrunched his face in confusion. "Hurt? He looked fine to me. He's inside."

I blinked. "Really? That's weird."

Falcon unhooked the velvet rope and made a sweeping gesture with his hand. "You should go ask him about it. Maybe he was just too afraid to lose to you."

I scoffed. "Unlikely. His ego is too big to even consider the possibility of losing."

The thought of Tanner faking an injury made my blood boil. He could've taken a healing tonic. So why didn't he? Was Falcon right? Was the infamous Tanner Woods too afraid to me face me? I seriously doubted it.

I followed Cala through the crowded dancefloor and up the stairs to a table on the second floor, where a few of our friends were celebrating their wins. And another few were drowning their sorrows after some crushing defeats.

"There they are!" Rocko called. The were-liger was one hell of a fighter. He was also one of my closest friends.

The guys at the table with Rocko scooted closer together to make room for us.

"How ya feeling, Cala?" Rocko asked, pursing his lips to suppress the smile tugging at the corners of his mouth.

"Like I got my ass kicked. The medics covered me in creams and gave me tonics. I'm all good. Now it's just my pride that hurts." She reached for Rocko's beer and took a long drink. "Not that I expected to win."

The server, a pretty water fae named Mary, came over with a bottle of champagne and a tray full of flutes. "First one is on the house," she said, looking in my direction. "Congrats, Brie."

"Thanks." I offered her a small smile.

Defeating Cala didn't feel like a big victory. I loved her like a sister, but my best friend really wasn't on my level. She didn't spend her free time in the gym the way I did.

She didn't put in extra practice sessions, and she frequently cheated on our strict diet. She fought in the arena because she had to—that was life under the dome. But she wasn't dedicated to the job.

I, too, fought because the casters made me. Honestly, though, I did love it. In the arena, I channeled all my rage into those fights. Oftentimes, instead of seeing my opponent's face, I saw the vampire who stole me from my home. The bloodsucker who'd bitten me. It was his face that I punched, his body that kicked. He was the one I really wanted to let loose on. One day, I would get my revenge. One day, the vampire called Mat would pay for what he'd done to me.

Mary popped the cork on the champagne bottle and poured some into each of the flutes. Cala helped her distribute them.

"Please tell Clive thank you from me," I told Mary before she departed. Clive owned the Hideout. Once upon a time, he'd been a fighter. He'd retired at his peak and used all his winnings to open the nightclub. Judging by the lines outside and the sardine-packed dancefloor, his gamble had paid off.

"Wanna say a few words, Brie?" Rocko asked.

"I'm good."

He grinned. "Then I'll do the honors. To all the winners at the table, which includes me, congrats! To those of you—looking at you, Rudy—who should be in bed because they have to fight tomorrow, thanks for coming out." Rudy nodded as though he'd done us a great favor by joining in the celebration. "To Lenny, who fought bravely and lost with honor," Rocko continued.

Lenny, a skinny were-lion with incredible reflexes, smiled at the acknowledgement. "To Cala, the most gallant loser I have ever met."

My best friend laughed. "Yeah, thanks."

"And, of course, to our favorite fire fae, Brie. Still undefeated, still as humble as ever."

We all clinked glasses. The champagne went straight to my head and warmed my insides.

"Why did you fight Brie today?" the were-bear named Rudy asked. His hazel gaze shifting toward me. "Weren't you supposed to deflate Tanner's big head?"

"Apparently, he got injured," I said dryly, and then took another sip of champagne. "But Falcon said he's here."

I looked around the at the nearby tables. From our corner booth, I had a good view of the dancefloor, as well as the other patrons on the second floor. Tanner's auburn hair made him easy to spot. He was sitting at the other end of our row, at the other corner booth. The prick didn't look hurt. He was laughing and chugging beer with a group of older fighters.

My feet must've had a mind of their own, because I was up and striding toward Tanner's table like I had a purpose. Which, I supposed, I did.

Hands on hips, I stopped in front of the table of male fighters. "You don't look injured," I snapped at Tanner.

His laughter died a quick death. "Hey, Brie. Nice match today," he said warily.

"Why didn't you fight?" I demanded.

Why I thought I had the right to confront him, I would never know.

"Oh, right. Yeah, I got sick during warmup. I must've eaten something that didn't agree with me." Tanner flashed me a grin that simultaneously fueled my anger and made me wonder if he had a girlfriend.

What is wrong with me?

"You must be feeling better, since you're drinking and all," I pointed out.

"Much better. Thanks for your concern." The smile widened, and I sort of wanted to punch him. "Want to join us?"

I shook my head. "No. I want to know the real reason you backed out today. Are you so afraid to lose that you faked an illness?"

"Woah. Brie, calm down." Kenoa, an ex-fighter and current bodyguard to the privileged Prince Kai, held up a hand to stop my tirade.

I ignored the water fae and concentrated on Tanner. His expression went blank, a sign I was onto something. He *had* faked his illness. I was certain of it.

"You are that confident you would've beaten me."

It wasn't a question. Nevertheless, I answered. "I am," I lied. I was so not confident that I could beat him. "Just like I'm confident you faked being sick."

Tanner hesitated, narrowing his pale blue eyes like he was studying me. Then, he asked me the last question I would've expected. "Would you like to dance?"

I wrinkled my nose. "Are you for real?"

He gave me a lopsided smile. "One dance," he said evenly.

There was something in his expression that led me to believe that he wanted to speak privately, something we couldn't do at a table full of gossipy fighters.

"Fine," I said shortly. "One dance."

The music was loud, a pulsing beat that shook the dancefloor. Tanner took my hand as we navigated our way through the crowd of sweaty people. His fingers were warm against mine, and a weird sensation climbed up my spine.

Don't get romantic notions, I told myself.

We found a small patch of empty space and wedged ourselves in. Tanner's hands found my hips and he pulled me closer. I didn't resist, but I also wasn't sure how I felt about his nearness. He bent down to whisper in my ear, sending a shiver through me.

"How did you know I faked it?" he asked.

I pulled back from him. Tanner's light eyes held no expression. His jaw was set in a firm line. "I don't know," I practically yelled to be heard over the music. "It just seems obvious. I mean, you were fine this morning. You're out partying now. What illness only lasts a few hours? Plus, you only had a smoothie for breakfast, and there is no way that made you sick. The additives are meant to help our immune systems and speed healing."

"You really want to know where I was, why I didn't fight you?"

I hesitated. Suddenly, I wasn't so sure I did want to know. In fact, I wasn't sure why I'd made this a thing in the first place. But I had come this far, it felt weak to back down now. So, I nodded. "Yeah, I do."

Tanner licked his lips and looked around at the other dancers, none of whom seemed to notice that we weren't moving. Satisfied no one was listening, he leaned closer and spoke into my ear again.

"I had an emergency extraction." He pulled away just enough to look straight into my eyes. "For the rebellion."

I had heard whispers about the rebellion—a group that helped fae and shifters escape the dome. Truthfully, I had thought them an urban legend. Open defiance was something the casters took very seriously. And the repercussions if caught were pretty awful. Fae could be imprisoned. Or worse, drained of their magic and executed.

"You're part of the rebellion?" I asked softly.

Tanner nodded slowly.

Oddly, I wasn't as surprised as I probably should've been. Having a dimensional fae on call would make it so much easier to smuggle fae and shifters out from beneath the dome.

For a brief minute, I allowed myself to think of Fae Canyon. Of my father. Of my brother. Of Sienna and Gregory. Since accepting my fate, I had blocked out that part of my life. I loved my family and friends, and I wanted more than anything to be back with them. That wasn't possible. To survive in the Hawaiian Kingdom, I had let go of the past.

Or so I'd thought.

"You transport people to the Freelands?" I asked Tanner.

Again, he nodded.

"Why are you telling me this?" I asked suspiciously.

His hands were still on my hips, making this moment more awkwardly intimate than necessary. The logical part of my brain wanted to pull away. Another part of me liked his touch. It was comforting. And since I wasn't a big hugger, Tanner was the first person in a long time to hold me.

"Because I think you feel the same way I do about the casters. You do everything right, and you're great at pretending. But you hate them. You hate the casters. You hate the royal family."

I bit my lip. Tanner was right. I did hate them. They were the reason I'd been kidnapped. Queen Lilli had wanted a fire fae. She was responsible for my current situation. Thinking these traitorous thoughts was one thing, voicing them aloud in public was dangerous.

"Are you trying to recruit me?" I asked uneasily.

Tanner shrugged. "I just think maybe I have some likeminded friends that you should meet."

A slow song came on. Tanner drew me closer. We swayed to the music just like all the other couples on the dancefloor.

My mouth suddenly felt very dry. "Have you been watching me?" I asked softly, our hips moving in unison.

Tanner wrinkled his nose. "A little," he admitted. "We like to vet people before we ask them to join our ranks."

"I'll meet your friends," I said slowly. "On one condition."

Tanner made a face. "What's this condition?"

"I want to go home. I want to go back to Fae Canyon. You can take me, right?"

Once again, Tanner looked around to make sure we didn't have eavesdroppers nearby. "I can." He shook his head. "But I won't. I'm sorry. Truly. I only use my magic for extreme cases. I'm sure you miss your family, but your situation here is one of the best for fae. You have money, fame, and you're about to own a condo. You're doing pretty well by most standards."

Admittedly, he had a point. My day-to-day life wasn't so bad. I had the freedom to come and go as I pleased. I did have quite a bit of money in my bank account. I didn't have to share my magic with some jackass caster. On the surface, my life was pretty great compared to a lot of fae. Still, the witches and warlocks forced us to fight, sometimes to the death.

"Do you consider being terrified that I will meet my end every time I step in the arena a good situation?" I asked softly.

Tanner sighed. "I get what you're saying. Really, I do. But fae like you and me—the rebellion needs us. We have a lot of freedom compared to others."

"And a lot more money," I pointed out.

Was that the reason the rebellion wanted me? Because I was financially well off?

"That's part of it," Tanner conceded.

I appreciated his honesty. "When? When do you want me to meet your friends?"

Oh, Gaia, what am I doing?

Was I seriously considering joining the rebellion? Was I really prepared to take such a huge risk? This was all happening too fast. I needed time to contemplate the pros and cons.

He squeezed my hips and smiled. "Tonight. Christina is very eager to introduce herself."

Tonight? That's so soon.

"What are you afraid of?" Tanner asked softly, clearly

sensing my hesitation. "The casters get away with murder, literally. They force us to fight. They force us to share our magic just so they can perform spells for stupid shit like fetching a pen from across the room. I know a house fae that has to follow her mistress around like a shadow so the vain woman can wear a constant glamour because the crazy old bat doesn't want anyone to see her wrinkles. That's no life. And her story isn't even close to the worst I've heard."

I had heard the stories too. Everyone under the dome heard the whispers eventually. Nonetheless, even meeting with rebellion leaders was extremely dangerous. If I was caught…. I shook my head. I couldn't think about the consequences. Not in that moment. On the dancefloor with Tanner, there was no choice. Not really. I did hate the casters. I hated everything they were and everything they stood for. But that was not why I finally bobbed my head up and down. I agreed to the meeting for the same reason I'd stopped to help the caravan of captives that night in Fae Canyon—the night Mat had taken me. For the same reason I had instead insisted on being the one to provide the distraction so that Sienna could get help and so that the vamps wouldn't find Gregory.

"Okay. Tonight," I agreed with more confidence than I felt.

Tanner grinned. "Christina will be so pleased."

CHAPTER ONE

DOMED CITY OF LOS ANGELES, KINGDOM OF THE AMERICAS
PRESENT DAY

BRIE

AMANDA RAMONE, DIRECTOR of Hawaii's
Royal Bureau of Investigation, was a smug bitch. She
wore a satisfied smile the entire time her cronies marched
me downstairs and through the service entrance at the
back of the hotel like they were herding cattle. My silver
gown swished with every stilted step; it was preposterous
attire for the occasion, but Ramone had refused to let me
change into something more appropriate. The fact I was

wearing heels made walking with my hands magically bound behind my back particularly challenging.

Not exactly the victory party I'd anticipated when getting ready.

A white van was waiting at the loading dock, and several dark SUVs idled nearby. The back door of the van opened, and a guy from Ramone's team shoved me forward. His meaty palm was sweaty, and I recoiled from his touch on the bare skin of my back. My knees scraped against the metal as I tried to climb in without the use of my hands. The guard pushed me forward again, and I flopped unceremoniously onto my side in the van's sparse interior. A metal grate separated the front with seats from the cargo space. The driver didn't so much glance at me in the back as the doors slammed close.

My shoulder bumped against the hard metal floor during the short drive. The same guard with the damp hands and a greasy mustache dragged me out by the arm. We were in front of the Los Angeles Kingdom Justice Center. So was a gaggle of photographers. Flashes went off continuously as I was steered up the steps of the building by a dozen of Ramone's guards.

Seems like overkill, I thought. With my hands bound by whatever spell Ramone cast on me, I wasn't a threat to anyone. I also wasn't resisting; I didn't want Kai to suffer the repercussions of my actions. Even though I was flooded with shame inside, I held my head high as I strode past the paparazzi. They wanted the money shot? I'd give it to them.

At least you look good, I thought, hysterical laughter bubbling in my throat. Biting back the tears that threatened to fall, I breathed a sigh of relief once we entered the building and left the vultures behind.

My picture was taken one more time by an intake officer, and then I was thrown into a sparse cell. The cinderblock space was small and contained only a metal slab that was supposed to pass for a bed. The infusion of magic from Kai was waning with all the adrenaline rushing through me. Suddenly, I was exhausted. Hands still bound behind my back, I slumped down on the bed that lacked a mattress and curled into myself.

Memories of my first weeks in Hawaii flooded in, but I shoved them back. While I'd been certain those would always be the worst days of my life, I'd somehow managed to find myself in a predicament that was even worse.

You're being tried for murder and treason tomorrow, I told myself, trying to will my brain into understanding that this was the new reality. No more worrying about Kai's advisors or the rebellion or anything at all. *The sentence for a guilty verdict will be death. You have to accept that.*

My hands were numb from lack of circulation. Laying on my side, the shoulder that bore my weight was losing feeling as well. The rest of my body ached. Sienna was supposed to perform the counter-spell before we fled with the rebellion. Without that, the gift of magic from Kai was only a temporary fix.

Don't worry, I thought as my eyelids drooped. *You might not live long enough for the poison to kill you.*

Without any sense of how long I'd been asleep, I awoke to the cell door sweeping open and banging against the wall behind it.

"On your feet," an older man said as he stepped into

my cell. His guard uniform was tight around the middle, and he gave off an air of utter indifference. Ramone was waiting in the hallway behind him.

Struggling to sit up, I glared at her. "Any chance you can unbind my hands?" I asked, straining to temper the venom in my voice. "I seriously can't feel the upper half of my body."

Ramone rolled her eyes. "Someone got used to the royal treatment." Despite her words, the Director waved a hand in my direction and muttered an incantation.

My arms slumped forward to my side where they belonged. It took a full minute of shaking them to feel the pins and needles that indicated my circulation was restoring.

"For heaven's sake, just stand up," Ramone demanded. "Follow me. Do not try anything, or I will bind more than just your hands."

"Where are we going?" I asked as we walked down the narrow hallway with cells on either side.

The guard who'd opened my cell walked behind me. He jabbed a finger into my back. "Just shut up and walk."

Humiliation flooded through me. They were treating me like someone unworthy of the respect every living being deserved. My fingers curled into fists by my side, still tingling.

We went out the back of the building to another white van idling by the door. At least we were avoiding the paparazzi; I didn't need a second public perp walk. This van had benches bolted to either side of the cargo area, and I sank onto the hard surface with a sigh of relief. I hadn't been looking forward to another ride slamming around the floor of the vehicle. The van pulled away, and I tried to peer through the windshield to get a sense of where we were going. The combination of the metal grate and the darkness outside made it impossible to tell. Resigned, I leaned back against the side of the van.

We'd been on the road for about ten minutes when the driver suddenly swerved to the right. The vehicle's back wheels skidded until we were nearly sideways. Headlights shone brightly through the windshield, but I couldn't see anything more. Even with my hands unbound, I flew across the space and into the bench on the opposite side. My ribs connecting with the metal didn't hurt as much as my finger that jammed into the corner and bent left. Before I could recover, the transport van swerved hard again, this time to the left. I slammed into the wire divider, my head connecting with it before I could catch myself. An abrupt halt made me swear out loud as I hit the divider again. Spots of light danced in my vision. In the next instant, the van doors swung open and I was being yanked out by my ankles.

"What the hell?" I demanded.

In the darkness, I didn't recognize the face of the man who lorded above me. Fear rushed through me with a dash of panic that I couldn't shake. Despite my terror, I kicked and screamed. Drawing my legs in, I gathered energy and then shoved out with my heels. Without any idea who he was or what he wanted, I wasn't going anywhere without a fight. My kick had the added advantage of the impractical stilettos, and the man pulling me out of the transport van doubled over with a cry of pain.

Who the hell is after you now? I wondered, taking the brief time to wrack my brain. *Who would want you badly enough to hijack a transport?*

My body went cold as I considered the very real possibility that it was a bounty hunter who was after my fire magic. Again. No matter what, I wouldn't allow cowboys to take me for a second time. I'd be damned if I let them drag me off to servitude in a new land. I drew in the deepest of breaths and prepared myself for what was coming. Despite the aches of my body, I was ready for a physical fight.

Don't use your magic, I reminded myself. *The poison's effects increase with use.*

Two more figures appeared at the back of the van. Before I could react, they yanked me from the vehicle and dropped me on the ground. My abductors obviously weren't in the mood for a vicious fight. With the asphalt crunching into my skin, I contemplated the path that had brought me to this moment.

I'd been kidnapped by a vampire while in the safety of Fae Canyon, and then I was sold to the Kingdom of Hawaii for entertainment. After adapting to life within the fight pits of the island, I'd become so proficient at kicking the ass of other supes that there was a certain ease to it. Sure, falling in love with Kai had been a heartbreaking misstep. There was no room to let it define me, though. I had to move forward with that in mind. Survival was the only goal.

A silhouette peered down at me. He was flanked by more men dressed in all black who were poised for action. Though they watched as I glared from my prone position on the road, no one touched me. No one held me down, and no one restricted my movements. Still, almost like a reflex, I kicked and spat. Once my efforts against the concrete had been exhausted, I struggled to my feet and returned the stares of those who were looking at me.

"Are you sure this is the one we want?" an innocuous looking guy asked. He looked so unremarkable, I found myself questioning if my earlier assumption was wrong; he certainly didn't look like a cowboy.

"They said to take her," another voice replied. "Whether or not it's the right girl is their call. This is the right transport, so this should be the right girl."

Were these people who wanted to help me? Or was it the rebellion, who could've wanted to save *or* kill me? Was it a team from a different kingdom, whether friend or foe to the Hawaiian Islands, looking for extra fae magic to power their dome?

"Whether or not it's her, she's brimming with power," a younger guy said as another vehicle pulled up on the deserted road. Headlights shone on our faceoff, the sudden brightness painful on my eyes. One of the doors opened and shut as I blinked rapidly.

A figure stepped out into the light. A grisly, jagged scar ran down one side of his face. "You were supposed to save her, not hurt her," he growled at the crowd around me.

"Harry?" I blinked.

It was Botto's friend, one of the two mercenaries supposed to smuggle me out of the dome.

"Yeah, it's me, kid." He smiled as the other man I'd

met at the gym in West Hollywood climbed out from the opposite side of the vehicle. Harry cocked a thumb in his direction. "Tye's here, too."

"Where's Botto?" I called.

Just because I'd met these before didn't mean I trusted them.

"You'll see him—Run!" Harry cried as a dark SUV screeched around the corner and barreled down the road toward the front of the van. A second vehicle came hot on the wheels of the first.

Ramone was undoubtedly inside of one of them. Being taken back by the Justice Department would lead to my trial and inevitable execution. My gaze turned to Harry's crew climbing into the vans.

"Brie, come on!" shouted the mercenary.

Uncertainty is better than certain death, I decided.

Turning away from the rapidly approaching SUVs—two more were rounding the corner—I ran after the people who'd broken me out. As I reached the open side door of their van, I turned back for a moment we couldn't spare. Calling forth every ounce of energy left within me, I conjured fireballs and flung them at the lead vehicle. Instead of blowing it up completely, I simply aimed for the tires. The smell of melting rubber filled the air as the first car skidded to a stop. After flinging enough flames to disable the other vehicles, Harry grabbed my shoulders and yanked me into the van.

The door slammed closed, and I peered out the back window as we fled. The vehicles were blocking the road entirely, making it impossible for their back-up to pursue us. We sped away, leaving Ramone and her people behind. As the distance between us grew, my exhaustion grew as well.

Shouldn't have used your magic, I thought as darkness crept into the sides of my vision. The poison's effects were taking hold of me again and spreading. Using my magic to repel the guys trying to take me had been one thing; it didn't take a ton of energy to make it uncomfortable to touch me. Melting the tires of our pursuers was another thing entirely. The fact I'd refused to blow up the vehicles and sent the fireballs only at the tires had cost me dearly.

With an acrid smell in my nostrils, surrounded by people I didn't know, I struggled to keep my eyes open. My head hit the seat back. Apparently, I wasn't capable of holding it up on my own.

You did too much.

Harry sank down beside me, his scar appearing even more gruesome through my hazy vision.

"How'd you know to come get me?" I mumbled suspiciously.

He smiled. "We got eyes and ears everywhere, sweetheart."

"Where's Botto? Shouldn't he be with you?" My words ran together to form a very incoherent question.

"Rest, Brie. You're safe now." Harry patted my arm.

I didn't feel particularly safe, but I was too exhausted to do anything about it.

Can't be worse than an execution, I thought as everything went dark and my body pulsed with pain.

The next time I opened my eyes, I was in a bunker of some sort. The cement walls weren't the same as the ones in the jail cell, and it was a much larger space, but the feeling was still just as desolate.

"Water?" a voice called. I felt an instant flood of relief. *Botto.*

The moment I'd taken two sips from the glass, I collapsed back on the cot and passed out again. I felt the glass being pulled my hand just as I went back to sleep.

I wasn't sure how long I was out of it, but the time was filled with feverish dreams of worst-case scenarios. I saw Kai and I being executed side-by-side. I saw all my friends lined up to face a trial of the caster justice system. I also saw Ramone cackling with laughter as she watched it all. Finally, I saw my father and my brother. As much as I longed for their presence, I didn't feel comfort from the vision. Instead, dread filled me. Something bad was going to happen.

"Brie, we need you to wake up," Botto's voice said, cutting into the weird scenes playing in my head.

"You promised me a trip out of here," Sienna's voice added. Hearing her brought a flood of relief. I might've been hallucinating Botto earlier, but my old friend was definitely there when I opened my eyes. "It's time I held up my side of the deal."

The idea of getting rid of the curse on my magic, even if it came from Sienna and was dark in nature, made me fight to sit up. I wouldn't be any good to Kai and my friends if I couldn't use my magic. And I had to help them. My alleged crimes would fall back on my friends, that much was certain.

My eyelids drooped while Sienna set up candles around me, lighting them in turn while she spoke quiet incantations. The last thing I remembered was Sienna standing at the foot of my bed and the candle flames flickering at an unnatural height. She spoke words I'd never heard before, and then I was out again.

It had to be another day that passed before I woke again. This time, Botto was shoving a snowsuit at me.

"You need to change out of that ridiculous dress," he said, as if I'd thought a silver sequined backless gown was the ideal outfit for being a fugitive.

It was a struggle, but I managed to swap my victory gown for the clothing that was much more appropriate. Still exhausted, I leaned against Sienna as I changed into the new outfit and pulled my hair up into a ponytail.

"The spell will take," she assured me. "I promise you."

Getting changed had taken every ounce of energy within me. Although the counter-curse was taking effect, it was utterly draining to have so much conflicting black magic swirling inside of me.

Once dressed in the puffy snowsuit, I passed back out on the cot.

The next time my eyes opened, I felt like an entirely new person. Botto was in a corner of the bunker room filling a backpack with supplies.

"You gonna be up for a little haul?" he asked once I sat up.

The world still felt slightly off kilter, but my body felt a million times better. "Absolutely," I answered, ignoring the dizzy feeling that threatened to lay me out on the cot again.

"We're made you a makeshift bed in the back of the transport," Botto said, his tone almost apologetic. "We're doing our best to keep you comfortable, but this is the window for us to leave. We have to go."

"I'm fine," I assured him. "I don't need anything special, let's just get the hell out of here."

When I followed him up the bunker stairs and into a warehouse, I breathed deeply. The stale air of the bunker had been claustrophobic. Evidently, I wasn't cut out for living in a post-apocalyptic world. The night sky above my head when I approached the transport truck waiting outside was a huge relief. Staring at the stars, I thought of all the different scenarios where I'd done the same thing—Fae Canyon, my apartment on Oahu, the balcony of my room at Iolani Palace. This was the same view, which tugged at my heart.

You're never going back, I reminded myself. *Get used to it.*

Head tucked down, I swiped at my cheeks as I climbed into the space hidden behind boxes of medical supplies. Though it appeared to be a full load from the outside, the cargo area had been left empty in the middle to accommodate our group of fugitives. The thin mattress that lay against the back of the driver's cabin was suddenly the most appealing thing I'd ever seen.

Harry and Tye's people stacked more aid boxes behind us and closed our group in. I collapsed onto the thin cotton slab. I didn't know where we were going or who we would encounter at our next stop, but I knew my choices were limited. Eyes closing again, I managed to look over to where Botto and Sienna were huddled a few feet away.

I'll be fine, I thought as I drifted into unconsciousness. I didn't trust Sienna in the least, but I knew Botto would never betray me.

Or will he? The question bounced around my head as I succumbed to the darkness again. *Your fate is in the hands of other people. Accept that. Deal with it.*

SOPHIE DAVIS

CHAPTER TWO

DOMED CITY OF LOS ANGELES, KINGDOM OF THE AMERICAS
PRESENT DAY

Kai

"AND WHAT ARE you doing to find her precisely?" Kai barked at the people surrounding him. The gathering included not only his advisors, but half the Californian royal family.

"Your Majesty?" Director Ramone started. Before continuing, she rose slightly from her chair and offered an awkward, half-hearted curtsy.

Kai rounded on her and quirked an eyebrow. "Yes, Director? Would you like to detail the measures you are taking to recapture my mother's murderer?"

If not for the years of diplomatic training, he would never have been able to say those last words without grimacing. In the seventy-eight hours since police had stormed his hotel suite and taken Brie into custody, Kai's emotions had been on one hell of a rollercoaster ride. He'd wanted to scream her innocence from the roof of Calypso Palace but wasn't that stupid. He knew that if he remained resistant to what many believed was the truth about Brie, he would be cut out of the investigation into her disappearance. Kai couldn't have that. Needing to be kept in the loop, he'd erred on the side of not saying much.

"We have received numerous tips, sightings of the fae," Director Ramone began again. Her eyes didn't quite meet his as she cleared her throat and clutched her hands in her lap beneath the large conference table in one of the Calypso Palace's meeting rooms. "We are assembling teams to investigate the legitimacy of these claims." She hesitated a beat too long, giving King Ronald the chance to interject.

"Why have you not already sent out investigative teams?" he asked. "The girl has been gone for three days. If we let her gallivant about any longer, she might manage to escape the dome altogether. In the meantime, we cannot have a rebel assassin running about the city."

California's reigning monarch sat on a raised dais, on a smaller version, though no less gaudy, of the throne inside the palace's official throne room. King Ronald wore a navy suit much the one Kai wore, though not quite as slim fit, and a dark red tie that the older man kept smoothing.

"Well, you see, Your Majesty…." Director Ramone glanced around the conference room as she tugged at the cuffs of her black blazer like the sleeves had suddenly shrunk. Many in the room refused to meet her eyes. Like Kai, they had to know that Brie had already left the domed city of Los Angeles. No one wanted to deliver that message to King Ronald.

"What? Spit it out," Queen Katherine snapped from her post beside her husband's throne.

The California royals were old-fashioned; they liked formality, pomp, circumstance, and etiquette. Those were all the things Kai wanted to phase out from his own lands, or at the very least update for modern times now that he was king.

"All our intelligence suggests the fae is already in the Freelands. That is where she has been sighted, that is where you need to pursue her," Ramone finally admitted.

Though his expression remained impassive, Kai's heart beat a little faster upon hearing confirmation that Brie had escaped the confines of the dome.

King Ronald shook his head and waved a hand dismissively. "That is absurd. There is no way a foreign fae could cross the border."

"We have reason to believe that the female air fae you also had in holding is with her. Credible intelligence links both women to the rebellion, there's not much left to figure out or surmise," Ramone replied.

They have names, Kai thought with annoyance. Yes, it was normal for casters, particularly royal casters and high-ranking government officials to refer to non-casters as "the fae girl" or "that male shifter", but he found that hearing a roomful of uptight assholes talking about Brie like that made him see red. He'd never considered himself violent—he'd never even been in a real fight—but he *really* wanted to punch King Ronald in his jowly face.

"Fine. For argument's sake, I will concede the fae may have been able to leave the dome." King Ronald narrowed his gaze, zeroing in on Director Ramone. "That does not explain your delay in sending out search parties to investigate any and all sightings."

How have I never realized what a moron this guy is? Kai wondered. Too impatient to wait for Director Ramone to sputter out an explanation, he snapped, "The Freelands aren't safe for casters. We don't fare well in subzero climates."

"Ah, yes. Of course. This is not a task for casters, though, is it?" King Ronald looked to a woman three down from Kai at the conference table.

Her name was Paula Sanchez. Her title was something like Secretary of Dungeons. Kai knew little else about her except that she was taking a lot of heat for Brie's escape.

"Have you spoken to our fanged friends, Paula?" King Ronald asked.

Paula's dark gaze shifted to Director Ramone and her mouth tightened. "There have been some disagreements on whether vampires are the right group to send."

"They're professional hunters. Who would be better to send?" King Ronald scoffed.

"Not those who murdered my mother," Kai

interjected. "Vampires cannot be trusted. Don't forget, it was vampires conspiring with the rebellion in my kingdom." Both statements were true. Both were reasons that Kai had been adamant that vampires not be called in. But the reason his blood ran colder than the average temperature outside the dome was solely about Brie. Though she could definitely outrun and outlast casters, and she stood a good chance against shifters and other fae, vampires were a different story. Especially the ones who specialized in capturing fae and shifters and selling them to the domed cities.

"We do not need to trust them. Trust plays no part in our business transactions with those fanged beasts," King Ronald spat. The elder royal's tone implied that he was a naïve child, and Kai's fists clenched. "Money, blood—those inspire loyalty in those undead heathens. Both of which we have to offer. The vamps on my payroll are not stupid enough to wage war against the kingdom that feeds them."

Kai was on his feet. The mood in the conference room shifted from tense to oppressive. It seemed no one, neither Kai's people nor Ronald's knew what to do when two kings butted heads. *Keep calm,* Kai lectured himself. *You cannot let them think you are too emotionally invested.*

He took a deep breath and exhaled slowly. "Vampires are unnecessary. Brie is sick. She won't make it far without help. What she needs isn't the type of help the rebellion can provide."

Kai had planned to hold on to this bit of information for as long as possible, and it seemed the time had come to show his hand.

"Brie was poisoned by someone in *your kingdom*." He held up his hand to stop the rush of questions about to be launched his way from every direction. "We do not know by who or how the poison was administered."

It wasn't quite the truth and not quite a lie. Kai had a lot of theories about the how and a few about the why. The who was harder, though. A lot of people wanted Brie dead, including members of the rebellion.

As he'd tried to figure out where she'd disappeared to, Kai had learned a lot in the days since his girlfriend's escape. Very few had the ability to pull off the type of powerful dark magic that had gone into the spell that poisoned Brie. Kai wanted to devote more resources to tracking down anyone with such capabilities; it was the most solid lead they had available, and it was easily the simplest to track. Magic that held those capabilities wasn't commonplace. Kenoa had been making discreet inquiries, but the water fae was the only one Kai could trust to do so. The Hawaiian king worried that his other advisors, and even some of his longtime bodyguards, might run back to his sister and tell her what he was up to. And that was the last thing that Kai could afford. Whatever Sarah's reasons for arresting Brie were, nothing would excuse the fact she'd ordered the treason charges without Kai's approval.

"There are plenty of fae in the Freelands capable of brewing antidotes to most any poison," Queen Katherine said dismissively. "And if not, then the assassin did our work for us."

Kai was still standing, and he felt the blood rush into his cheeks. Still, his stoicism didn't allow his face to betray the feelings of anger and frustration. The queen's tone had him questioning whether or not to let the fury fly. But it was what Kai said next—what he had to say next—that pained him to the core.

"Queen killers cannot be allowed to die an insignificant death. We must make an example of anyone who commits such a heinous act. Otherwise, we are all vulnerable. If we allow this act to go unpunished, the same could happen to any of us."

When the meeting finally dispersed, the ride back to the hotel from Calypso Palace was quiet, save the faint sound of the tires rolling over the paved roads. Lara and Makani, two of Kai's bodyguards, rode in the back of the SUV with him and Kenoa. It was a big factor in the silence; neither was a fan of Brie and anything they said would've just been all the more awkward. It was more than their simple disapproval of the royal relationship with a lowly fae, though. With Kai and Sarah at odds, the king couldn't be sure where anyone's loyalties lied. For all he knew, his team could've been planning a mutiny.

Speaking of his sister, they were scheduled for a chat that evening. It would be their first conversation without eavesdroppers since he'd seen the princess' signature on Brie's arrest warrant. Kai wasn't looking forward to the conversation. He wanted to confide in Sarah, to explain things to her the same way Brie had explained them to him.

It's too risky, he told himself. *She doesn't love Brie the way you do.* The thought made Kai miserable. He hated that he couldn't trust his own blood. Never in his life had Kai felt so lost, helpless, and hopeless. With the power of running a kingdom, he should've had the power to save the woman he loved. Instead, he had to toe the party line and pretend that he at least understood the decision to arrest her.

Unfortunately, there were more unpleasant meetings on the king's schedule before his face-to-face with Sarah. Los Angeles had gone into lockdown after Brie escaped. Even the visiting royals had been told they couldn't leave until every attic, basement, and cubbyhole beneath the dome was thoroughly searched. Many were using the time for private meetings with one another, but Kai worried that their displeasure with the situation might make them more likely to become displeased with him. To keep up appearances, Kai had agreed to do the same and engage with the other royals.

"You have Prince Felipe in thirty," Kenoa reminded him on the elevator ride to the penthouse suite. Kai had been staying there for a week now, and he was sick of it. When he'd arrived at the hotel, he'd felt happy and excited with Brie by his side, ready to fight in the Interkingdom Championships. Now, the suite felt empty.

"He wants to discuss trade, is that right?" he said, silently thanking the part of his brain that was still tuned into the world around him.

"Seafood," Kenoa replied. "His mother is a big fan of tuna, and their current supplier just raised prices again. They're hoping to negotiate a better deal with you."

Fish. No one knew where Brie was, and Kai was about to discuss fish with a Spanish prince over eggs benedict. *What a ridiculous use of my time,* he thought.

The meeting proved to be a complete waste of Kai's

time and energy, just as he'd suspected. As if seafood wasn't a ridiculous enough conversation, Prince Felipe was more interested in pitching the idea of international sports leagues similar to the ones that existed during the human age. In Kai's opinion, the whole idea was outlandish given the growing tensions beneath the domes. They needed real solutions to the tensions, not facades of everything being great and happy.

They did talk tuna briefly, at least. Even though it still felt frivolous, Kai did appreciate a conversation that wasn't nearly as flippant as ball sports. "Send over your terms, and I will take a look," Kai promised as he walked Prince Felipe to the door.

"Think about the sports leagues. It could really boost morale." Felipe held out his hand to Kai. "I was very sorry to hear about your girlfriend. Though many people question how you didn't know she was a traitor this whole time, I do understand."

Kai stiffened and dropped Prince Felipe's hand. Unfortunately, the action didn't dissuade the other royal from plunging forward.

"Three years ago, my older sister was the ringleader in a plot to kill our mother. We never suspected her." Felipe shook his head. The admission stunned Kai, and he wasn't able to conjure a response before Felipe continued. "Not once. Even when she confessed, I didn't believe her capable of murder."

Kai swallowed thickly and wracked his brain to remember what he knew about the tragedy. If memory served, Princess Isabel, eldest child and heir to her mother's throne, had died in an airship crash. At least, that was the public story.

As though reading Kai's mind, Felipe continued, "My mother thought it would make us look weak if the world knew Spain's heir apparent had aligned herself with the rebellion. My sister was executed in private. The airship crash was the story we gave the news outlets."

"Why are you telling me this?" Kai asked uneasily.

A small, sad smile crossed Felipe's lips. "You know, not a day goes by that I don't wish I had gone to Isabel before the executioner took her. She might have done something terrible, but she was still my sister. I will always love her."

Kai stood in the doorway and watched Prince Felipe walk away. The departure had been so abrupt, he wasn't sure what just happened. Was he for real? Had there been more to the other royal's story? Was Felipe trying to tell him something? Or was the prince just trying to be nice, to remind Kai that love has a way of blinding people?

"You have another appointment," Kenoa said softly. "Karl Hooper, the Director of Dome Maintenance for Chicago. Do you want to reschedule?"

How much did he overhear? Kai wondered.

Instead of dwelling on the concern, Kai waved at his friend in acquiescence. "Send him up."

The meeting with the Chicago caster dragged on for close to ninety minutes. Hooper would've gladly talked Kai's ear off for the foreseeable future, but the king's next appointment arrived and finally cut him short. By early evening, Kai had met with another handful of people. By the time they'd finished, his eyelids were drooping, and his head was pounding. He was used to spending his days in meetings, many that were way more tiresome and boring than any he'd sat through in L.A. The difference that day was that even matters of state no longer mattered to him. Finally alone in his hotel suite, or at least as alone as Kai ever was, he admitted something to himself: only Brie mattered.

"You look like you need this." The voice of his best friend brought Kai's thoughts back to the present.

In the suite's sitting room, he had the shades down over all the windows to block out the setting sun and rising city lights. When he looked up, Kenoa held with two tumblers with one extended toward Kai. The king accepted the drink and toasted his friend. "Thanks."

Kenoa sank down in one of the armchairs. "They made it out of the city last night in a medical supply caravan. It's headed for that mini-dome in the middle of the frozen desert."

"Why the delay?" The ice in Kai's glass clanged with the question, an involuntary twitch of annoyance. Looking down, he saw that both of his hands were shaking.

Kenoa shrugged his broad shoulders. "If I had to guess, Brie's health was probably the reason for the delay. They would've needed to get her the counter curse before she was strong enough to travel. My source didn't know the reason, although it's possible that was always the plan."

"Are you ever going to tell me who this mysterious source is?" Kai asked. Sipping his drink, he noticed the scrapes on Kenoa's knuckles for the first time.

Kenoa caught him looking. "The less you know, the

better it is for all of us."

Kai understood the need for plausible deniability; the less he knew, the less he could be blamed for later. Still, he also felt that the actions of any proxy working on his behalf were his responsibility. He was the king, after all. Regardless, Kai was too tired to press the issue. Instead, he asked, "Where are they headed now?"

"My source didn't know for certain. There are at least a dozen fae communities within a few hundred miles of here. Including Fae Canyon."

Kai swirled the contents of his glass. "Do you have any contacts there?"

"Not personally. But I can probably get a message to the elders."

The king considered it. As much as he wanted to reach out to Brie, if the message was intercepted…. No, it was too dangerous. He wouldn't risk Brie's life just to give himself peace of mind. That was the only thing to be gained by reaching out to the communities where she might seek refuge—his own mental comfort.

"Not yet," Kai said finally. "Home is the first place Director Ramone will send people. Did you get the list of credible sightings?"

Kenoa laughed softly. "Yeah, but they really aren't very credible. Someone claimed a fae matching Brie's description was spotted about an hour north of San Francisco the day before yesterday. I know for a fact that's not possible. An outpost worker near Phoenix says they saw her riding in the passenger seat of a supply caravan. Also not possible. The list goes on."

"Any reports that we should be worried about?" Kai

cocked an eyebrow.

Kenoa hesitated a beat. "One. There's a pack of were-coyotes not far from the mini-dome. Just before the meeting this morning, Ramone received word that two female fae and a large male hybrid were spotted by the pack's night patrols. The timing checks with what my source told me. If it was Brie and company, they're long gone by now."

Kai blew out a long, relieved breath. "Keep tabs on the situation. Try not to be too obvious."

His best friend laughed. "I've been doing your dirty work a long time. I know how to be discrete."

It was meant as a joke, but there was truth in Kenoa's words. He had been cleaning up after Kai for years. Whether it was girls that couldn't accept that they weren't going to be the next queen of Hawaii or paparazzi snapping photos of Kai stumbling out of bars in the middle of the night, Kenoa had always had his back. He'd even stepped in with Sarah when Kai forgot her tenth birthday. But this, helping Kai thwart an official government investigation? It was next level.

"You don't have to do this. You don't owe me anything. You know that, right?" Kai met his friend's troubled gaze.

Kenoa sighed heavily. "I know. I also could've turned Brie in weeks ago. I didn't. I made that choice. Not because of our friendship." With his glass he gestured to first Kai and then himself. "But because Brie's my friend too. She made mistakes, sure. That doesn't make her a mass murderer. I know she had nothing to do with your mother's death, I know that in my soul."

"Thank you." Kai reached out and touched his tumbler to Kenoa's. "For better or worse, whatever comes next, we're in it together."

"Just like always," Kenoa agreed.

CHAPTER THREE

FREELANDS OF THE AMERICAS

Brie

"IS IT POSSIBLE for you to be any louder? It's not like the casters of the world are searching for us or anything." Small, white cloud puffs came out of Sienna's mouth with every breath she took. She tossed her glossy blonde ponytail—how she managed to have flawless hair while a fugitive was beyond comprehension—and glared at me over her shoulder. "You've gone soft living in paradise."

"Sorry the fact my teeth chatter is bothering you," I snapped. "Some of us could stand to be a bit warmer."

"Ladies. Please," Botto said wearily.

In the days since my trainer and his friends broke me out of the dungeons beneath Calypso Palace, those were the two words that he kept repeating. In fairness, Sienna and I weren't exactly the best company. We did tend to bicker. A lot. The two of us couldn't agree on anything. Every decision I made drew nasty commentary from her. Everything she uttered made me fire back with a contrary response. In all, we were kind of a nightmare to deal with.

If I was being honest with myself, Sienna wasn't completely off base with the dig about my lack of immunity to the cold. I'd spent seventy-five percent of my life outside the domes in the frozen tundra. Nevertheless, it seemed the last five years had spoiled me. In the Freelands, even indoors, cold permeated the bones right down to the marrow. Outside, with the wind gusts were strong enough to make me stumble on occasion, every breath was a slice to my lungs.

You endured this for most of your life, I reminded myself. At the same time, my brain screamed, *How did you endure this for so long?* The cold was unnatural; ice lived within my veins, and I questioned whether it would be possible to ever be warm again.

"How much longer to the next stop?" I asked aloud. It felt like we'd been walking for days straight, but I couldn't be sure how much time had truly elapsed. The medical supply caravan had dropped us off twenty miles from the mini dome under the cover of darkness. From there, the walk to our second rendezvous point had only taken about thirty minutes. That bitterly cold half hour ad felt much longer.

Two female were-bobcats picked us up in an old pickup. Botto gallantly offered to ride in the back since his hybrid genes made him more resistant to the extreme climate. Unfortunately, the heater inside such a tired vehicle didn't pump out a lot of warmth, and the hour inside the truck didn't do much toward defrosting my insides. On the bright side, the rusty metal can on wheels did keep the wind at bay.

"Not long. Less than a mile," Botto promised.

Snow and frozen branches cracked beneath his boots as he scurried up an icy embankment. I followed closely behind. For all her bitching about me and my inadequacies, Sienna was the one who struggled up the slippery slope. Her heavy boots, identical to the ones I wore, couldn't find purchase. As her feet slid from beneath her and Sienna pitched forward, I held out an arm to break her fall. She swatted me away like a pesky fly.

She's lived in warmth as long as you have, I reminded myself. *It might not have been the most comfortable warmth, but it was still under a dome.* Sienna peered up at me from beneath lashes dotted with melting snowflakes. Her brow narrowed suspiciously. Our gazes locked, and she again smacked the hand I held out to her like an olive branch.

"I'm fine. I don't need your help," she snapped.

I rolled my eyes. "Whatever."

Sienna climbed to her feet—the fall could've been avoided if she wasn't so resistant to help—and brushed the snow off her thermal leggings. "Let's just go. I'm starving. The sooner we get wherever we're going, the sooner I can eat." She cleared the top of the embankment and blew out a sharp breath. "Where are we going, exactly?"

It was a question she'd asked a lot in the days since we'd been on the run. As many times as she'd asked, Botto continually refused to give a straight answer. It was safer that way. My time in the rebellion had taught me that as much as anything. Few, if any, single individual knew every piece of an extraction plan. The less information one knew, the less information they could give up if caught.

"For now, we're going right there." Botto pointed ahead to a break in the tree line that I would've never noticed if he hadn't said something. "I'll go first to check things out. I'm not sure we're really alone out here, and we need to know. You two stay put and be quiet."

He didn't wait for a response before tightening the straps on his backpack and setting off toward the shelter.

The sun had been up for almost an hour. I tipped my head back and let the rays warm my face.

"I forgot how beautiful real sunshine is," I murmured.

The artificial light beneath the domes was great and all, but nothing manufactured was ever as good as the real thing.

"Playing house with a caster made you forget where you came from," Sienna scoffed.

Recovering from magic poisoning was exhausting business, and my patience was short. Particularly where Sienna was concerned. But I also didn't want to expend the little energy I had left fighting with her. Instead of engaging, I took the high road and stalked off after Botto.

It was a good thing his boots had left prints in the snow, because he was nowhere to be seen. I was about to call out his name when I felt someone come up behind me. The cold slowed my reflexes just enough that I was able to catch myself before punching Sienna in the face.

"What's wrong with you?" she hissed.

"Me?" I squeaked. "What's wrong with you? Don't you know better than to sneak up on a fighter?"

"What's wrong with both of you?" a loud, disapproving voice interrupted.

My eyes did a quick scan of the immediate area. It took me a minute to locate Botto, or rather his disembodied head protruding from a snow pile. I did a doubletake. Then I blinked, numerous times. It took another minute before I understood what I was seeing. From a distance, it had looked like the break in the trees was due to a hill. That wasn't the case. The mound of treeless snow was a building buried so deep on all sides that only a few windows were visible—that was where I found Botto's annoyed face poking out from.

"Come around to the other side, there's a door," he added and then disappeared from sight.

Botto must've used his air magic to clear away the snow from the door, which he'd left open for us. I had no qualms about charging inside, but Sienna hesitated.

"What? Are you going to prove you're a real fae and stand watch outside while we rest?" I asked flippantly.

Her lack of immediate snide response gave me pause and a sudden need to apologize.

"I'm sorry. I'm really tired," I told her.

Her lip snarled. "Gaia, didn't they teach you anything

useful on that stupid island of yours?"

"What does that even mean?" I threw my hands. "Whatever. Come in, don't come in. I don't care." Spinning on my heel, I started inside and collided with Botto's broad chest.

He merely cocked an eyebrow and said, "There are fireplaces on each wall. Can you do the honors?"

"Huh? Oh, yeah. Sure."

Dust particles danced like dirty snowflakes in the thin white light coming through the windows on the east side of the building. The structure consisted of exactly one long, rectangular room and several dozen cots. Bookcases were arranged along each of the long sides, each shelf lined with hardbacks. A colorful wooden box marked toys and another marked quilts were in the middle of the room. I skimmed my fingertips along the lid of the toybox, unsurprised to see dirt on my white gloves.

"It's freezing in here," Sienna scoffed loudly.

"Brie, the fires?" Botto prompted.

"Yeah, sorry." I shrugged off my backpack and then removed my gloves, dropping both on one of the cots. I called the magic and made the rounds of the fireplaces. Each time I tossed a fireball, I cast an everlasting spell so the flames would continue to burn without assistance.

It was the first bit of magic I'd used since Sienna broke the curse on me, and I was a little nervous that I wouldn't be pleased with the results. She'd warned me there could be some aftereffects, but that they should fade in the next week or so. Of course, I only had her word that any issues I might encounter were from the curse and not some new hex Sienna had placed on me.

Nothing seemed amiss with my fire magic. I felt fine using it. *Only time will tell, I guess.*

"So, what is this place?" I sank down on a cot close to one of the fireplaces and started loosening the clasps on my boots.

"Some sort of outpost." Botto had already stripped off his outer layer of clothing and was spreading the items out in front of the fire to dry.

"There's a toybox," I pointed out.

Botto shrugged. "These were the coordinates I was given. Smugglers get squirrely when you ask too many questions."

"How long are we here?" Sienna called from across the room. She'd selected the bed farthest from mine and stretched out on top of the blankets while still fully dressed. Her eyes were already closed. It might've been the exhaustion, but it definitely felt like she was blocking out my mere presence.

"Someone is supposed to come for us after dark. Then, I can only assume it's going to be another long night," Botto told her. He sat down across from me and dug around in his backpack until he came up with bottles of water. He handed me one. "Stay hydrated."

I laughed softly. "Do you ever switch out of trainer mode?"

Botto didn't crack a smile. "This is serious, Brie. You haven't lived outside the dome in years. Your body will expend more water trying to stay warm, just trust me." With that, he drained another bottle of water in six gulps.

"Ugh. Not you too. I get it, okay? I did get used to the sun and the trees and bathing suit weather. And, okay, I'll admit I don't remember freedom being quite so cold," I huffed as I unscrewed the cap on my water bottle.

Botto watched me for a minute without speaking. Then, he reached inside his backpack and retrieved a sandwich. "Here. Eat this. You need to keep your energy up."

"I hate you," I said without any real heat and snatched the sandwich from his outstretched hand.

It was nothing special, only ham and cheese on soggy white bread. Regardless, in that moment, it tasted just as good as anything Chef or Sarah had made for me at the palace. The thought of Kai's sister put a sour taste in my mouth, and I could barely swallow the half-chewed food. Aside from sniping back and forth with Sienna, the long walk to this weird little orphanage-style outpost in the middle of nowhere had been quiet, providing me ample time to brood over the princess' betrayal.

She didn't betray you, the empathetic part of me insisted. Sarah was sixteen and had just lost her mother. The poor girl was hurt and wanted justice. I shouldn't begrudge her for it. And yet, I did. Sarah was my friend, and she'd gone behind her own brother's back to have me arrested.

She's young and easily manipulated. While I mostly believed the thought, I knew that it was probably only half true. Sarah was young and much less emotionally attached to me than her brother. To her, family had been everything. While Kai was a source of love and semi-stability, their mother had been her whole heart and an absolute rock in the world. In sum, without the guidance of their mother, Sarah had been an easier target to convince of my guilt for Kai's advisors. They must've thought they won the karmic lottery when Kai gave her the power to make decisions on behalf of his kingdom while he was traveling. But Sarah was strong-willed, and I had a hard time believing anyone could have forced her to do something she was staunchly against.

Why didn't she just come to me first? I wouldn't have blamed her if she still wanted to arrest me after we spoke, but I could have at least explained my side of the story. At least then she would've known I didn't show up to the luau with the intention of murdering the queen. At least then I could've told her my friends had no part in Christina's plan. *Oh, who am I kidding? The word of traitorous fae means nothing to a caster princess,* the cynic in me thought.

Botto cleared his throat loudly, like he'd been trying to draw me out of my own head for a while.

"They can take care of themselves, Brie," he said when I met his gaze.

I narrowed my eyes. "Who?"

He shrugged. "Whoever you're all torn up about leaving behind. Kai is the king. He gave his sister her power, he can take it away again."

"If only it were that easy."

Yes, as king, Kai's power should've been absolute. It was, but it also wasn't. When he made decisions that even a slim majority of his advisors and caster subjects liked, his word was law. Should his views become unpopular to the masses, there were several loopholes that allowed another to take over, if only temporarily. With Sarah already warming her brother's throne in his absence, it wouldn't be that hard for his advisors to prolong her reign. At least until her mother's murderers, including myself, were dealt with.

Was there a real chance this would happen? Honestly, I had no idea. But I at least knew Kai's life was not in danger. People might not agree with his politics, but his subjects adored him as a person. And so did Sarah. Not all my close friends were so lucky. Particularly the non-caster set.

"Do you think Cala's been arrested yet?" I asked Botto.

He took a deep breath, expression impassive. "You want the truth?"

Why did people ask that?

"I guess I already have it," I grumbled, flopping back on the cot. The springs squeaked loudly, and dust flew up from the bedding, making me sneeze several times.

"A warrant was issued for her arrest. Same with Rocko and Everly. And your caster friend, Samira."

As I pounded my fists on the flimsy mattress, I managed to suppress the urge to scream. This was the fear that had plagued me for weeks; that my friends would pay for my mistake.

"What will happen to them?" I asked in a small voice. "I mean, I know what will happen. But is there a chance they'll be released?"

"You mean, will they be released if you turn yourself in?" Botto guessed.

That wasn't where I'd been going with the question, but the thought had crossed my mind.

He shook his head vehemently. "No. Surrendering will do them no good. They haven't been caught yet."

SOPHIE DAVIS

Chapter Four
DOMED CITY OF LOS ANGELES, KINGDOM OF THE AMERICAS
Kai

THE SPELL WAS simple, one that Kai and Sarah used to perform whenever they got in trouble as children to get their stories straight before their mother's interrogation. At the agreed upon time, Kai stood in front of the mirror in his bedroom at Riggs Hotel and pressed his palms flat against the glass. His lips began to move as he murmured the incantation. The glass shimmered and swirled like a reflective whirlpool. Then, the mirror started to vibrate. It was a struggle for Kai to maintain contact with the movement. He chanted louder as he slammed his hands harder against the glass.

Just when he began to wonder if his sister was going to show, Sarah's slim fingers slid between his. An instant later, he was staring into her bright blue eyes. The mirror stopped shaking. Kai dropped the princess' hands and stepped back.

"Hello, Kai."

It was late, nearly midnight in Hawaii, but Sarah still wore a black sheath dress and sheer stockings. Evidently meetings had gone late back in the kingdom.

"How are you, Sarah?" he replied curtly.

She rolled her eyes and slumped into the chair she'd pulled in front of her own mirror. "I'm too tired to pretend with you right now. You summoned me to this meeting so you can yell at me, so let's just get to it."

Some of Kai's anger dried up at the sound of her weary tone. "I didn't ask for this meeting to yell at you."

His little sister leveled him with a skeptical look. "You aren't pissed at me for having your girlfriend arrested?"

"I didn't say that." Kai placed his hands on his hips and shook his head. "Why didn't you talk to me first?"

Sarah averted her gaze. "They said you wouldn't believe me."

Kai had figured her answer would be something to that effect.

"You're too close to the situation to be objective," his sister continued, repeating what was undoubtedly another soundbite from the advisors. "Be honest, Kai. If I'd come to you with the evidence, would you have believed me?"

"Yes," Kai said simply.

Her head whipped around so fast that her blonde bun came loose in the process. "Really? Love hasn't blinded you completely?"

"I would have believed you, because I know Brie was involved with the rebellion. She told me everything, Sarah."

Sharing this revelation with his sister was something he'd debated with Kenoa. Neither guy thought the admission would surprise Sarah. Still, Kenoa had argued that much like any secret, the less people who knew the truth the better. Kai agreed with the notion but trusted his sister, despite recent events.

The princess jumped to her feet and glared daggers at him through the mirror. "She told you she murdered our mother and you're just cool with that?" Sarah snapped.

"Brie did not murder our mother," Kai replied calmly, clasping his hands behind his back.

"She's an active member of the rebellion!" Sarah hollered back.

"Was. Brie was an active member," he corrected her.

Sarah actually stomped her foot, which would've made Kai smile under different circumstances. "Semantics."

"Brie didn't know the rebellion was working with vampires. She had no idea they planned to kill Mom at the luau."

His sister's eyes looked like they were about to pop out of her head. "Are you stupid? There's no way she didn't know, Kai."

Few people dared speak to him in that tone or use those words. Only his baby sister and heir apparent would be so bold. Kai's demeanor turned frosty. "Like there is no way I didn't know that you planned to have my girlfriend arrested?"

The princess paled and lowered her eyes to stare at her feet. "That's different," she mumbled.

His laugh was humorless. "It's hardly different."

Silence fell between the royal siblings. The matter they'd been discussing was so delicate. Normally, when Kai wanted to end a fight with Sarah, he pulled the big brother card. But they'd never fought about anything truly important before. Signing Brie's arrest warrant behind his back was the type of thing that split apart families. He didn't want that to happen, and yet, he wanted to shake the teenager in the mirror until she saw sense.

"She escaped anyway, so what's the big deal?" Sarah asked finally, still refusing to meet Kai's gaze.

He inhaled deeply to give his temper time to simmer down. "You do realize by publicly naming Brie as a murderess, you have made her a very wanted criminal. Now, instead of continuing to investigate what really happened to our mother, all our resources—manpower, time, magic—are going toward hunting parties."

Sarah's head whipped up, fire flashing in her blue irises. "She was there, Kai! Your precious little fae was there! She watched them kill Mom!" Tears poured down her flushed cheeks. "She ruined everything. Now you're king, and I have to marry some stupid prince and spend my days knitting dollies!"

His brow furrowed. His sister did have a flare for the dramatic, but this outburst seemed excessive even for

Sarah.

"Is something else bothering you?" he asked carefully.

Most women Kai had dated over the years wanted only to please him, so he wasn't accustomed to dealing with emotional people. Until Brie. Ever since their first real conversation, it seemed he was always putting his foot in his mouth. As a result, Kai had quickly learned that not every argument was about the obvious.

"Ugh!" Sarah let out a guttural snarl as she stomped her foot again. "You don't get it! You don't know what it's like to be me, Kai. I'm not free. You wouldn't understand."

"So this is about something else besides Mom." He nodded slowly and racked his brain in case his sister made him guess.

Sarah let out another annoyed scream, this one so high pitched that the glass mirror actually cracked—and, as Kai realized too late, the spell along with it. The last image he saw of his sister was her shaking shoulders as she sobbed openly into her hands. Kai tried calling her using technology instead of magic, but her phone went straight to voicemail. He knew if he called the palace someone would bring her the phone. He also knew his sister wouldn't have turned off her cell unless she was avoiding him.

Resigned to the fact that not only had nothing between him and his sister been resolved but instead become more confusing, Kai poured himself a whiskey and carried the drink into Brie's room. It had been his ritual—if doing something three times constituted a ritual—since Brie's arrest. All her clothes still hung in the closet. He ran his fingertips over the silky fabrics and smiled. The scent of her perfume clung to the dresses she'd worn while in L.A. Kai leaned closer to the red jumpsuit Sarah had lent Brie for the airship ride from Hawaii. The color was made for Brie, he decided, like a public declaration of her inner strength.

Gaia, I wish I could talk to her, he thought as buried his face in Brie's laundry.

There *were* ways to get in touch, spells to cast as he'd done with the mirror to talk to Sarah. He could use an astral projection spell to send his consciousness to Brie's location. His physical body, however, would remain in L.A. in a meditative state, which was dangerous. If someone found him and figured out what he was doing, Kai's astral location could be traced. If that happened, he would lead an army straight to Brie's doorstep.

There's one thing I can do, he told himself. It wouldn't satisfy his own need to know the woman he loved was safe, but at least she would know that he was thinking about her.

Kai took his drink over to Brie's bed and sat against the pillows piled near the headboard. He took a long swallow of whiskey to bolster his confidence. Sending Brie a message wasn't as risky as an actual conversation. Still, he was under heavy scrutiny, and any magic use of his would probably be traced. He needed to choose his words carefully.

The king composed at least a dozen messages in his head while he finished his nightcap. When he finally removed the chunky metal watch from his wrist and flipped it over, the three words he magically inscribed were simple: I love you.

Those were the words Brie would read on the inside of her bangle. Without her knowing, he'd charmed it with a tracking spell and magical note passing capabilities right after he'd first learned of her involvement with the rebellion. At the time, Kai had wanted to keep an eye on her movements—an act that would surely piss her off once she learned of it. The bangle was how he'd found her in Sienna's apartment the first time she'd succumbed to the magical poisoning. He wasn't sure whether the tracking spell was strong enough to locate her now that she was outside the dome, but the message function should still work. All he needed was for Brie to look at the bangle.

That night, Kai fell asleep in Brie's room. With his watch clutched in one hand, he waited on a reply that never came.

That was where Kenoa found the king the next morning with one of Brie's t-shirts balled beneath his head like a pillow. Under different circumstances, the water fae would have teased Kai about his pathetic mooning behavior. But one look at the hard set of Kenoa's jaw, and Kai knew his best friend was in no joking mood.

He sat up in the bed, suddenly very awake. "What?" he demanded. "Did they find Brie? Is she okay?"

"Brie's fine." Kenoa reconsidered. "Well, as far as I know. She's still in the wind. No updates on that front. The problem is the Domed City of Austin. Fae and shifters marched on the palace in the middle of the night. They've taken the royal family hostage."

Hearing news like that so early in the morning was enough to turn Kai's stomach. He wished it came as more of a shock. After his mother's assassination and the brief crashing of the dome, Kai had known it was only a matter of time until the rebellion struck again. He'd had a feeling they'd hit another kingdom, one that wasn't on the same high alert as Hawaii.

Swinging his legs over the side of the bed, Kai slumped with his elbows on his knees and rubbed his eyes. "Have they been hurt? Has the rebellion made demands?"

"The king and queen are alive. No word on the king's sisters. As for demands," Kenoa sighed heavily, "we're about to find out. King Ronald has requested your presence at Calypso Palace to be there when he talks to the rebels."

Kai ran a hand through his hair and wracked his brain for information. "The Texas queen is related to Ronald, if I remember correctly?"

"By marriage. She's Queen Katherine's much younger half-sister," Kenoa reminded him.

Kai slid from the bed and started toward the bathroom. He caught sight of his reflection in the mirror and winced. His dark hair was sticking up and out from his head like porcupine quills, except for the flat patch above his left ear where his head had rested against the makeshift pillow. The heavy bags under his eyes served to enhance the red splotches on his cheeks.

Some king you are, he thought as he passed by.

"Do you want to tell me what happened in your bedroom?" Kenoa called after him. "A small hurricane come through in the night?"

Kai paused in front of the bathroom door and glanced back over his shoulder. "My sister."

Kenoa grinned. "Sounds like Sarah. I'll have someone clean up the mess."

"Don't worry about the mirror. I need you to do something else for me."

"Your sister?" Kenoa guessed.

Kai nodded gravely. "Find someone you trust, someone who can get her out of Hawaii if need be. I don't want to wake up tomorrow to you telling me she is the rebel's newest hostage. Secure Sarah."

CHAPTER FIVE

FREELANDS OF THE AMERICAS

Brie

AS DAY FADED into night with no communication from the outside world, we took turns keeping watch. The temperature inside the cabin dipped considerably once the sun set. It was uncomfortable as hell, but we didn't freeze between the fires and blankets.

I woke from my nap sometime around midnight. Once my eyes adjusted to the dim lighting, I found Botto sitting beside the door, dozing in and out of consciousness. Sienna was asleep but still fully clothed, of bed and padded over to my trainer on bare feet.

"Hey, go lay down." I placed a hand on his shoulder. Botto blinked up at me, eyes slightly unfocused. "I'm awake now. Your turn to sleep."

He stood and stretched, joints cracking as his spine realigned. "How ya feeling?" he asked around a yawn.

"Good," I replied, a little surprised to realize it was true. My muscles were still a little sore from our snowy hike, but it felt like recovery after a solid workout and nothing I couldn't handle. The pounding in my head was gone, as was the crippling nausea. It was the best I'd felt since we'd left Hawaii.

"Wake me up when our friends arrive." With that, Botto moved to a cot near a fireplace and promptly passed out.

Though I moved to the spot he'd vacated, I was too restless to sit, too anxious over our next move. I needed to refuel. My backpack had enough food for one week if I rationed. After grabbing an apple, I dug around for a bottle of water. Most of the stuff in my bag was warm from sitting so close to the fire, so I was caught off-guard when my fingers brushed something cold.

The bangle from Kai, I thought, pulling it from the bag. The gold bracelet was even more dazzling in the firelight. The metal warmed beneath my fingers, and then it began to glow. I dropped the shining hoop as if it had singed my hand. It landed on the ground with a soft thud, still radiating. I looked around the room like I might find someone standing there who could confirm that I wasn't seeing things. Everyone else was still asleep.

Cautiously, I picked up the bangle with two fingers. *It's*

enchanted, I realized. My heart skipped a beat. This was so not good. Had an enemy in LA managed to track me with it? I needed to figure out the spell immediately. Then I needed to figure out how to break it. With a deep breath, I placed the glowing bangle in my other palm. The magic was palpable, which meant a very powerful caster was the culprit. *Why didn't I notice this before?* I wondered.

I considered taking it out to the woods and burying it. Though that wouldn't mask my location, I could buy time by leaving it behind. Just as I eyed my boots sitting by the fireplace, I noticed words scrawled on the inside of the bracelet: I love you.

My breath caught. *Kai.* He'd placed a spell on my bangle. *You should've known. That's the only way he could've found you at Sienna's apartment.* Did that mean he knew where we were? I ran the tip of my finger over the three words. *I love you, too,* I thought. The glow faded, as did Kai's message. Clasping the bracelet around my wrist, I fought back the tears stinging my eyes.

The past few days had been so overwhelming, my mind had blocked out everything besides our escape. Now that we were in the Freelands and relatively safe, I couldn't deny the fact that leaving Kai had created a fissure in my heart. My chest ached at the thought of a future that didn't include him. For a minute, I thought I might have a panic attack.

Will I ever see him again?

We hadn't even said a proper goodbye. There was no last kiss, no promise that we would find our way back to each other. Instead, I'd been dragged away from him by a crew sent by Sarah with an arrest warrant. That thought made my heart crumble impossibly further. I loved Sarah. I'd even allowed myself to believe that we were building a sisterly relationship.

A faint sound drew my thoughts back to the present situation. The noise was dim, like the popping and crackling of a fire. Except, there was no wood in the fireplace; the flames were magical and silent.

Should I wake Botto and Sienna? I wondered. Were the friendlies here to take us to our next location? There was only way to find out if it was a friend or foe. As I hurried over to put on my boots and jacket, another cracking noise rang out in the still cabin. My muscles tensed. We definitely had company. Instead of taking chances, I shook Botto awake.

"What? What's going on?" he asked groggily.

My finger flew to my lips in a shush motion. I didn't whisper a reply until he signaled that he comprehended the gesture by mimicking it. "Someone's here."

Botto rolled out of bed and started getting dressed. I headed over to Sienna, but she was already awake and sitting up in bed. She rubbed sleep from her eyes.

"I'm ready," she said so softly that I shouldn't have been able to hear her. The words carried on a small gust of wind that ruffled my hair.

The three of us grabbed our packs and huddled in the middle of the cabin. Without hesitation, I moved beside Botto so that Sienna was behind us both.

"What's the plan?" I asked quietly.

Botto's gaze panned the room as he spoked in a voice just above a whisper. "Let's hope that it's just our next contact out there. Still, we need to be prepared to run."

He nodded toward the door. "This place isn't defendable. If we stay, we're trapped."

As I opened my mouth to speak, the windows exploded. Shards of glass rained down on us. Botto swore loudly.

No longer worried about the volume of his voice, he bellowed, "Go!" When he pushed me toward the door, it took two steps to catch my own balance and rush forward. Sienna conjured a gust of wind so powerful that the door flew off its hinges.

Cold air filled the cabin as the three of us rushed to the exit. We didn't get far. Three pale faces were waiting for us outside. A dark-haired woman stepped forward, dressed in a skintight white-and-gray camouflage getup. Sharp fangs flashed when she smiled.

"Maybrie Hawkins," she said in a melodic voice.

Botto stepped in front of me again, and even Sienna moved so that our shoulders were touching. "I suggest you all go on your way," my trainer growled in a guttural voice.

The woman laughed. "Calm down, hybrid." Her dark gaze shifted to me, and I inhaled sharply. There was something about her, something familiar. "We're here for you, darling. Come with us, and your friends can go free."

Flames bursting from my fingers, I shook my head. "Not a chance. Do you really want to dance with a fire fae?"

The two other vamps, both male, moved from the shadows to flank the woman. Botto let out a primal yell, and the change was almost instantaneous. One second, he was a man. The next, a giant bear stood on all fours in his place. The jarring growl that followed echoed in the frozen woods.

"There is no reason for bloodshed," the woman said calmly. She extended her arm and waved me over. "Come with me, darling. You can't outrun—" Her words were cut short by an arrow that lodged on the right side of her chest. It wasn't a kill shot, but the woman crumpled to the ground.

My head whipped around, searching for the shooter. A girl about my age stood on top of the cabin with a crossbow. A second shifter flashed through the woods to my right. Then, I saw the pack of wolves speeding toward us.

Acting on impulse, I let my years of training take over fully. The other two vampires hadn't moved. I hurled two fireballs, one for each bloodsucker. The recipients were too fast for me, and they easily dodged my assault.

Botto, in were-bear form, charged after the vampire with bleached blond hair. I sent more fireballs at the other one but only managed to hit trees. The crossbow wielder fired one arrow after another, the projectiles raining down on all of us.

"Kill the vamp woman!" Sienna yelled. "Light her up, Brie."

The ringleader struggled to her knees and groaned as she pulled the arrow from her chest. Our eyes met. Her pale face was expressionless. *Why does she look so familiar? I wondered. Do I know her?*

"Brie! Take her out!" Sienna demanded.

Another arrow struck the vampire, this time in her shoulder. Her body jerked violently, yet she managed to stay on her knees. The crossbow girl fired again as the woman rose to her feet. Our eyes locked for a brief instant. Then, in a blur of motion, the vampire disappeared.

"What's wrong with you?" Sienna demanded, stomping her foot like a child throwing a tantrum.

"I don't know," I admitted. It wasn't like I hadn't killed a vampire before. I didn't have qualms about choosing myself and my people over the life of an enemy. Why had I hesitated?

"She could've killed us," Sienna scoffed. White puffs of air came from her nose and mouth as she huffed indignantly. "You get that, right?"

"Yeah, I get it," I snapped.

Sienna gestured wildly. "Then why didn't you kill her?"

"I don't know," I growled. "I'm sorry, okay? It wasn't some convoluted way of spiting you or whatever you think. I messed up. But…maybe it's for the best. Leaving a trail of bodies behind us is a surefire way to get caught." The excuse was lame but still true.

"Try telling them that." With one gloved hand, Sienna pointed to the pack of wolves that were in the process of tearing the two vampire lackies limb from limb.

The crossbow wielding shifter leapt from the roof and landed in the snow beside me with a soft thud.

"You two plan on fighting the whole way to Revival?" the shifter asked lazily. She holstered the bow over one shoulder in a sling beside the one for arrows.

"They've been arguing since L.A.," Botto answered from the tree line, once again in human form. Blood was smeared from the corner of his mouth down his chin, and one of his eyes was swelling rapidly.

Ignoring his snide tone, I focused on our new friend.

"What's Revival?"

"It's a shifter colony that's about ninety miles from here," she informed me. "We—"

"Livie!" a deep voice interjected. "Information is on a need to know basis."

One of the wolves had shifted back and fallen in step with Botto.

"I didn't tell them which direction," Livie defended herself, rolling big brown eyes. "And everyone looking for them knows about Revival, so it's not a big deal."

Everyone looking for us might have heard of the shifter colony, but I was utterly clueless. "Why are you taking us to a place where people will think to look?" I demanded. "That's asinine."

Livie, Botto, and the wolf exchanged meaningful looks, but it was Sienna who answered me. "Even vamps won't get anywhere near Revival. Not without an engraved invitation from the Dresden clan."

At the risk of sounding just as naïve as I was, I asked, "And who is the Dresden clan, exactly?"

"It's the first family of crime in the Freelands," Botto said gravely.

I blinked as if that would help me make sense of his reply. It didn't. The Freelands were no man's land. There was no police force, no army, and no law. That made it pretty easy for criminals to thrive. Most societies like Fae Canyon kept to themselves, only trading with other groups when necessary. Aside from the abductions at the hands of cowboy vampires like those that had taken me, there weren't a lot of crimes against people. Theft and vagrancy, sure, but no personal harm.

"What does that even mean?" I asked my trainer.

Botto's face scrunched up as he considered my question. "You'll see soon enough."

"All you need to know for now is that they are really excited to meet you." The wolf strode forward on two human legs clad only in camo pants and boots, though he didn't seem cold at all. "I'm Buck, Alpha of the White Plains wolves."

"Brie," I replied, "but I guess you already know that."

We shook hands, and then he turned and repeated the introduction with Sienna.

"Let's get on the road," he declared when the formalities were done. "I want to be in Revival by sunrise."

"She said it was ninety miles. Are we walking?" Sienna demanded, clearly annoyed.

Buck chuckled. "Only part of the way."

It turned out we were only trekking the first leg. Buck, Livie, and a third wolf called Macon walked on two legs with Sienna, Botto, and me. The rest of the White Plains pack remained in animal form and fanned out around us like a protective guard. Livie had a lot of questions about life beneath the dome. Like, a *lot* of questions. She didn't seem envious of the life I'd experienced so much as baffled by the luxuries I'd come to take for granted.

"You slept inside every night? What about the shifters?" she asked at one point. "They do the same?"

"Yep, we were all indoors," I huffed. The wind had picked up, and we were walking right into the gusts, making the trek slower and more exhausting.

"Don't they need fresh air?" Livie pressed.

"That's enough, Liv," Buck said kindly but firmly.

Neither had said so, but I was pretty sure the two wolves were father and daughter. They had the same sharp features and athletic build, though Livie's skin was much paler and less weathered, like maybe she didn't spend as much time outside as the Alpha.

"They still go outside. They just don't sleep out there," I replied. Though I lowered my voice, it was a pointless gesture since the wolves twenty yards in any direction could hear our conversation.

"I read that you have a job," Macon chimed in.

"*You* have a job, Macon," Buck reminded him.

"Yeah, but Brie serves people food at a restaurant," Livie added.

"How do you know about Pele's?" I asked uneasily.

"Caster Gossip," Livie and Macon replied in unison.

If my face hadn't been frozen from the frigid temperatures, I might've smiled. Cala loved Caster Gossip. For her, there was no greater pleasure than reading the scandalous details of someone else's life. Personally, I thought she also liked the validation that came from the fact a lot of the stories on the site were only slight less crazy than Cala's real-life escapades.

Less inclined to make small talk after the admission they read the tabloid that loved to follow me around, I retreated into my own head. Livie and Macon shifted their focus to Sienna and started peppering her with questions.

Between the wind and the cold, I had very little sense of how much time was passing. I thought Buck might've been leading us in circles to ensure we weren't being followed, but it was hard to be sure since the blowing snow obscured our footprints as fast as we made them. At one point, visibility became so bad that I couldn't see my own hand unless it was wiping ice from my eyes. Botto pulled a rope from his backpack, and we each held onto a section to keep from getting separated.

There were some tense moments once we reached the spot where the wolves had stashed our transportation for the next leg of the journey. Buck sent the pack in first to make sure there wasn't anyone waiting to welcome us with an ambush. While we were all good on that front, there was evidence someone had been there recently; they'd slashed the tires of nearly all the four-wheelers Buck had hidden beneath white tarps.

"How worried should we be?" Botto asked.

"Could just be vandals," Buck replied, running a hand over dark, military-style hair. "I don't want to take chances, though. Let's move." The Alpha pointed to me and then Sienna. "Which one of you wants to drive?"

"You're kidding, right?" Sienna's lip curled into a snarl.

I glared at her. "It's fine. I'll drive."

"Do you even know how to drive?" Sienna demanded.

Actually, I didn't. Fae, even wealthy fae, in the Hawaiian Kingdom weren't permitted to drive. And there had never been cause for me to learn in Fae Canyon; we didn't have vehicles other than a couple of emergency junkers.

"Sienna is driving," Botto announced, making the executive decision and saving me the embarrassment of admitting I'd never operated a vehicle of any sort. The were-bear leveled a pointed glance in my direction. "Play nice, Brie."

"Fine. What about the rest of you?" I asked, looking

around as though more drivable four-wheelers would miraculously appear.

"We'll run with the pack," Botto told me.

He moved closer on the pretense of helping Sienna and me get ourselves and the backpacks arranged on the snow mobile. I felt his large hand slip inside my coat pocket, his breath warm against my cheek as he leaned over my shoulder.

"No matter what happens, do not stop," he muttered in my ear. "That's an order."

"You're not really my trainer anymore," I tried to joke around the lump in my throat. "I don't think you're in a position to give me orders."

He didn't crack a smile. "When you reach the gates of Revival, tell them that Delancey is expecting you. Do not give your name. If the guards give you trouble, show them what's in your pocket."

"Okay," I said uneasily, unsure of what Botto had tucked in my pocket but knowing better than to pull it out and look. "But, I mean, everything's going to be fine, right? I'm sure it was vandals, like Buck said."

Botto's gaze shifted to Sienna, who gave him a subtle head nod in response.

"Promise me, Brie," he demanded. "No matter what, you two keep going."

I'd left too many people behind already, I didn't want Botto's name added to that list. Decision made, I levelled him with a stare. "Only if you promise that you'll see me in Revival."

"I promise," he said without missing a beat.

Guess we're both bad liars.

Chapter Six

Kai

"I DON'T CARE what they want. They have my sister."
The Californian queen paced back and forth in the throne
room. Her husband sat atop his gaudy gold chair watching
her.

Iolani Palace did have a throne room, and his mother
had used it on occasion for meetings with important
dignitaries. Feeling like an imposter, Kai had never sat
upon the royal chair himself. By comparison, King
Ronald seemed to use the throne room at Calypso Palace

for everything, including, it seemed, a pre-meeting meeting with his own wife, Kai, and Kenoa.

"*Half*-sister," Ronald corrected, sounding bored. "Georgina is your half-sister."

The queen stopped pacing long enough to glare up at her husband. Despite the dire circumstances, she'd taken care to select a black and white striped pants suit that flattered her frame. Her dyed blonde hair was smoothed back in a neat bun, showing off the half-inch diamond studs weighing down her earlobes. She looked as regal as Kai had ever seen her, until her eyes flashed annoyance.

Kai and Kenoa exchanged glances. The queen rarely showed emotion. She *never* shared her opinion when it contradicted her husband's, especially not in front of foreign royals and their advisors.

Katherine placed her hands on her hips and glared up at her husband in challenge. "Georgina might be my half-sister," she began coolly. "But at least she's fully royal. A *full* caster." The queen's voice increased in pitch with each word. "That's more than I can say for your bastard hybrids running around this dome."

A muscle in Kai's neck twitched. He didn't care about Ronald and Katherine's marital problems, but he did take offense to the queen's callous tone. His children with Brie would be hybrids: half caster and half fae. Personally, Kai thought children in that situation would get the best of all worlds. They'd have the constitution to survive the cold without suffering from the same depletion issues as full-blooded casters. They had the widest range of magical powers, to boot.

"Those people are terrorists," Ronald said flatly.

"Terrorists that have my sister!" Katherine threw her hands up. "My baby sister."

King Ronald rubbed his temples with the thumb and forefinger of his left hand. "Half-sister, Katherine. Don't make me remind you again."

"Ronald," Kai said the other king's name sharply as he stepped between the throne and Queen Katherine. He thought he heard Kenoa groan but ignored his friend. "Let us save all this animosity for the rebels, shall we?"

The tension in the room ratcheted up several notches. King Ronald sat up straighter in his shiny gold chair, nostrils flaring. Kai refused to look away. He didn't care that he was a foreign king in a foreign land with little more privilege and freedom than the fae and shifters populating Calypso Palace's dungeon.

One of the doors at the back behind King Ronald's throne opened quietly, and someone cleared their throat. Neither king wanted to be the first to look away, which left Queen Katherine the task of addressing the newcomer.

"What is it, Leonardo?" she demanded.

"I apologize, Your Majesties. The rebels are here."

Egos flew out the window as everyone turned to look at King Ronald's top aid.

"Here? Where?" Ronald sputtered, glancing around the throne room like he expected to find rebellion leaders hiding behind one of the ceremonial flags lining the walls.

"In your private office, Your Majesty." Leonardo kept his eyes downcast while he spoke.

"In my office?" King Ronald's eyes went wide with

outrage. Kai wondered if the older monarch might be on the verge of a having a stroke. "Guards!"

The doors at the front of the throne room burst open, and the California royal guard rushed inside.

"Sir, they aren't physically here," Leonard said quickly.

King Ronald held up his hand and gestured for the guards to lower their weapons. "Explain," he demanded of his aid.

Kai didn't have the patience for this conversation. "Magic, Ronald. They obviously used a projection spell."

"Yes, exactly." Leonard flashed Kai an appreciative smile. "The insurgents request an audience with you at your earliest convenience."

"I'm sure those were exactly the words they used," Kenoa mumbled under his breath.

With a shooing gesture from King Ronald, the royal guard retreated into the hallway. Everyone else followed Leonardo in the opposite direction.

Three translucent forms were waiting in King Ronald's private office. All the shifters were dressed in camo suits and heavy snow boots. Not one of them looked happy.

"Where's my sister, you barbarians?" Queen Katherine shouted, lunging for the trio of shifters. Without their actual bodies to stop her, she collapsed in a heap between the shifters' feet. Fists balled tightly, she pounded the carpet and let out an inhuman screech. "I want to see my fucking sister!"

Kai and Kenoa each grabbed one of the queen's arms and helped her to her feet. When her knees buckled again, they lead her over to a leather couch along one wall. Katherine sobbed openly. Through the cries, she mumbled, "Georgina, please be alive."

King Ronald barely acknowledged his bereft wife as he strode over to sit behind his desk. It was a power move meant to show the shifters they weren't important enough to stand for. What Kai knew and Ronald didn't understand was that it was only an insult to people used to respect. Few fae or shifters were used to civil treatment from casters, so the slight went unnoticed.

"What is it you want?" King Ronald asked the shifters, his tone bored.

"Nothing." The shortest of the rebels, a man in his mid-twenties, stepped toward Ronald's desk. "We didn't come to make demands."

Kai and Kenoa exchanged looks. They both knew this was not a good sign.

"Then why did you come?" One of Ronald's bushy eyebrows winged upward. "Why bother?"

"We came to warn you," the man replied. Though he held no weapons, and his tone was mild, an ominous chill ran through Kai. The shifter's gaze panned the room as he propped his hands on his hips. "Overpowering Austin was like taking magic from a caster kid. We can and will do the same anywhere we choose—in L.A., New York, Chicago."

"Why are you telling us your plans?" Kai interjected, though he was certain he already knew the answer.

"So you can live in fear, just as we have for so long. Fear of someone coming into your home and tearing apart your families—just like we have for so long. Tonight, when you're comfortably lying in your feather beds, sipping tea prepared for you by your fae and shifter servants, you'll know you're on borrowed time. When you're eating lavish meals prepared in the formal dining room of your palace, you'll wonder if this one will be your last."

The lone female cleared her throat. With an icy smile on her thin lips, she spoke in a flat voice. "The time of the casters is nearing an end. Just like the humans before you, you will all be nothing more than a footnote in history."

"What have you done with my sister?" Katherine screamed back at the woman.

As much as Kai wanted to know the answer, he realized it would probably be best if the queen left beforehand.

The shifter's smile became more genuine and all the scarier because of it. "I think you mean caster 0002. She is alive." The woman shrugged her thin shoulders. "At least, for now. I can't say what will happen after her trial."

"Trial?" King Ronald scoffed. "For what crimes?"

Of course, Kai already knew the charges the rebellion would levy against the Austin royals. Georgina and her husband would be tried for torture, kidnapping, false imprisonment, murder...and those were just the beginning. He knew because it was what happened in the last fae uprising, when rebels marched on the Painted Desert Palace in the Domed City of Santa Fe.

"Don't worry," the short shifter drawled, a vengeful gleam in his eye. "There will be a formal reading of the charges at the start of the trial, which will be televised." He winked at Queen Katherine. "Thought you might appreciate that touch."

The queen let out a primal scream. Kai had no doubt that if the shifters had been more than magically projected images, Katherine would have torn them limb from limb on the spot. The frosty female shifter gave a deep, mocking curtsy.

"Sleep well, Your Majesties," she said. With that, all three visages vanished into thin air.

****

Kai spent most of the morning at Calypso Palace with King Ronald, meeting with the other monarchs of the Americas using the same sort of projection spell that the shifters had employed. Chief among most of the royals' concerns was perimeter security. Most cities already had strict protocols for entering and exiting the domes, so it was just a matter of increasing the number of guards. Oahu was one of the exceptions, however. Being an island that was surrounded by a frozen ocean, there wasn't a lot of worry about fae and shifters crossing the dome boundaries on foot in either direction. For Kai, the biggest fear was the rebels who were already beneath the dome rising up against the casters—namely, his sister.

There was a lot of talk about the punishments that would befall rebels once the casters doused the sparks of this uprising, but not one monarch posed the most important question: What if we lose? The possibility was unfathomable to Kai's fellow rulers. Not long ago, the idea would've been just as farfetched for Kai. But that was before his mother was murdered in their own home. Since then, Kai wholeheartedly believed there was a chance that the rebellion might triumph. The fact other royals were dismissing it as a possibility made it all the more viable; underestimating an opponent as treacherous as the rebellion was dangerous. When he finally did voice the risk of a successful overthrow, no one else would even entertain the notion.

"They think what happened in Austin can't happen in their cities," Kai lamented to Kenoa over lunch that afternoon. They were back at the hotel after the meeting, and Kai's frustration spilled forth freely with his best friend.

The water fae watched him closely, noting the ever-deepening creases in Kai's forehead. "Based on what, exactly? A false sense of safety that stems from entitlement?" Kenoa asked.

He was always honest when Kai asked for his opinion on political matters, but the fae rarely showed open disdain for casters, even royal casters. The fact he was doing so now only bolstered Kai's belief that war was inevitable.

"Yeah, basically," he told his best friend, running one hand through his dark hair as he loosened the knot on his tie with the other. "They brought up Santa Fe."

Kenoa washed down a mouthful of bacon cheeseburger with a swig of soda. "Santa Fe was different. Only fae rebelled. A lot of shifters fought and died for the royal family. Vamps didn't even come into play. And, if I'm remembering our history lessons right, calling it a win for either side is a stretch. The rebels were defeated, but the city was destroyed, the royal family executed, and the dome came down."

"There also weren't subsequent uprisings in other

cities," Kai pointed out. He reached for a fry on his plate. Instead of eating it, he just twirled the crispy potato in a bowl of mustard.

"I see." Kenoa wiped his mouth with a cloth napkin. "Your counterparts are assuming the Austin royal army will quash the rebels."

"Pretty much." Kai submerged the fry beneath the surface of the yellow pool and then wiped mustard from his fingers. "You don't even want to hear what Ronald said when I suggested we send aid to Austin. It's like the logic of helping to destroy the rebels before they reach our kingdoms is totally lost on him."

Kenoa offered him a wry smile. "I can imagine. The king doesn't seem particularly fond of logic. Or strategy. Or anything other than his whims."

"How did things go on your end?" While Kai had spent the morning in the unproductive meeting, he'd tasked Kenoa with a much more meaningful job.

The water fae sighed. "I wish I had better news on that front. I have some leads on smugglers willing to transport human cargo out of Hawaii, but nothing definitive yet."

"Let me guess," Kai interjected. "That kindness doesn't extend to casters?"

"It doesn't," Kenoa confirmed. "Particularly not your sister. It seems by signing Brie's arrest warrant, Sarah may have also signed her own death warrant. A lot of the smugglers we'd heard of knew either Brie or Tanner. They aren't going to help us, regardless of how much you offer."

Kai leaned back in his chair and blew out a long breath. Admittedly, he'd thought getting Sarah off Oahu would be challenging. Despite that, he had not anticipated this hurdle. What did you offer a person whose loyalty wasn't for sale?

"Look, I'm not saying all hope is lost. I'm working on it. But I won't lie to you." Kenoa shook his head sadly. "It's going to be extremely tricky."

I'm completely useless, Kai thought. He'd been helpless to do anything for Brie except stand aside and let her go. Now there was nothing he could do to help his baby sister. *No, not nothing. There's always something that can be done. What's the saying, where there's a will there's a way?* Sheer willpower it would have to be, Kai decided. Because he wouldn't lose another person he loved. He was a king. It was time to start acting like one.

"I do have some other news you might want to hear," Kenoa hedged, bringing Kai out of his maudlin thoughts.

"Good or bad?"

"You'll have to be the judge."

Kai sat up straighter, curiosity piqued. "What is it?"

"While I was out making discreet inquires on your behalf, I received a message for you." Kenoa's expression remained annoyingly blank. "More like a request, I guess. For a face-to-face meeting."

Kai's stomach turned over. "From who?" he demanded.

"For the record, I think this is a really bad idea," Kenoa hedged. He looked his friend directly in the eye before answering. "Illion Hawkins. Brie's little brother."

Kai took a full minute to digest the new information. Illion Hawkins, Brie's little brother, wanted to meet with him. He wasn't sure how he felt about that.

"Why?" he asked Kenoa simply.

The water fae shrugged. "No clue. Honestly, I didn't want to tell you. I don't want you doing something stupid. Meeting with Illion Hawkins is too risky, Kai."

Several minutes of tense silence followed.

"It's a risk I'm willing to take," Kai said finally. He smiled at his best and oldest friend. His only real friend. "You understand why I have to do this, right Ken?"

Kenoa gave as small nod of agreement. "I'll get word to Illion. I'll tell him the both of us will meet with him."

It was pointless to argue, Kai knew that. Not that he would have. Kenoa wasn't just his best friend—he was the king's protector. And Kai always felt better with the water fae by his side. Plus, everything with his sister had taught him just how dangerous teenagers with power could be.

"Thank you, Kenoa. For everything." He reached over and placed a hand on the water fae's arm. "Honestly, I don't know what I'd do without you."

Kenoa smirked. "Let's hope this meeting doesn't make it so you have to find out."

CHAPTER SEVEN

FREELANDS OF THE AMERICAS

Brie

"HEY!" I SHOUTED in Sienna's ear to be heard over the collective noise of the wind and the roar of the four-wheeler. "When's the last time you saw the pack?"

My old friend flinched as though the sound of my voice grated her nerves. Which was probably the case. "Calm down. They're out there."

"Have you seen them, though?" I insisted. Peering over first one shoulder and then the other, all I could see was blowing snow in all directions.

"I smell them," Sienna called back to me. "You need to calm the hell down. You're making me anxious."

Pursing my lips, I fought the urge to say something that might cause Sienna to toss me from the snowmobile. We'd been driving for hours, and the snowy landscape finally started to brighten with the early rays of morning.

Ninety miles, my ass. By my estimation, it had been at least thirty minutes since I last saw hide or hair of a wolf, and even longer since I'd seen Botto's bear form. Maybe I was worrying for no reason, but the whole goodbye scene at the stash site had left me with a pit in my stomach.

Something whizzed past my ear, making me jump in my seat. Sienna swerved sharply to the left in response. As it turned out, the maneuver saved our lives. An orange blur shot across the gray backdrop and landed several feet to our right, exploding into a great ball of flame. The next whizzing streak flew over our heads and detonated directly in our path. Sienna yanked hard on the handlebars. The four-wheeler swung back right so hard that two of the tires left the ground. Then, we were airborne.

In the fighting pits, many opponents had sent me flying through the air. This time was different from those experiences, slower somehow. It felt like every second stretched for minutes as I tumbled high above the ground. Gravity inevitably took over, and my shoulder slammed into the frozen earth. My ears rang from the impact and the exploding fireballs that rained from every direction. Instinct had me on my feet in no time, head swiveling from side to side. Where was the four-wheeler?

Where was Sienna? I caught a flash of movement as two shapes barreled toward me from the darkness.

Wolves, I thought with only a measure of relief. It instantly turned to panic when the duo didn't slow as they neared.

"Brie! Run!"

Sienna didn't have to tell me twice. I followed the sound of her scream since I couldn't actually see her. With all the snow and smoke and howls, I was too disoriented to know which way was up. I felt a nudge on the back of my knees and nearly fired off a blast in Buck's wolf face before realizing it was him.

"What's happening? Who's attacking us?" I demanded.

Buck shifted to human, and I noticed the blood smeared across half of his face. "You need to run. Get as far from here as possible. We'll keep them off you as long as we can."

"What?" I pleaded. "No! Who are they?"

A high-pitched squeal pierced the air, followed by a thundering roar that I knew belonged to Botto.

"Go!" Buck shouted.

"I don't even know where I am!" I snapped. *Don't panic. You've been in stressful situations before. You can do this.*

"Follow me!" Buck was on all fours an instant later. He shot forward like a dart. I hesitated. *Botto. Sienna. I can't leave them.* But Botto had made me promise that I would keep going no matter what happened. He'd known an attack was likely when extracting the promise from me, I was sure of it.

Something smacked me hard in the back of the head. *Shit.*

"What's wrong with you?" Sienna grabbed my arm roughly, forcing me into motion. "Do you have any survival instincts?"

"Huh?" I rubbed the back of my head.

"You were just standing there with a dumb look on your face. Do you want them to catch you?" she panted. Our jog turned into a run.

I yanked my arm free of her grip but maintained pace with her. "Where's Botto?"

"No idea."

"Who are they?" I demanded.

"People who want to capture you," Sienna replied. The tone suggested she'd rolled her eyes while answering, even though I couldn't see her face.

Buck's black tail was fading in front of us, and I kicked up the pace another notch. Though my endurance training helped, sucking in the cold winter air wasn't something I was accustomed to. My chest heaved with each labored breath. "What…people?" I wheezed.

"Save your breath. We don't—"

A mountain lion came out of nowhere, teeth bared and claws out. He went for Sienna's ankles and managed to knock her legs out from under her. Fire poured forth from my palms without conscious thought. The smell of burnt hair filled my nostrils before I realized what I was doing. The screeching roar in response to my attack filled the still night, making me wince.

Sienna rolled away from the hurt shifter and onto her feet in one fluid motion. Ice pellets littered the ground around us. We both took off. The bullets followed us, narrowly missing their marks. I stumbled on the uneven terrain but managed to stay on my feet. My only goal was to keep moving.

Then, the chorus of whistling projectiles ceased. The only noises I heard were the pounding of my heart and the crunching of snow and leaves beneath my boots. Still, I didn't slow until Sienna did. When we stopped to catch our breaths, I looked around the us at the odd frozen trees.

Where are we? Is that a house up there?

"Do you still have the medallion?" Sienna demanded, breaking the silence.

"What medallion?" I asked uneasily.

"The one Botto gave you." She pointed to my coat. "In there."

"Oh, right." Reaching into the pocket, I felt the small package left by my trainer. "Yeah, it's here. Why? Are we close?"

Sienna eyed me like I was a moron. "How do you think we escaped the firing squad?"

Honestly, I hadn't given it a whole lot of thought yet. "Luck?" I replied dryly.

She scoffed. "We're in Dresden territory now."

"Is that supposed to make me feel safe?"

Sienna shook her head. "No. But at least they'll do us the courtesy of a face-to-face meeting before they try to kill us, if that helps."

Yeah, I definitely didn't feel safer.

"What about Botto and the wolves?" I asked. "Will the Dresdens send help for them?"

She laughed humorlessly. "No. They're not exactly the heroic, white knight types."

I stopped in my tracks and whirled back in the direction we'd come. "We need to go back. We can't leave them to whoever that was chasing us."

"No," Sienna said firmly, moving to stand in front of me. "He knew what he got himself into. That's why he gave you that medallion. Going back now is a suicide mission, and probably a pointless one."

Her bluntness stung. On one level, I knew she was right. Botto and the others were probably dead already, but I couldn't let myself believe that was true. In my heart, I wasn't ready to accept it was even a possibility.

Sienna sighed heavily and placed her hands on my shoulders. Though I leaned away from her, I didn't step back.

"They won't kill Botto," she reasoned. "He's too valuable."

I held her gaze. "To whom?"

She hesitated a beat too long. "A lot of people. I mean, he's a wealth of knowledge to the royals. To you, obviously, since you want to risk your life for him."

Both of her points were valid, yet neither felt like the one she had in mind. There seemed to be something she was withholding, something she wasn't saying. Yet.

"If you don't tell me the truth, I am going back right now," I snapped. The adrenaline was wearing off, and I found I was very annoyed with all the secrets.

"I honestly don't know, okay?" Sienna shook her head and shrugged. "It's got something to do with the pack he's from. Like who his parents are, I think."

A trickle of guilt leaked through my worry. I didn't know much about Botto's pre-dome life. Our pasts weren't really a hot topic of discussion among fae and shifters taken from the Freelands. Nonetheless, I felt like a crappy friend for not knowing more.

"You mean his mom's pack?" I clarified. While I may not have known much about Botto's past, I did know his mother was a shifter and his father was a fae.

Sienna's brows drew together. "I guess. I don't know specifics. I just know that he's important to someone who's important." She shook my shoulders gently. "Can we please go now? The sweat on my skin is freezing."

"Yeah. Okay."

We walked in silence. It turned out I'd been wrong about seeing a house in the distance earlier. It was something stranger—an outpost. *Where are we?* Things became even weirder when the frozen earth gave way to slick, paved streets beneath our feet. A red farmhouse appeared like a drop of blood beyond snowy fields. *Why isn't it buried in the snow? Or at least frozen over?*

From one side, I heard the soft hum of an approaching snowmobile engine.

"Don't." Sienna grabbed my arm. "Don't provoke them."

I looked down at the twisted flames dancing on my palms, which had been gloveless since I attacked the were-lion. The fire snuffed out between my fingers as three four-wheelers surrounded us.

"You two lost?" a male fae called, his cloudy blue eyes darting back and forth between Sienna and me.

"We're headed for Revival," Sienna responded evenly.

"Oh, yeah?" The fae looked at his two companions, all three laughed, and then he continued, "We're not accepting applications."

"Delancey is expecting us," I interjected impatiently.

"Oh, yeah?" The guy said again. "What makes you so special?"

I shrugged. "Depends who you ask."

Sienna nudged me hard in the ribs with her elbow. "Give him the medallion."

I reached in my pocket.

"Keep your hands where I can see them," barked the fae.

"Believe me, I don't need a concealed weapon." Rolling my eyes, I quickly tossed the package from Botto toward the man.

The fae nodded to one of his fellow guards, and the werewolf scurried to collect the medallion. He flipped it over in his gloved hands, studying both sides with a critical eye. All the color drained from his cheeks.

"Sir, you're going to want to look at this yourself."

Sienna and I exchanged glances as the two guards conversed in low voices. They both kept an eye in our direction, their expressions more wary than suspicious.

"Alright." The fae waved us over. "Let's see if you're really who you say you are."

When he gestured to the back of his snowmobile, I climbed aboard to ride with the fae. Sienna followed suit with the shifter, while the third guard sped ahead, presumably to warn the Delancey person about our arrival. We passed another five outposts, all of which were manned by guards who waved us past. Tall iron gates opened as the snowmobiles approached. We passed run-down apartment buildings that looked like they were still occupied. More guards in military issue camo patrolled the area on foot, and quite a few stopped to stare openly at the four-wheelers.

The second set of gates was more substantial, made of heavy wood and reinforced steel beams. This section of Revival was all winding streets and subdivisions of ranch-style houses. Other snowmobiles were on the roads, but the people driving them didn't look like guards. One woman zoomed past us in the opposite direction wearing a bright red fur jacket and knee-high black boots that Cala would've given a year's salary to own.

I knew we'd reached the center of the weird, wintery city when I spotted the third gate. It was thirty feet high and made of electrified metal. Ancient fae ruins were carved on the surface. The magic was so strong that the air vibrated. Inside the gates, the temperature was noticeably warmer. Not tank top and sandals weather, a decent jacket was still necessary, but gloves and hats suddenly weren't essential. I even spotted a woman pushing a stroller in heels. The shopping district of the city—a luxury I'd previously thought exclusive to domed cities—had many of the same pricey stores as the one on Oahu. Restaurants bustled with the early breakfast crowd.

The next leg of our journey took us through the center of the city and out to a more residential section. These homes weren't cookie-cutter. They were large and windowless, like fortresses, and yet no two looked anything alike. We followed the very curvy road through a mountain pass. When we came out the other side, a great icy castle sat in the center of the valley.

The patrol guards took us all the way to the palace steps. Stiff and sore, I climbed from the snowmobile. A tall man in dark jeans and a black leather jacket eyed me from the entranceway, his salt-and-pepper hair blowing in the light wind.

"Who're you?" he demanded gruffly.

"Are you Delancey?" I called back.

"You first." Crossing muscular arms over his chest, he leaned against the door lazily.

I shook my head. "Sorry. I was told not to give my name to anyone but Delancey."

The man pursed his lips, highlighting a thin scar that ran from one side of his mouth all the way to his ear. "The way I see it, you need me. I don't need you, whoever you are. You're in my territory—Dresden land. So, you can answer my questions and enjoy our hospitality, or you can get a taste of what we do to our enemies."

Before I could decide whether to call his bluff, the doors burst open. A woman in sky-high suede heels marched down the steps. She spared a glance at Sienna but focused her furious glare on me.

"Where is my brother?"

"Your brother?" I repeated numbly.

"Yes, Botto. My brother," she snapped, tapping her foot impatiently. "Where is he?"

It was embarrassing how long my brain took to fit all the pieces together. "You're Delancey?" I guessed.

"Delancey Dresden." She didn't offer me her hand. "And I want to know where my brother is."

Delancey Dresden was definitely a woman used to

getting answers, so I was a little nervous to admit that I didn't know what had happened to Botto. Sienna and I explained the ambush, and how Botto and the pack kept the attackers busy so we could escape.

"Were-lions?" Delancey asked.

"I only saw the one for sure, but yeah. Possibly a fire fae, too, or maybe casters," I replied.

She shook her head. "No casters this close to Revival. It sounds like nomads."

I opened my mouth to ask what the hell a nomad was, but Sienna's not-so-subtle headshake made me clamp my lips shut again.

"At least that means my brother is alive. Lucky for you." Delancey spun and marched back up the stairs. Before she entered the palace, she called back to me over her shoulder. "Come on. War doesn't wait for anyone, not even the famous Maybrie Hawkins."

CHAPTER EIGHT

SOMEWHERE OVER THE PACIFIC OCEAN

Cala

THERE WERE A lot of advantages to being a serial
dater: nights out at fancy galas, premiere restaurants, and
the hottest nightclubs. Then there were the nights in with
prospects, drinking imported vintage wine and watching
classic movies. Shopping for these romantic interludes had
always been one of Cala's favorite pastimes. The activity
had become even more fun once her best friend became a
royal consort. Cala had never cared about the gifts from
her wealthier suitors, especially since they were given only

in the hope of locking down her affections. Until now.

"I can't believe you brought that thing," Rocko grumbled under his breath.

The two shifters, along with Everly, were squashed in the cargo bay of a pineapple airship bound for a runway outside the Domed City of Austin. It had taken a lot of bribing and begging and bartering, but the trio had finally found a trade pilot willing to fly them to the mainland. Texas wouldn't have been Cala's first choice, or even her second, but fugitives didn't really get to be picky.

"Good thing I did. Otherwise, we'd be screwed," Cala muttered, not bothering to disguise her annoyance.

Her stomach growled audibly, and it occurred to her that she couldn't remember when she last ate. *What day is it?* she wondered. Cala didn't know the answer to that question, either. Time had become a very abstract concept since she first went on the run.

"What's the deal with that?" Rocko stabbed a meaty finger toward the object clutched in Cala's arms.

She swatted his hand away. "Gabriella is a collector's item, don't mess with her."

"She has a name?" Rocko laughed. "She's a doll. Why do you even have her?"

Everly cut her dead eyes toward her boyfriend. "Gabriella is one of the four Princesses of the Americas," she said flatly. "She's the only human one, and they only made fifty."

Cala and Rocko put their respective bad moods aside and shared an uneasy look. Of the three of them, Everly was having the hardest time dealing with their reversal in fortune. Their lives beneath the dome hadn't prepared them for the harsh realities of the world outside it, and it was only going to get worse. Fae could survive outside domes, of course, but the journey ahead wasn't just going to be cold; it would also be physically and emotionally demanding. They would go without food and without sleep. The likelihood of injury was more of a certainty, and even death wasn't out of the question. Everly wasn't cut out for that type of stress.

That wasn't to say she was weak. In many ways, the earth fae was the strongest of the three. Fighting in the pits was dangerous and took a toll on the body, but at least the job paid well. House fae like Everly spent long hours on their feet and did work that was even more soul-crushing than being a competitor in a blood sport. Nonetheless, Everly had survived the life for years, even through the death of her older brother.

"Why do you know so much about dolls?" Rocko asked his girlfriend.

Everly stared straight ahead as she replied. "The first family I worked for had three of the four princesses. They were only missing Gabriella. That's when I learned how valuable one of these would be."

They fell silent as the airship started its initial descent into Texas. Cala's leg bobbed up and down. This was it—the last obstacle before true freedom. Getting out of Oahu had been the easy part. Hiding out on the frozen island of Maui had been okay; at least they'd had warm shelter there. All in all, the flight from the islands hadn't been too bad, just a little bumpy. As long as the airport attendant kept his word—the doll in exchange for keeping his mouth shut—the trio would set out into the

Freelands once they landed.

"Hey, guys?" the pilot called over the intercom system.

Cala's heart skipped a beat. "What's up?" she asked tightly.

"We've been hailed, which is normal. It's not the guy we expected, though. My info must be outdated, because I don't have a call-response."

Rocko swore loudly. "What do we do?" he asked no one in particular.

"Don't look at me," Cala snapped.

"What's the call-sign they're using?" Everly asked the pilot.

"It's a riddle, I think. I don't know," he said, sounding weary. "'We before I, you before me, and me before you.' Does that mean anything to any of you?"

"Loyalty to the cause above all," Everly replied quietly.

"You sure?" asked the pilot.

"Positive," she said with a tight nod. "It's part of the rebellion's motto."

The pilot repeated Everly's words, and Cala sucked in a breath in anticipation. Over the years, Cala had never come closer than the fringes of the rebellion. Though she knew a lot of the major players and contributed financial support, she wasn't part of the inner circle. On occasion, she'd passed messages and helped procure passwords for sensitive data that Christina had then used to blackmail unwilling accomplices. But she'd never been privy to the innerworkings, the greater plan. She had no knowledge of the different factions within the rebellion, or any specifics on how the networks operated.

Nevertheless, Cala knew the response Everly gave was

the right one when the airship started losing altitude.

"So, what does this mean?" she asked, eyes darting between her two friends. "Why would they be using that as a call?"

"Hopefully that the rebels have taken over this airstrip," Everly replied. There was an undercurrent of excitement in her voice that Cala hadn't heard in a very long time. Was it possible that the rebellion was actually making progress in overthrowing the casters?

A few moments later, they finally touched down on the mainland. Cala's relief that they'd made it safely out of the Hawaiian Kingdom was abruptly cut short when the cargo bay doors burst open. A blast of cold air smacked her hard across the face like a harsh dose of reality. At least a dozen soldiers waited on the other side, guns trained on her and the others. Were these the good guys, or the bad guys? Which side was which anymore?

"Who are you?" a woman demanded. Standing at the front of the group, she seemed to be a de facto leader of the armed men. The cute white jacket she wore with a fur-lined collar practically had Cala salivating, and not just because it looked warm as hell. Who knew that fashion outside the domes was so chic?

"We came from Oahu," Everly spoke up, her voice strong and clear.

"I can read a flight plan," the woman snapped back, tapping one toe of an adorable pair of gray boots. "Surprise, surprise, you three aren't on the manifest. Who are you?"

"My name is Everly Woods. These are my friends Rocko and Cala."

Cala wasn't sure how she felt about giving their real names, but she didn't have time to protest before Everly did it. Though their names wouldn't have meant much to anyone outside of the Hawaiian Kingdom, it was still a risk to go around blurting out their identities. They weren't normal refugees; there were outstanding arrest warrants with their names in association with a queen's murder. Even if no one cared about the justice aspect of the hunt for killers, a lot of people would gladly turn them over to the casters for the reward money. Was there any way that the world at large wasn't aware of the fact there was a band of fugitives running from the Hawaiian royals? Unlikely, considering the huge bounty on their heads.

"Woods?" the woman repeated, appraising Everly with renewed interest. "Are you related to Tanner?"

Cala watched as her friend and the other fae studied one another. The question was a test, she was positive, but what happened next depended more than Everly giving the correct answer.

"He was my brother," Everly said after a long pause. "He passed away last year."

The woman's eyes flashed as though the news of Tanner's death was painful to hear. Or maybe it was a reminder, since she didn't seem surprised. Either way, she lowered her weapon and extended one leather-gloved hand to Everly. Cala let out a long, relieved breath.

"Nya Dresden." The way she said her own name suggested they should have recognized it, like she was someone famous. Though it meant nothing to Cala, a spark of recognition passed over Everly's features.

"Follow me," the woman continued. "I'll explain more on the ride. We don't want you three dome babies freezing to death out here." Nya pointed to two of her silent companions. "The pilot," she said simply. The duo trotted off to the plane they'd taken over from the islands.

Nya spun and started marching down the runway in the opposite direction. A male shifter used the barrel of his rifle to motion Cala out of the cargo hold. Honestly, she wasn't sure she wanted to go with these people. When she heard the distinct sound of a gunshot pierce the air, Cala knew for certain she didn't want to go with them.

Everly and Rocko had already climbed out of the airship, and the latter held out a hand to help her out of the craft. "Are you coming, Cala?"

"Seriously?" She hissed back, cocking her head to one side. Was she the only one who'd heard the gunshot?

"We don't have a lot of options right now," he said in a low voice. "Let's just hear what this Nya woman has to say."

Cala hesitated a moment longer. While she didn't care what Nya said about anything, the mainland was a lot colder than Cala remembered. Her face was already frozen, muscles too cold to be expressive. If the choice was refusing to go and dying of hypothermia or possibly being shot, the latter was the logical choice. *What has my life become?*

"Fine," she relented, taking Rocko's hand even though she didn't need any help. "But only because I'm really freaking cold."

No one put them in chains, but there was no doubt they were prisoners. *We just traded one captor for another,* Cala thought. She wasn't naïve enough to believe the casters would've treated her fairly if she'd stayed in Hawaii, but at least there were laws and protocols that had to be followed. Out in the Freelands with the rebellion, Nya could kill with impunity and there was no recourse.

Cala and her friends were led to a shiny black SUV with enormous tires. It was worlds nicer than the caged transport truck she'd expected Nya to throw them in, so at least that was a bonus. The seats were buttery smooth leather, and the interior was warm and toasty. For the first time since leaving the dome, Cala's teeth stopped chattering.

"Where are you taking us?" she asked Nya, not really expecting a response.

The other woman smiled. "I think it would be better to show you. I don't want to ruin the surprise."

Cala and Rocko exchanged uneasy glances. Only Everly appeared at ease as the vehicle rolled over snowy Texas roads. Cala watched the landscape pass by through one of the tinted windows. It had been so long since she'd set foot on the mainland, and she'd never been to Texas. It looked a lot like where she was from—white and frozen. *That's how everything outside the domes looks,* she reminded herself.

Unlike a lot of fae and shifters, Cala hadn't stayed up at night dreaming of escape from Oahu. It wasn't that she supported the hierarchical caste system the stuck-up casters put into place. Who'd given them the right to rule over everyone else? It wasn't some divine decree bestowed from Gaia like so many pretended. But Cala had learned to live with their rules in their society, because she loved living beneath the dome. Under the dome, she was never hungry, never cold, never scared. That wasn't true for all fae and shifters, of course, but it was a huge improvement over Cala's previous life.

Twenty minutes or so into the car ride, she saw the signs for the Austin city limits. Most were simply leftover from the human civilizations and severely damaged from exposure to the elements. A few were encased entirely in ice, perfectly preserved for generations.

"Is it really wise to be driving us right past a domed city? What about checkpoints?" Cala asked, breaking the tense silence in the SUV. "I *knew* getting in this stupid warm car with you was a bad idea. Are you going to turn us in for reward money?"

Nya smiled as though Cala was an adorably foolish child. "Do I look like I need caster money?"

Admittedly, the other woman was wearing very expensive clothes. The suede boots alone looked like they cost more than Cala made in a month—which was a lot by most standards. The SUV turned at a marker that read *Dome Border Checkpoint: 10 miles.*

Everly shifted in her seat, visibly shaken. She'd really believed Nya was going to help them. Or at least she's hoped so. The possibility of that happening was growing smaller with each mile they traversed on the way to a domed city.

"You've had your fun, Nya," the driver called over his shoulder. "Stop torturing them."

He'd already been in the car when Cala and the others

climbed inside, so she hadn't gotten a good look at him. The fact he'd spoken up against her—hell, speaking at all, considering no one else had—suggested he wasn't just one of Nya's foot soldiers. Maybe he was closer to her equal? Maybe he could help them survive?

Nya rolled her eyes and flicked the snow from her leather gloves at the back of the driver's head. "No one asked for your opinion, Ryun."

With a shrug, he gave Cala a reassuring smile in the rearview mirror. "No one ever asks. That doesn't stop me from giving it," he told Nya. Then, in a louder voice so everyone in the SUV winced when he spoke, Ryun added, "We've taken the city. Austin is no longer under caster reign."

Cala sat up straighter, her eyes widening. She glanced between Rocko and Everly, who wore identical shocked expressions that surely matched her own. She knew they were all thinking the same thing: *And so it begins.*

The drive from the dome border to a warehouse the rebellion was using as their base of operations was a stark contrast to the frozen tundra outside the magical bubble. Cala had expected the Domed City of Austin to look a lot like the Domed City of Oahu, but it was an entirely new world. From the architecture to the vegetation, everything in Austin was just different, and Cala couldn't stop staring. The most noticeable difference was more of an absence, she quickly realized. An absence of anyone out and about on the streets. An absence of anyone who wasn't wearing a military-style uniform.

"Where is everyone?" Eyebrows drawing together, she looked to Nya for answers.

"Martial law. No one is permitted to leave their home unless they've been explicitly cleared by us."

"What's up with that flaming pitchfork thing?" Cala asked. She pointed at a house where the symbol burned bright against the white front door.

"It represents the rebellion. Members inside the city put the symbol outside their houses so we know they are friendly to the cause," Everly explained.

"Can't anyone put up the symbol, though?" Cala reasoned. "What's stopping the casters from doing the same once they realize you guys aren't bothering the people with the symbol?" In her opinion, this method of marking friend from foe was extremely flawed.

Everly smirked. "Casters can't see it. Only fire fae can cast it, and you need shifter blood to make it."

Cala wasn't sure how she felt about the development, so she pursed her lips and reserved comment. Once they arrived at the warehouse, Nya and Ryun gave them a quick tour of the public areas. Both skirted around the need for so much security around the restricted ones.

"You all are welcome to stay here with our people as long as you like." Nya placed her hands on her hips. "Unless Revival says otherwise, of course."

Ryun rolled his smoky gray eyes. "Give it a rest, N."

Maybe it wasn't the time or the place, but Cala couldn't help staring at the hybrid who'd been driving them once she could actually see his face. His dark blond hair was held back in a messy ponytail, and his scruff was in desperate need of a shave. Or maybe just a trim, she decided. The facial hair definitely worked for him.

Their tour ended in one of the makeshift dormitories,

where Ryun managed to find them three bunks together. He handed each of them a booklet with meal and clothing tickets and a cuff-style bracelet that he insisted they put on immediately. Cala did as instructed. The metal bracelet clamped shut around her wrist, with a click that filled her with dread. It wasn't so tight that it hurt, but the cuff was tight enough that it couldn't slide off.

"Relax," Ryun told her just as her pulse quickened. "It's merely for identification."

"Identification?" she repeated, gaze shifting to Rocko and Everly. Only the former looked as bothered as Cala felt.

Ryun's smile was perfunctory at best. "It's not a big deal. The bracelet will get you into all the areas where citizens are permitted."

"And keep you from being arrested," Nya added. "Only those who've been vetted get the ID bracelets."

"We've been vetted?" Rocko cocked an eyebrow, his tone only mildly curious.

Nya laughed humorlessly. "What a ridiculous question," she mused, turning and sauntering out of the dorm on her gorgeous boots.

A moment of awkward silence passed before Ryun cleared his throat loudly. "Sorry about my sister. She's...well, she's Nya. You guys should go get something to eat, I'm sure you're eager for something other than pineapple. I have a few things to deal with, but I'll come find you after."

"Sounds good," Cala replied, trying to keep her tone strong and assertive. It was probably a lost cause to flirt with him after spending countless hours in the cargo hold of a plane, but damn if he wasn't hot enough to at least try. Looking down at Cala, the corners of Ryun's eyes crinkled with amusement.

"What's the deal with doll?"

Right, she was still clutching Gabriella like her life depending on it. *Smooth.*

CHAPTER NINE

REVIVAL, FORMERLY KNOWN AS THE DOMED CITY OF SANTA FE,
KINGDOM OF THE AMERICAS

Brie

THE FIRST THING I noticed once inside the palace was the grandeur. The building wasn't as old as the Hawaiian royal residence, nor did it share the classical features. The architecture suggested it had been built after the time of the humans and was likely occupied by casters until the Dresden Clan took possession. Nevertheless, the rebels had definitely put their own spin on the décor.

"This is the Painted Desert Palace, right?" I asked as

Delancey led us down a hallway. The walls on either side were adorned with portraits of were-bears in animal form wearing crowns atop their furry heads.

"Someone paid attention in history class," Delancey replied, managing to sound both bored and annoyed. "We have renamed Revival Palace."

"They neglected the part where a shifter clan moved in," I replied. Sienna nudged me in the ribs with her elbow. "What?" I demanded, eyes widening in my most innocent expression.

"You've lived with casters for too long." Delancey stopped in front of a purple door, which snapped open beneath her touch. She gestured Sienna and me through first. "After you."

The magic inside smelled like burnt oranges and made my stomach turn. I hesitated. Delancey wasn't giving us a choice, but I wasn't big on the idea of entering a room with such powerful, dark magic swirling inside. Sienna nudged me again. "Go," she hissed.

"It's only a sealing spell," Delancey promised.

That's an awfully strong sealing spell, I thought, trying to peer inside. I could only see darkness beyond the room's threshold. *Oh, whatever.* Resigned to whatever fate awaited me, I entered the room. Surprisingly, I was slightly disappointed that it was merely a stairwell on the other side. Sienna followed right behind me, with Delancey resealing the passage before joining us on the stairs.

"We're going all the way to the top," Delancey called, gesturing for me to keep moving.

With an annoyed sigh, I started up the wide stone stairs. The magic grew stronger, denser, the higher we climbed. In turn, I grew more uneasy with each step. We were in rebel territory, which should've made me feel safe but didn't.

"Where are we going?" I demanded when I could no longer stand the suspense.

"I told you, there are people who want to meet you," Delancey replied.

"What about Botto? Are you going to send people to rescue him?"

Delancey narrowed her eyes as I turned to ask the question. "You seem awfully concerned about my brother, considering you left him behind."

"It's more complicated than that," I protested, my voice too squeaky. She'd hit a sore spot and likely knew it.

"My brother is for me to worry about now." The note of finality in her tone muted any further questions on my part. "You abandoned him in the thick of enemies." Guilt weighed like lead in my stomach at the reminder.

Several minutes later, we reached the top of the stairs and another purple door. This one opened on a sensor of some kind. A man in cowboy boots stepped into view, chewing a small stick like it was a toothpick. He looked me up and down with watery bronze eyes.

"You're the fire fae?" he asked, his forehead crinkling. "Thought you'd be bigger."

"What does that mean?" I retorted. Straightening to my full height, which was not that much less than the shifter in front of me, I shot him a hard look.

"Move, Swiss." Annoyed, Delancey pushed past both me and the shifter. "Come on, you two. Granite is waiting."

I wasn't sure what I expected a man named Granite to look like. Thoughts of a large rock man, like the one from an old comic book, were quickly supplanted when I found an older version of Botto with the pointy ears of a pureblood fae. It was my trainer's father—that much was obvious. It took me an extra beat to remember that also meant Granite was Delancey's father.

The burly water fae sat on a couch by the window, watching the snow falling outside. His hair was a shade darker than his son's but no less curly. When he spoke, however, his accent was thick and not immediately identifiable.

"It is very nice to meet you finally, Maybrie." Granite didn't bother to stand for the greeting. "And you, Sienna, darling. I am so pleased to see you again."

I shot her a glare. "Seriously?" I hissed.

My old friend shook her head tightly. "Not now, Brie."

"Come, sit." The elder fae gestured to one end of the wraparound couch.

Delancey joined her father in the center of the sofa, while Sienna and I sat where Granite had indicated. It was warm inside the castle, much too warm for all the clothing I was wearing. Still, I didn't dare strip off layers without being invited to do so. I didn't know what the protocol was in their world.

"Would either of you care for a drink?" Granite asked.

"No, thank you, sir," Sienna said, casting her eyes downward. I'd only heard the reverent tone of hers when we were children addressing the elders in Fae Canyon.

I wasn't feeling quite so polite. "What is this place?

Why do you want me here?"

Delancey's face turned an unhealthy shade of purple and for the first time I really saw her resemblance to Botto. I thought she might deck me, but then her father chuckled.

"You're just as I have heard," he told me.

That probably wasn't a good thing, I decided.

"I only wish to keep you safe," Granite continued. "That is why I invited you to Revival."

"You *should* be grateful," Delancey added.

No one commented on that, not even her father.

"I imagine you have many questions." The elder fae gave me a fatherly smile. "Sienna can give you many of those answers. Right now, I am sorry to say, we do not have the luxury of time. There's business that needs our attention."

"*Our* attention?" I repeated numbly.

Granite smiled tightly. "The rebellion has taken the Domed City of Austin. We are preparing to make our first formal statement to all the Kingdoms of the Americas. It would be wonderful if you were there, to represent fae everywhere."

I looked from Granite to Delancey and finally Sienna. The sinking feeling in my gut intensified by the second. "Wow. You guys are serious. Look, um, I don't know that I'm the right person for this job. I mean, I've been living beneath a dome and, you know, dating a caster. A caster king, no less. I'm not spokesperson material."

"Spying on a caster king," Granite corrected pointedly.

Technically, he was right. But while I'd started dating Kai for the rebellion, I'd continued to date him for me.

That fact would certainly not gain me popularity points with the rest of the rebellion members.

"You were instrumental in bringing down the dome over Oahu," Granite added.

"No. No, no, no." I shook my head back forth fast enough to give myself whiplash. The conversation was moving in a direction that made me exceptionally uncomfortable. Maybe it wasn't wise to correct him, but I wanted to make it abundantly clear that the mass murder of casters was not cool with me.

"You aided in the successful assassination of a sitting monarch, which hasn't been done in decades," Granite continued over my protests. "Maybrie, darling, you don't even realize how valuable you are to the cause."

Springing to my feet, I realized too late that the move would be considered aggressive. Delancey jumped up and positioned her body between her father and me. She bared her teeth in an angry snarl. Like Botto, Delancey was a hybrid. She looked to be some sort of were-cat that I couldn't quite pinpoint crossed with the fae genes from her father.

"Sit back down," she snarled.

Granite reached up and placed a gentle hand on his daughter's arm. "Heed your own warning, dear." With a slightly firmer touch, he pushed her aside. "Maybrie wouldn't be the one we need if she took orders blindly. She wouldn't be *our* fae."

It was meant as a compliment, yet I didn't feel flattered. I didn't want to be their fae. "I really appreciate your protection or whatever, but I'm not interested in helping to further your agenda." My eyes were fixed firmly on Granite's weathered face.

"Brie," Sienna hissed. The plea was so urgent, it was almost like her life was tied to my compliance. Wait....

Had she told them I would help? How did they know each other? What the hell was going on?

"I'm sorry, but I don't work with vampires," I insisted. "I will not side with the same vile creatures that kidnapped me and sold me to the casters."

"Yet you'll forgive the very caster who bought you?" Fury flashed in Delancey's irises as she hurdled the accusation. "The one who purchased you from the vampires you so detest? You will forgive him? You will marry him?"

The words stung more than they should have. It wasn't like I didn't know who Kai was. What Kai was. I'd always known. Still, hearing the accusations—the realities I'd been ignoring for so long—made me wince. Botto's sister hadn't called me a traitor. Not exactly. She didn't have to; I already felt like one.

"Vampires are a necessary evil in this war," Granite said gravely. As he spoke, he pulled Delancey back onto the cushion beside him. "They have access to casters. They have access to the domes that we in the Freelands do not. Our fae and shifter allies beneath the domes do not have the access either. I do not trust the vampires. I will never forgive or forget what they have done to our people." The older fae met my gaze with the same determined expression I'd seen on Botto's face so many times. "One day soon, they will pay for their crimes against the Freelanders. You have my word on that. For now, the enemy of my enemy is my friend."

Raking a hand through my hair, I took a deep breath and exhaled slowly. "What is it exactly you want from me?"

It was Delancey who answered. "Your face." A slow smile parted her lips. "All you have to do is stand there."

"Please, Maybrie. Sit." Granite gestured to the couch again. "Hear me out. As I said, time is of the essence."

I opened my mouth to say, "thanks but no thanks", but Delancey raised a hand to silence me. "There's something you will want to know. Three of your friends arrived on the mainland earlier today. Cala, Rocko, and Everly, I believe. They're with my sister Nya in Austin."

My blood ran cold. Had my friends escaped one threat only to walk right into another? Both of which were on account of their friendships with me.

"I want to speak with them," I told Delancey in the calmest voice I could muster. Her threat hadn't been subtle, but I couldn't afford to be equally as brash with my friends' lives on the line.

"After we address the kingdoms," she promised.

My gaze shifted to Granite, who'd seemed like the more reasonable of the two previously. *He's head of a crime family, whatever that means,* I reminded myself. *Reasonable is absolutely skewed in this situation.*

The fae held his hands palms up and shrugged. "If only there were time. We are addressing the world shortly."

"Fine," I bit back, nearly choking on the single word. "Just tell me where to stand. I have nothing to say, but I will stand in the background."

Gaia, what did I just agree to?

Despite Granite's repeated claims that there wasn't time to explain everything beforehand, there was plenty time for me to shower and change.

My body was bruised and battered from the snowmobile crash earlier. Adrenaline had masked that fact previously, but it was shockingly apparent once my clothes were stripped away and I saw the evidence with my own eyes. One of my ribs had a visible lump, which I knew from prior experience meant it was more than likely broken. *Awesome.* My left shoulder was already a deep purple with the promise of becoming bluish-black by morning. *Super.* And if not for my many layers of winter clothes, I would've had a stick lodged in my kidney. Even still, there was a three-inch scrape on my back that needed either stitches or a good healer. While I didn't have access to either, I did have a healing tonic in my backpack.

There probably should've been more consideration of rationing Samira's potion, but it also wasn't like my life expectancy was all that great these days. For now, I needed to use what I had at my disposal. For now, I could only survive one day at a time. To move forward, I needed to be as close to full-strength as I could muster. If that meant depleting my only source of medical care, so be it. Taking a small sip of the healing tonic, I felt some of the ache in my muscles ease as the liquid magic spread through my body.

Feeling slightly more like myself, I finally took in the room I was shuffled off to. The room Delancey sent me to shower and change was nothing particularly special. It was neat and tidy, though, with two double beds, a small closet, and a mirror. There was a fireplace in the corner, which someone had been nice enough to light while I was in the shower. The en suite bathroom was a study in beige, from the walls to the countertop to the compact shower. There was a small window, not wide enough to escape but just wide enough to look out over the former caster kingdom now covered in snow and ice.

Someone had left a small stack of clothes on the bed, probably the same someone who'd started the fire. I slipped on a fresh pair of long underwear, warm wool socks, a thick white sweater, and white and grey camo pants. I dried my hair with heated hands and studied my appearance in the mirror. My under eyes were in serious need of some concealer, and my cheeks would've benefited from a little rosy blush.

These aren't the royals, I reminded myself. The rebellion wasn't going to dress me in silk gowns and paint my face with makeup. They needed me to look tough, not like some doll on parade.

Three sharp knocks on the door brought me out of my thoughts. Delancey entered without waiting for an invitation. Her intense gaze raked me from head to toe. "Put your hair up," she ordered, spinning on one heel and crooking her finger for me to follow.

Hastily, I pulled on my own less glamorous boots and hurried after her. "Any word on Botto yet?" I asked hopefully.

She didn't even look my way. "I told you: my brother, my concern."

We met Granite in a study on the first floor of the palace, and he wasn't alone. The water fae stood in the center of the room with three other men and a teenage boy sporting Botto's wild curls. All five looked over when Delancey and I entered. I glanced around the study uneasily.

"Where's Sienna?" I asked.

She wasn't high on my trust list, but at least she was a familiar face. Even though it made me instantly annoyed, I did feel a little better with her around.

"She will rejoin us after the address," Granite assured me. Unfortunately, his tone wasn't reassuring in the least.

A wizened old earth fae with wisps of snow-white hair beckoned me forward. He sucked in a sharp breath as I approached. When he spoke, his words were directed to Granite.

"The girl's magic is strong," he muttered.

Awesome, now people were talking about me right in front of my face. As I bit back a snappy retort about his lack of power, Granite gave a curt nod of acknowledgement. He made quick introductions between me and the others. The earth fae was called Gil. The two leather-clad shifters were Bunt and Mic, and the boy was named Brach. Unsurprisingly, the latter was indeed Botto's younger brother.

Gil arranged all of us into a straight line spread across the space, including Delancey. He stood in front of us, clutching a perfect stone sphere that he'd retrieved from a hutch in the corner. Its magic filled the room with raw energy that Gil fought to channel. He began to chant. My casting education was severely lacking, yet even I recognized the incantation for a projection spell. It was the same one my father had used on the rare occasion he needed to speak with fae elders in other communities. If I wasn't mistaken, the spell also concealed our location. All in all, it was the perfect charm for meetings with enemies.

The smell of damp grass filled the study as Gil wielded more and more of his magic. Just as I began to wonder if he might not fall over before he finished the spell, a current of earth magic shot through me. Disoriented, I blinked rapidly. Opening my eyes again, it was like I was inside a picture that had been doubly exposed. The study in the Painted Desert Palace was overlaid with a sight I knew all too well. A place that felt comfortingly familiar while bringing nauseating anger. It was a fight pit.

My eyes shot to Delancey, who stood on my left.

"You'll see," she muttered before I could even ask. She was simply annoyed by my very existence and wasn't making a show of hiding that fact.

I blinked several more times and concentrated on the arena. After a minute, the study faded away completely. Our group seemed to stand on a platform high in the stands that looked down on the pit below. A spotlight trained the attention of everyone on us. At least four similar set-ups around the arena also held projected fae and shifters, most wearing fatigues that were identical to mine.

The royal box was also illuminated. When I'd been a champion fighter on Oahu, Queen Lilli had sat atop a throne to watch her favorite blood sport. In L.A., King Ronald was no different. In the grand tradition of the Los Angeles royals, his throne was far more ostentatious.

It stood to reason that at one time in Austin there had been at the very least a decorative chair in the royal box, but no seats where in sight. They'd likely been fixed right where the two very disheveled casters stood hunched over. On either side, half a dozen bulky shifter guards flanked the couple.

The sight made me feel like I'd swallowed a mouthful of sand. I didn't keep up with caster gossip the way Cala did, but I spent enough time on the tabloid sites to recognize King Joaquin and Queen Georgina of Austin. Theirs was the fallen kingdom. Both were relatively young, just a few years older than Kai. Looking at Queen Georgina in a pair of tattered silk pants that had probably once been beautiful, her long hair hanging in greasy clumps down her bent spine, I would have sworn she was still a teenager. Her expression was terrified and guileless—a dangerous combination for her own wellbeing.

The stands were packed to capacity with fae, shifters, and casters alike. Only the casters' sections had guards patrolling to maintain the order, which was a reversal of roles that I had longed to witness many times over my years beneath the dome. So why did the spectacle make me so feel so ill?

"Good day, people of the Kingdoms of the Americas!" a man's voice boomed. A spotlight winked on in the center of the arena, revealing a good-looking guy that I swore I recognized from somewhere. He oozed charisma the way others oozed sweat. He held no microphone, choosing to magically amplify his voice instead.

"My name is Hale Dresden," the man continued. "It is with great honor that I address you tonight. But also great sorrow."

Shooting another glance in Delancey's direction, I hissed. "How many of you are there?"

"No bond is stronger than that of family," she replied without taking her eyes off Hale.

"Earlier today, the great Domed City of Austin was liberated from the tyrants who have ruled for too long without being checked," Hale went on.

Loud cheers and raucous applause sounded in the crowd, though not all fae and shifters joined in. They were scared, I realized. This was not the first fae uprising. It also wasn't the first time a domed city had fallen. The last time my people had gained ground in a war against caster oppression, those who'd sided with the rebels had been treated harshly. I didn't blame people for being wary of showing support in public for the people working against the casters; cameras were recording everything. Odds weren't in our favor to win independence, not if history was any indication. Still, that didn't stop the enthusiasm radiating from certain parts of the stadium. A lot of people were ready to ignore survival instincts in favor of mutiny.

"No longer will we bow to the casters," the evangelist continued. "They are the weakest among us, and it's time they were reminded of that!" Hale's words were doing a great job of working up the parts of the crowd who were unafraid to show their allegiance to the rebellion. The more he said, the more people he won over. More and more bodies joined those standing, until half of the stadium was on their feet to cheer.

Admittedly, I was moved by his statements. Hale reminded me of Tanner. He reminded me why I'd joined up with Christina and the rebellion in the first place; the absolute principles of knowing the casters were wrong to assert dominance over others. Still, there was something about the whole scene that made my skin crawl. Probably because I couldn't stop picturing Kai standing on that dais in King Joaquin's place.

"From this moment forward, all citizens of Revival Colonies will be treated equally. That includes casters, although...," Dresden continued, leaving the sentence open for a long, ominous moment. "But before you can become an equal citizen, you must pay for your past crimes."

It felt like I'd swallowed a slug. I'd known from the instant I laid eyes on the royal couple that this was some sort of public trial or shaming. Still, that knowledge didn't make the confirmation any easier to digest.

"Today, we begin the citizenship trials." At Hale's pronouncement, a fiery pitchfork lit up in the air above his head. The cheers were much louder this time. The magical flames broke apart and fell to the ground like stars during a meteor shower. The embers reformed the symbol of the rebellion and branded it into the earth.

Hale made a sweeping gesture toward the royal box. "Caster 0001, you have been accused of treason against the citizens of Austin. You are also charged with the unlawful murder of citizens of Austin and unlawful imprisonment of another without proper authority...."

The offenses continued to be read, and the list was

long. It included a few obscure charges that even I thought were laughable, like the crime of indulgence. What did that even mean? When Hale was done reading of King Joaquin's purported crimes, he moved on to Queen Georgina and the crimes she'd allegedly committed. Hers were nearly identical, save the charge called theft of ancient artifacts. I had no idea what that was all about, but I was giving up on trying to figure it out. For all I knew, the queen had chewed a piece of gum that came from the days of humans; there was nothing to explain the charge further.

"You have a choice," Hale said gravely once he finished with the queen's many offenses. "Caster 0001, you may choose to face a tribunal of your accusers. In conjunction with the temporary council assigned to the Austin colony, they will decide your fate. Alternatively, you may choose to participate in the citizenship trials and be absolved of your crimes."

The young king stared down at Hale with contempt. "You have no authority here," he spat.

"Given the rejection of the alternative, the tribunal it is," Hale declared. He gave a nod to the shifter guards, and they started leading King Joaquin away. He struggled, even managing to escape the guards long enough to throw his magically bound arms around the queen. As they were ripped from the embrace, she sobbed openly and shrank back as the guards went for her husband again.

Hale waited until Joaquin's shouts died out before turning to Queen Georgina and posing the same options. Silence fell as though the entire arena was holding a collective breath while waiting for her answer. My gaze panned across our little row of virtual delegates. Most wore impassive expressions, including Granite. Only Delancey appeared to feel any joy at witnessing the demise of the royal family; she kept muttering under her breath, something that sounded like, "Pick the trial. *Please* pick the trial."

What does this so-called citizenship trial entail? I wondered numbly.

Finally, the beautiful young caster queen from Austin raised her head. Through watery eyes, she glared at Hale. In a loud, clear voice, she called down to the expectant faces below. "Trial."

"Yes!" Wicked delight flashed across Delancey's face. She smiled over at me. "I think you're going to like what comes next."

The fact she'd said it made me think I wouldn't enjoy what came next one bit. I was right; Hale's next order confirmed as much.

"Tonight, at nightfall, caster 0002 will be brought to the dome border to begin her citizenship trial."

"What?" Georgina screeched. "No. No! I change my mind!"

It was too late for regrets, though. The guards carried her from the dais to a symphony of cheers from the crowd below. I rounded on Delancey. "Casters can't survive in the cold. This trial is a death sentence," I snapped.

Botto's sister smiled indulgently. "Sometimes in order to move forward, you have to eliminate the dead weight and weed out the weak."

I swallowed thickly. "Casters are the weak? All of them?"

"They always have been, Brie. It's time we started treating them accordingly. Otherwise, we will all go the way of the humans."

Chapter Ten

DOMED CITY OF LOS ANGELES, KINGDOM OF THE AMERICAS

Kai

KAI WATCHED THE original broadcast of King Joaquin and Queen Georgina's indictment at Calypso Palace with the California royals. Even a few of King Ronald's illegitimate children were there—everyone had turned out for the transmission. He'd managed to keep his expression impassive through the entire spectacle, which was a huge feat once Kai caught sight of Brie standing on a platform high above the crowd. It was harder to remain outwardly neutral when King Ronald saw the same thing and shot him a meaningful look.

"See?" It said. "She is nothing more than a lying, traitorous fae."

The gesture proved Kai's suspicions that Ronald knew he was bluffing when it came to Brie. The other king wasn't nearly as stupid as Kai had previously thought; the other king clearly wasn't buying Kai's sudden change of heart or professed innocence in Brie's escape.

Once back at the hotel, Kai replayed the broadcast several times just to see Brie's face. The camera was only on her for a few seconds in the background, but it was enough to allay his fears about her wellbeing. She looked okay, he decided. Although there were no visible injuries, it was hard to tell if she was bruised and battered through all her layers of winter clothing. It was hard to know for certain exactly how she was doing when he only had four seconds of footage to go on. Dark circles suggested that Brie hadn't been sleeping much, but her color was much better than the last time he'd laid eyes on her. The tight set of her jaw could've been stress or disgust for the proceedings.

"Hey, you okay?"

For such a big guy, Kenoa was extremely light on his feet. He'd managed to enter the suite without Kai hearing him. Kai paused the broadcast, leaving Queen Georgina's terrified face frozen in front of him.

"I honestly don't know," Kai told his friend. "I don't know how I am. I feel numb."

Kenoa eased his large frame into an armchair beside the couch where Kai sat. "Do you want to talk about it?"

"Why couldn't she have stayed hidden?" Kai answered

the question with a question. "Would that have been so hard? She swore to me she was no longer involved with the rebellion." He gestured angrily to the television. Until that moment, Kai hadn't realized just how upset he was that Brie had gone running back to the very organization that she had supposedly denounced for killing his mother.

"What is she thinking?" he continued ranting. "Does she know how this looks? Did she even consider what might happen to me before showing her face on television? Did she consider the scrutiny I'd be under for dating someone who is openly a face of the rebellion? I mean—"

Kenoa's snort of laughter cut him off. "Really? That's your biggest concern here, how her public appearance alongside the heavy hitters in the rebellion reflects on you?"

Annoyance flashed through Kai's dark eyes. "It looks like she's supporting them," he fired back. "I didn't help her escape so that she could lead an uprising against my people."

All traces of amusement fled the water fae's expression. "Careful, your royal privilege is showing," he said evenly. "I love you like a brother, but not everything is about you."

No one, not even his little sister would've spoken to him in such a manner. Especially not when he was already worked up. Jumping to his feet, Kai glared down at his best friend and jabbed a finger dangerously close to Kenoa's face.

"I've been tormenting myself thinking that she was

hurt," he defended. "Or worse. What if the search parties hunting her would find her? Or what if she had no food and was starving? Or cold, what if she was freezing out there?" He trailed off, throwing his hands up in the air. "This whole time she's been with the rebels! Was that her plan all along? Was her sob story about not knowing their plan for my mother, her *queen,* a lie?"

Even as he gave voice to the accusations, Kai knew how ridiculous they sounded. He felt more than a little stupid, but that didn't seem to stop the barrage of doubts flying through his mind. Kai's only defense was that he wasn't accustomed to feeling powerless in situations, especially those of a romantic nature. He'd never had his feelings hurt by a girlfriend. Seeing Brie with his enemies was the biggest kick in the pants he'd ever experienced.

Kenoa's posture remained relatively relaxed in the face of Kai's outburst. When he spoke next, his words were measured. "Brie isn't that good of a liar. You're pissed, I get that. I can't say I'm not a little miffed, too, but I'm also not surprised. You think the royals are the only ones who sent hunters after her? The rebellion wants her badly. Brie is an accused queen killer. She is gold to them, even to those who'd prefer a revolution that's a little less bloody. The Freelands are their territory. They know every inch of this snow-covered country better than your people ever could; it's not surprising that they found Brie."

"You think she's in Austin against her will?" Kai demanded. Most of the fight had gone out of him, so the question just sounded weary and defeated.

"I think she might be doing what fae do best," Kenoa

replied carefully. "She's trying to survive in a very unforgiving world. You think you're under pressure in here?" He made a sweeping gesture meant to encompass the entire domed city of Los Angeles. "You have no idea what the rebellion leaders will do to her for falling in love with a royal caster. Being branded a traitor to the Hawaiian Kingdom is nothing compared to being branded a traitor to our own people. The fae stick together, and they're vindictive as hell."

The last statement made Kai sway on his feet. *Gaia, I really am an asshole,* he thought numbly. His best friend was right. Kai's royal advisors and the other monarchs thought he was naïve. They wanted him to do more to distance himself from Brie, something along the lines of a public denouncement of their relationship. Even with that, he wouldn't face any real consequences. Long lectures and a slightly stunted freedom to choose his own bride in the future would likely be the sum total of his punishments. Brie wasn't so lucky.

"Also, Brie isn't in Austin, for whatever that's worth to you," Kenoa continued, his tone slightly gentler than before.

Kai flopped back down on the couch in a very undignified move. "Why do you say that?"

"Her clothes," his friend replied, as if Kai should've realized it. "The fact her hair wasn't blowing in the breeze like Queen Georgina's. She's not outdoors, she's somewhere inside. It's also a gut feeling, but that's an easy tell."

The king cocked an eyebrow and gestured for Kenoa to continue. Sighing, his friend pressed on reluctantly.

"I don't know much about the rebellion," he admitted. "What I do know is they're extremely secretive, and there's an obsessiveness when it comes to the privacy of their leaders. They're also not stupid. They remember what happened in Santa Fe. They learned from it." The water fae shook his head. "The top dogs aren't in Austin while the takeover is happening, it's too risky. They know there's a chance the other kingdoms will send troops to go after them if a location is known. Brie is likely in a secure stronghold somewhere. A *very* secure stronghold. If you want, I can ask around and see what's up with the other people on the platform with her. That might help us figure out where she is right now."

Kai swallowed his anger and his pride. "I'm sorry, Kenoa, you don't deserve me acting like a dick toward you. It's no excuse, but the last few days have been hard. I have never felt so lost."

"Right now, I'm your only friend. Don't forget that." Though Kenoa's tone was playful, Kai still took the words to heart. This was the only person he could trust; it made no sense to alienate the water fae who'd been with him through thick and thin.

"I will never forget that. You are, and always will be, my most trusted friend." Kai cleared his throat. "If you wouldn't mind finding out whatever you can about Brie's location, I would be grateful."

"Of course," Kenoa said without hesitation. Whatever else, the guy had never held a grudge. "I'm actually about to go meet with someone who might have intel, I'll see what he knows."

Kai scrubbed a hand over his face. The stubble that bit

back against his hand was a reminder that he'd forgotten to shave that morning. "Thanks. I have that monarch meeting." He hesitated before asking, "Any word back from Illion about our face-to-face?"

Kenoa averted his gaze. "Yeah. The kid wants to meet at midnight."

"Midnight tonight?"

Kenoa nodded. "The message said to dress warmly and be ready and in your hotel room at midnight."

"He's coming here?" That was a horrible idea. The kid was free, being seen in L.A. could change that.

"Seems so," Kenoa replied evenly. "Unless, of course, you've changed your mind."

"I haven't," Kai responded bluntly.

His best friend shook his head as if already saying I told you so. "I'll let Illion know."

Kenoa left shortly thereafter. Kai tried to make himself coffee with the in-room machine, but found he was about as incompetent with the simple task as he was at quieting the tensions of a tumultuous nation. Giving up, he ordered a pot from room service. Kai would've preferred a stiffer beverage for the meeting of monarchs, something that would numb his nerves, but he needed to keep a level head for later. He knew nothing about Brie's brother and didn't want to be impaired in the slightest when he met Illion.

King Ronald had wanted Kai to join him in person at Calypso Palace for the meeting, and he'd been perturbed when Kai refused. Though he didn't regret his decision one bit, especially as Kai sat alone in the hotel suite and summoned the magic required to cast a projection spell, he knew it might've been a tactical error. An instant later, the king of Hawaii was transported to the conference room. He greeted his fellow rulers with solemn nods and waited while the rest of the attendees trickled in.

Like the previous meeting, there was a lot of talk about border security measures, which Kai found redundant and boring. When the discussion switched to possible military responses to the events in Austin, his interest was piqued. Most of the rulers were still against the idea of sending aid to help the casters there. Even worse, some of them were in favor of sending a strike team to wipe out the entire domed city.

"If we bring the dome down, the rebels will have gained nothing," King Ronald said breezily. "It's the most expedient way to end this situation and discourage anyone who's considering trying their own mutiny. We strike quickly, and then we're done with it. It will only be a matter of time before the city freezes over and everything is covered in snow like the rest of the wastelands."

It was common among casters, particularly royal casters, to refer to the Freelands as the wastelands. Many believed that all societies outside of the domes were uncivilized, even primitive. It was laughable that they held such strong opinions of the world outside, considering none of them ever left the safety of the domes. Royal casters didn't visit enclaves like Fae Canyon to see how the rest of the world lived. Instead, they stayed in their privileged bubbles and made up stories meant to inspire enough fear that those fae and shifters born inside the dome never wanted to leave. Heaven forbid the casters actually venture outside the safety of their magical boundaries and try to understand what it was like for everyone else.

I sound like a rebel, he thought wryly.

"All the casters would die, too," Princess Edwina pointed out in response to King Ronald's callous comment. "That's something you're comfortable with?"

Kai was a little surprised to see her in attendance. The Alaskan royal princess was half fae and not in serious contention for her kingdom's throne. She did represent the family in certain matters, but those were usually the trivial ones that weren't so delicate. Nonetheless, Kai was glad to have her in the meeting. Edwina was a voice of reason that was sorely lacking among this bunch. His own position was so precarious that no one else seemed to have any interest in Kai's opinions on anything.

"The good of the majority must outweigh the wellbeing of the minority," King Ronald said dismissively. "We must set an example. We cannot give them the appearance of a victory. This stunt with televised trials must be stopped."

"You're suggesting mass murder. Mass murder of casters, no less," Kai interjected, unable to hold his tongue any longer. "That is not a viable option. We bring down the Austin dome, and we run the risk of our own people turning on us."

"That's absurd," Ronald scoffed. "Casters will never side with the rebels." He made a flippant gesture in Edwina's direction. "Even a hybrid knows which half of her is better than the other one."

It was probably a good thing that Kai was incorporeal, because he had a strong urge to wipe the smug look off the older king's face. The man was so out of touch with reality, it was both disgusting and a little sad.

Edwina said nothing in response to the dig. She sat straight and prim like the good princess she'd been taught to be. Kai would've given a fistful of family heirlooms to be able to read her thoughts. The princess might have been as poised and polished as any royal caster he'd ever met, but she was also a strongly opinionated woman who was proud of her fae heritage.

"I say we give it a few more days. Let's see how this plays out," said Queen Maxine from the Kingdom of the Carolinas. She was the oldest sitting monarch, and the others respected her opinion above all others. "Fae are not born leaders. It is not their fault, of course. Their power comes from nature, which makes it difficult for them to understand and control it properly. It also makes them weak. Shifters are rash, impulsive creatures who so often give in to their animal halves. That combination will burn out quickly."

Kai neither agreed nor fully understood this argument, though this wasn't the first time he'd heard it. A lot of casters believed fae were weak because their magic was driven by external forces. They were the same morons who never seemed to understand that external also meant there was an endless supply to tap into, while a caster's internally driven magic was finite. Without the fae to replenish caster magic, people like Queen Maxine would have died long ago. If he remembered correctly, the last statistic on caster lifespan without fae assistance was only about twenty years, even beneath a dome. That was also assuming the caster in question only performed simple spells that didn't deplete their powers. Of course, that wasn't a widely disseminated fact. Kai only knew because it was included in one of the many reports the royal researchers turned in every year.

None of you understand that we need fae more than they need us, he thought bitterly. He hadn't really understood that until recently. Really, if he wanted to be exact, the fall of the dome on the night his mother was killed was the frostiest wake-up call he could've imagined. So many of his formative years had been spent with people telling him that casters weren't kidnapping fae and shifters to bring beneath the dome. Instead, the elders had explained that they were saving the susceptible creatures from the frozen tundra and giving them a place to live where they'd be safe. His royal handlers had tried to drill it into his head that fae were weak, just as Maxine had said. That fae needed the leadership and wisdom of casters to survive. That shifters needed to be controlled in order to control their animal sides.

What a bunch of shit.

A knock on the meeting room door stopped him from saying so aloud. Leonardo, King Ronald's personal aid, stepped inside and bowed deeply. "Forgive the interruption, Your Majesties. I thought you might want to know that Queen Georgina's citizenship trial is beginning."

The meeting broke up, and Kai's was left alone inside the penthouse suite at Riggs Hotel. He switched the television from replay mode, and Hale Dresden's chiseled features filled the screen. Just as he had been that morning, the commentator wore an impeccably tailored navy suit and ridiculous pink bowtie with whales stitched on it in green thread. Hale's tone was solemn, but unbridled excitement danced his eyes. His true feelings about the proceedings were obvious to everyone watching.

"Kingdoms of the world, I am here with you tonight to witness the citizenship trial of caster 0002."

The camera switched from Hale inside what appeared to be the media room of the Austin palace to gates of the security wall outside the occupied domed city. Guards were positioned in two lines that extended as far as the eye could see, with a five-foot gap between them to form a gauntlet of sorts. Crowds of fae and shifters were gathered behind the guards, some standing on tiptoes and peering hungrily toward the closed gates. The heavy metal parted, and two tall people in heavy parkas emerged with a much smaller figure between them.

Kai sighed heavily as he took in Georgina's limp hair and tear-stained cheeks. He'd met her once or twice in passing and always thought she was very regal for such a young queen. Not anymore. Now she just looked like a frightened child. Her fancy clothes had been replaced with shapeless cargo pants and a puffy jacket. The extravagant, custom-made shoes that had made her the envy of other queens and princesses were gone, worn and dirty boots on her feet instead.

The queen's hands were bound in front of her with rope, though it was more for show than to restrain her. If the rebels really wanted to keep her docile, they would've used magic. Then again, maybe they had. It was impossible know via the broadcast.

"Caster 0002, this is the beginning of your citizenship trial." Hale's voice boomed like a voiceover, though the broadcast didn't switch back to him. "Over the next forty-eight hours, you must prove you are worthy of redemption. No help will come to you, but we are always watching. As are the eyes of the world."

Forty-eight hours was about the maximum amount of time a young, healthy caster could hope to survive outside the dome without assistance. That timeline assumed that she rationed her magic and was in decent shape, since she would have to keep moving to prevent hypothermia.

"Should you persevere, you will be rewarded with a place in our new world. Should you persevere, your past crimes against the fae and shifters will be forgiven," Hale continued.

Georgina's shoulders shook with silent sobs. Kai wanted to look away but didn't dare. It was horrific what they were doing to her, and it was only going to get worse. Despite the ache in his stomach, Kai felt as though this was something he needed to see, like a punishment for all the years he'd kept his head in the sand about the way casters treated others. If not for his friendship with Kenoa, would he be just as arrogant and elitist as so many of his counterparts? Would he have bought into the idea that casters really were superior?

The guards untied Georgina's hands. When she didn't start walking right away, one of them shoved her shoulder hard enough that the small queen stumbled forward and fell to her knees.

Barbaric, Kai thought automatically. But was it really

any worse than what his people had done to fae like Brie to get them to fight in the pits?

Georgina's head whipped around as one of her hands shot toward the guard who'd shoved her. A blast of green light hit the guy square in the face. He screamed and staggered backward, clawing at his cheeks. Instead of helping his colleague, the second guard pulled a long stick from the belt at his waist and prodded Georgina in the lower back. Her body bowed as she cried out in pain.

"Just remember, Caster 0002, your magic is limited," Hale's disembodied voice chuckled. "You might want to save it for the trials."

Georgina looked around with wide eyes, as if waiting for someone to help her up. Of course, no one did. A snowball sailed over the line of guards and hit her in the back of the head. Kai thought he was going to be sick to his stomach. Finally, after what felt like eons, Georgina climbed to her feet and started walking forward. She moved slowly at first. More and more snowballs pelted her from a multitude of directions, and her steps quickened. The young queen broke into a run not twenty feet from the gates of a city she'd once ruled.

CHAPTER ELEVEN

REVIVAL, FORMERLY KNOWN AS THE DOMED CITY OF SANTA FE, KINGDOM OF THE AMERICAS

Brie

"SPILL," I SNAPPED at Sienna.

The air fae sat on one of the two beds in the room we'd been given to share at the Revival Palace. Her long blonde hair hung in wet clumps, and she was trying to comb through the tangles. She looked up at me with wide, innocent eyes.

"What crawled up your ass now?" she asked.

"You've been here before. You've obviously met

Granite Dresden before." Hands on my hips, I glared down at my former friend with enough heat to make her flush beneath the scrutiny. "You acted like this was all new to you, like you didn't know who Botto was."

She sighed heavily and dropped the brush she was holding on the bed. "I met Granite through his son, Hale. Hale used to be a captive in L.A. He hosted a dating show for a while, and a cooking competition before that." One thin eyebrow arched upward. "Any of this ringing a bell?"

"That's why he looks so familiar," I muttered, more to myself than Sienna.

"I met Hale at a function. One thing led to another and, before I knew it, we were talking rebellion. I met his father a few months later. Never in the flesh, though. I didn't know Botto was part of the Dresden clan until Delancey said something. I've never been to Revival before now, so you can just chill with that accusatory glare."

I kicked the edge of a colorful throw rug with the toe of my boot. "You could have said something," I grumbled.

"Yeah, well, you could've chosen to not abandon me that night on the beach." She shrugged and resumed brushing her hair. The bitter quality to her words set my teeth on edge.

Are we ever going to get past that? I wondered.

There were a lot of things I wanted to say to her, none of which would've helped the situation. I needed her cooperation, not another fight. The Dresdens weren't particularly forthcoming with information about their plans or operation, and I wasn't about to make the same mistake I had with Christina. Though my involvement wasn't voluntary with the Dresdens, I still wanted to know Granite's planned endgame.

I perched on the edge of the second bed, facing Sienna, and started unlacing my boots. Taking a deep breath, I met her gaze. "Sienna, please. Can you please tell me what you know?" It pained me to plead with her, a necessary evil.

We sat in relative silence for several long moments. In the bathroom, a leaky faucet dripped water. Every drop grated at my nerves worse than the one before. Our bedroom door was open, and I heard two sets of footsteps in the distance. The whole time, Sienna and I stared at one another as though daring the other to blink first.

"What do you want to know?" she relented, tossing the brush on a small nightstand between our beds. Running both her hands through the strands, she started drying her hair with small bursts of air magic.

"Is Granite the head of the rebellion? The one at the very top?" Even after spending several years as part of the organization, I knew very little about them. All domed cities had a branch, though some were more active than others. I knew there were factions in the Freelands, but I'd thought they were more like helpers than leaders.

"He's a captain," Sienna replied simply, like I should know what they meant. "I don't know how many captains there are, so don't bother asking. Granite does have a lot of influence, maybe even more than the others."

"Probably because he's so fertile." The snarky comment just popped out.

Sienna snorted. "Yeah, I don't know the deal with that. Some say he was a big playboy when he was younger." Her brows drew together as she reconsidered. "I guess he still is, actually—his youngest is only a few months old."

"Does he purposely send his children beneath the domes?" Even as I asked, I was fairly certain I knew the answer.

"Yeah. He has at least one in every American kingdom. Supposedly there's a Dresden in Europe, too. Not sure if that's true."

"What's the plan for Austin?" I asked next.

She shrugged. "The casters in power will be arrested and put on trial for their crimes against our people. All others will be given the option to remain under the dome if they agree to abide by the laws of the new regime."

Nothing she said came as a surprise, but her blasé tone gave me chills. Particularly since I knew the little that she'd said was an oversimplification.

"What about the citizenship trials?" I narrowed my eyes and watched her face for even the slightest twitch to indicate she was lying.

Hair dried and styled in beachy waves, Sienna's hands fell back to her lap. She glanced toward the window where outside the sun was starting to sink below the horizon. "You should probably just see for yourself. It's hard to explain. The queen will be sent outside the dome soon, though her true test won't come until later."

My insides went numb. I really didn't want to watch a

caster freeze to death outside the dome. Granite had invited me to join him for a viewing party that night. I would've preferred eating rusty nails, but the invitation had truly been an order.

"What happens after Austin? Do they plan on invading other domed cities?" I asked, switching directions.

She squinted her eyes, studying me just as intensely as I'd been studying her a moment before. Languidly, like a cat, she stretched out on the bed. As she propped herself up with her elbow, Sienna's gaze never once left my face.

I brushed my cheeks with the back of my hand. "What? Do I have something on me?"

"Do you really expect me to believe you're just curious?" She laughed like the idea was ridiculous.

"As opposed to what?" I demanded, confused.

Her eyes darted back and forth around the empty room like the walls had eyes and ears. "I know you're talking to him," she hissed, voice barely above a whisper.

"Talking to who?"

Sienna gave a dramatic eye roll. "The king. I can feel the magic coming from your backpack."

The bracelet, I realized. Sienna had always been extremely sensitive to magic. Still, it made me nervous that I was walking around with an enchanted beacon. Since there was no point in lying, and I really didn't have anything to hide, I told Sienna the truth.

"It was a gift from Kai, I didn't know anything about it until last night. I think it can send messages back and forth, but I'm not really sure. I haven't sent him anything, I swear."

She held out her free hand. "Let me see."

I hesitated. It was just a bracelet, and it wasn't like she could run off with it, yet it was my only tangible reminder of Kai. I didn't know when or if I'd ever see him again. Losing that piece of him, of us, was more than I could handle just then.

"I just want to feel the magic up close. Relax," Sienna scoffed.

Reluctantly, I retrieved the bangle and handed it over. Sienna sat up and rolled the bracelet between her palms, closing her eyes and breathing in magic I could neither see nor feel. A slow smile spread across her face.

"Your caster is extremely powerful. And talented," she murmured, an almost dreamy quality to her voice.

Watching the scene with perverse fascination, I almost asked if she wanted to be alone with the enchanted bracelet.

Sienna's eyes popped open after minute. "There's a location spell on this, in addition to the messaging."

"Is the location spell strong enough to find me here?" I asked, hating that she was so much more knowledgeable.

I really should've worked harder on my magic, I thought.

"Not in Revival. The wards are too strong." With some reluctance, she handed the bracelet back to me.

"And the messages? Will I still get any from Kai?" I asked, slipping it back into my backpack.

She shook her head. "Not inside the wards. You won't be able to send him any, either. Just so you know."

"Seriously, I haven't," I snapped defensively.

"I know." Sienna smirked. "Because you don't know how."

Gaia, I hated that she was right.

"Whatever. Now will you tell me what happens next? I obviously can't tell Kai anyway."

"The Kingdom of the Carolinas," she answered matter-of-factly. "A faction of the rebellion is already near the Domed City of Charlotte. They invade at midnight."

This was exactly what I'd been afraid of. Admittedly, my true fear was that L.A. would be next. That Kai would soon be subjected to a fate worse than the one he'd saved me from. I couldn't allow that. I *wouldn't* allow that.

One problem at a time. While I didn't want the rebellion to get their hands on Kai, they already had Cala and the others in their grip. Until Delancey kept her promise to let me talk to them, I needed to be careful. My friends had already been forced from Hawaii because of me, I wouldn't let them be used as pawns by the rebellion, too.

"Look, Brie…I know you think you love him," Sienna began, her tone surprisingly gentle. "But he's a caster. A king. His family is responsible for everything bad that has happened to you. You need to remember that. This uprising isn't like any before. We will prevail. We will get justice against the casters. Don't you want to be on the winning side?"

Though I didn't dignify the question with a response, Sienna's words echoed through my brain as I finished getting ready for Granite's viewing party. Queen Georgina's citizenship trial was already underway when we arrived in the residential wing of the palace.

For someone who objects to royalty, Granite sure doesn't have a problem living in monarch quarters, I thought dryly. Fires burned in three separate fireplaces in the large living room. Portraits of Granite and his family hung in the gold frames on the walls—frames that I was willing to bet had once held paintings of caster kings and queens.

Shifters, fae, and everything in between were already lounging on heavy leather furniture, munching on racks of ribs and burgers. All eyes were on the screen above one fireplace, where the former Texan queen was crouched in a clump of frozen bushes, panting heavily.

"I'll bet guard duty tomorrow morning that she doesn't make it past this first test," a blonde shifter said to the guy next to him.

"She's a fighter," the other one replied, shaking his head. "I say she at least makes it through this one, but I'll take your bet."

"You might want to keep the looks of disgust to a minimum," Sienna muttered in my ear.

"Maybrie, Sienna, come sit," Granite called from a large leather armchair in the corner.

Several kids sat on cushions on the ground around the water fae, likely more of his offspring. A were-lion in head-to-toe leather hurried to find two empty chairs, and the children rearranged to make room for us. Delancey had been standing against the wall near the buffet table but joined us near her father.

"You're late," she said flatly.

"Sorry, I don't think this is a spectator sport," I snapped, gesturing to the screen. Georgina was whipping her head around as if searching for the source of a noise in the darkness.

"Brie," Sienna groaned my name.

Delancey smiled coldly. "The casters bet on your fights. Whether you win or lose. Whether you kill or are killed. What's the difference?"

My protest died in my throat. The words stuck, because they were true. I'd seen new fighters sob through their first match. House fae were subjected to far worse treatment than a night or two on their own in the cold darkness. Had I spent too much time beneath the dome? Had I gotten so used to the casters' shitty treatment of us that I'd become desensitized? That I sympathized too much with my jailers? Was this the justice people like Queen Georgina deserved?

Is this the justice that Kai deserves, too? The traitorous thought reverberated in my head and brought back Sienna's words from earlier.

Georgina's ear-piercing scream brought me out of my own head. A pack of wolves surrounded her, eyes glowing yellow in the darkness. One slow step at a time, they advanced in unison. The onlookers in Granite's private quarters leaned forward, literally on the edge of their seats with anticipation.

My heart raced in my chest. I wanted to scream at the stupid caster queen to do something. Most royals were extremely powerful, like Kai. Yet Georgina was just standing there and shaking. Where was her sense of self-preservation?

It wasn't until one of the wolves lunged for her that Georgina finally thought to use her witchy abilities. With a wave of her hand, she sent a barrage of icicles zooming toward the wolf's exposed underbelly. The shifter yelped in pain as he crumpled to the frozen ground. Dark red blood stained the snow beneath his body. A second wolf advanced with a low growl, and blue light shot from Georgina's outstretched hands. The wolf somersaulted backward through the air in a blur of grey fur.

Run, you idiot, I thought.

It took three more attacks before Georgina realized she needed to stop playing defense and go on the offensive. She threw her arms toward the inky black sky and cried out an incantation I didn't recognize. Sparks rained down on the wolves, singeing their fur on contact. The pack howled and scattered. The queen spun on her dirty snow boots and ran for all she was worth.

Back at Revival Palace, the onlookers let out a collective groan of disapproval. Well, except for the guy who'd bet guard duty that the queen would make it through the first test.

"She has two more trials tonight," Delancey informed me, studying me out of the corner of her eye.

"Then what?" I asked, curiosity getting the better of me.

Delancey shrugged and crossed her arms over her chest. "She'll have a few hours to rest if she can, eat if she can find food, and recharge if she knows how."

"What does that mean?"

I'd thought I understood how these citizenship trials worked. The caster was sent outside the dome and made to survive for forty-eight hours. But it wasn't quite so simple. The wolves didn't just happen by Georgina or vice versa. They were a test. An actual test that the queen needed to pass in order to keep going with the trial. Only, I was pretty sure Georgina had no clue about the rules of the very dangerous game she was playing.

"She's in a warded area," Delancey explained. "Others can enter, but she can't leave. If she reaches the edge, she'll be transported back to the center. There are edible plants and packs of dehydrated rations throughout the space, as well as hidden objects that have been infused with magic. All she needs to do is find them."

The knots in my stomach loosened. I still thought these trials were barbaric, but at least Georgina had a chance. Even if she wasn't aware of the fact.

"If she's strong, a survivor, she'll figure out what she needs to do to make it through the trial," Delancey continued.

"And if not?" I pressed, though I knew the answer.

"She'll die." Delancey leveled me with a hard look. "As the weak should."

For the next hour or so, we watched Georgina run around aimlessly in the snow. She didn't seem to realize she was going in circles, a fact I'd picked up on the third time she passed a weird rock formation. If she'd been smart, she would have ducked inside the enclosure to get out of the wind. Sleet started falling, undoubtedly summoned by a water fae.

"Another test?" I asked Delancey.

She shook her head. "Not exactly. The sleet is to make it more entertaining for us."

The pit in my belly grew.

"You think we're being cruel but give it time. Once you have more distance from your old life, you'll realize we aren't the enemy." Botto's sister leaned closer. Instinctively, I drew back. "Your precious King Kai is the one who deserves your anger," she hissed.

I gritted my teeth, ignoring the niggle at the base of my skull that reminded me I used to feel that way. It wasn't all that long ago that I would have relished the sight of a royal caster trying to survive in the frozen tundra that so many fae called home. That anger had lived and festered within me for years.

With a toss of my hair, I met Delancey's satisfied gaze. She knew her words had struck a chord, but I refused to give her the satisfaction of saying so aloud. "I might not consider you so much of an enemy if you kept your word and let me talk to my friends."

Straightening to her full height, Delancey laughed. "Well played, Brie. Well played." She cocked her head to the side. "Follow me."

CHAPTER TWELVE

DOMED CITY OF AUSTIN, KINGDOM OF THE AMERICAS

Cala

CALA PACED BACK and forth, chewing the cherry red polish from her thumbnail. Nya had pulled her from the dorm where the rebels who weren't part of the citizenship trial were watching the televised broadcast. After a day of sitting with rebellion leaders while they sentenced caster after caster, Cala had been left with a hollow, empty feeling inside. Sort of like hunger, except she didn't think she could stomach food. When Nya had come for her, Cala felt a flood of relief, even when the other woman refused to tell her where they were going.

But once she was left alone in a windowless room that reeked of magic, Cala would've given the contents of her bank account back in Hawaii to return to the dorm. The door opened, and Cala froze mid-pace. She'd expected Nya, but it was Ryun who slipped inside. His tan cheeks had two rosy patches, and his hair was slightly damp.

"Have you been outside the dome?" Cala asked curiously. She knew Ryun and Nya were related but couldn't figure out the power dynamic between them. Or anyone else for that matter. The siblings definitely held sway over the foot soldiers, many of whom went still when either of the duo passed by. Nya gave out orders like it was her job, which it probably was. More than one person had cowered in fear when giving Ryun less than awesome news. And yet, neither of the siblings had stepped in front of the cameras or even taken a lead role in the day's stadium proceedings.

"I'm overseeing the individual tests," Ryun said, his response a non-answer.

Unlike his sister and most of the of other rebels Cala had encountered, Ryun didn't seem to get any pleasure out of the so-called justice they were handing out to the casters of Austin. Cala wasn't sure how she felt about all these trials and tests yet, but she did know that Nya's smug smile made her feel ill. Caster after caster had been dragged into the center of the arena where Hale gave them the same choice as he had the royal couple, and Nya clearly enjoyed it.

"What's up?" Cala asked, fiddling with the ID bracelet around her wrist. "Why am I here?"

Ryun's lips quirked into a half smile. "Nervous?"

Obviously, she thought, not that Cala would admit that to him or anyone else in Austin. Instead, she frowned and repeated the question. "Why am I here?"

"Relax. Someone wants to talk to you." Ryun flicked his wrist toward one of the blank walls. The paint blistered and bubbled before sort of melting away. A shimmering hole grew, like a window to nothingness beyond.

Shifters didn't use magic the same way fae and casters did. Their transformations were magical, sort of, but that was very different than wielding power and casting spells. Witches and warlocks at Hideout, Cala's favorite bar on Oahu, often used simple spells for stupid shit like summoning their drink from across the table or impressing someone they hoped to take home for the night. Some of Cala's fae opponents even fought in the pits with magic. But whatever Ryun has just done was much more involved, much more advanced than anything she'd ever witnessed firsthand.

A girl's strained face appeared behind the window. Cala's eyes went wide, tears pooling instantly. "Brie!" she exclaimed, reaching out as though to touch her best friend's cheek.

Ryun pulled her hand back before she could make contact and shook his head. "No touching. It might interfere with the connection."

It took Brie's face a full thirty seconds to register Cala's appearance, almost like there was a time delay or something.

"Oh my, Gaia! Are you okay?" Brie demanded, leaning

forward like she was trying to get a better look at Cala's surroundings.

"Me?" Cala squeaked. A high-pitched giggle escaped her lips. "You're the one who was actually arrested. Are *you* okay?"

Brie smiled and ran a hand over her dark ponytail. "You escaped an island kingdom in the middle of a crisis lockdown."

"Okay, enough." Ryun stepped in front of Cala. He held up one hand toward her and one in Brie's direction. "We all get it. You've both managed to escape domed cities. You're both badass. Can we move this conversation along? I can't hold the connection forever."

With the look Brie shot him, it was a wonder Ryun didn't burst into flames on the spot. A snotty comment was on the tip of Cala's tongue, until she noticed the line of sweat forming on the shifter's forehead. Inhaling deeply, she took in the scents of perspiration and aftershave. The magical video conference was costing him a great deal.

"I'm fine. I'm in Austin, where are you?" Cala asked hurriedly.

Brie's scowl remained firmly in place, which made Cala smile. It was nice to know that recent events hadn't crushed her best friend's spirit.

"Revival," Brie replied. "I'm in Revival."

Cala's gaze shifted to Ryun. Throughout the day she'd heard numerous mentions of this mysterious Revival place. Every time she'd asked for specifics, people clammed up.

"I'll explain later," he muttered.

"Are you coming here? Am I going there? When do I get to see you, for real?" Cala asked, returning her attention to Brie.

Beside her, Ryun's strain was becoming more evident. Sweat dampened his shirt beneath his arms and down his back. There wasn't time for many questions, and most of what she wanted to know couldn't be asked in front of him.

"I don't know." Brie shook her head. "They ration their information even more sparsely than the food here."

Again, Cala looked at Ryun for answers. "You'll see each other soon," he promised.

"Okay, you've seen her. She's alive and whole," a female voice said on Brie's side of the wall, sounding extremely irritated.

Cala tried to peer around her best friend to locate the source of the comment, but Brie's shoulders took up the entire view.

"Hi, Delancey," Ryun drawled, his tone showing no hint of his physical discomfort.

"Hello, little brother," said the woman.

Brie cleared her throat loudly. "Where are Rocko and Everly? Are they with you?"

Cala nodded. "Yeah, they're good. Much happier now that we're with the rebellion." She tried to sound upbeat, like life really had improved drastically since the trio touched down on the mainland. Brie wasn't fooled.

"And you? Are you much happier now?"

Cala's gaze found her shoes—a pair of sneakers she'd been given along with new clothes. She was used to lying about all sorts of things, and she knew she was pretty good at it. But Cala found she couldn't lie to Brie. She also didn't want to tell the truth and risk being booted out of Austin or made to go through a citizenship trial like the queen. Instead, she shrugged.

"It's been a lot," she hedged. "The last few days have been a lot."

"I'm sorry, Cala. For everything," Brie said softly. "I wish there was something I could do to make it up to you." Her voice cracked. "I don't know if that's even possible."

Cala didn't know either. She didn't know anything anymore. Well, she did know one thing. "I'm pretty sure I have you to thank for the bed I'm about to sleep in and the food I've eaten, so we're even."

Ever since she'd seen Brie standing on the platform inside the arena, Cala had known why the rebellion took them in without much fuss. Nya wasn't being nice. The word probably wasn't even in her vocabulary. The rebellion needed Brie, if only as a symbol of change. Cala had overheard rebel soldiers talking about the fire fae who'd infiltrated the royal family and murdered a queen. The rebellion had spun the facts to fit their own narrative, and now they needed Brie's cooperation to keep the story going. Knowing Brie as she did, her best friend would've required great incentive to perpetuate that lie. Cala, Everly, and Rocko were that incentive.

"I'm so sorry," Brie repeated, her voice suddenly more distant than before.

Cala didn't need to look at Ryun to know he was losing his hold on the spell. Her super sensitive nose easily picked up on the unique aroma of fatigue and pride that she usually only smelled in the arena.

"Don't be," Cala told her best friend. "Just make sure you pick the right side in all this."

Brie's pretty face faded from view. An instant later, the wall was back to its pre-conversation appearance, without so much as a paint chip missing. For a long minute, Cala stared at the spot where Brie's face had been and wondered which was the right side. She didn't like bowing to casters any more than the next shifter, but they weren't all bad. Not even all royals were bad. She'd dated one of Kai's distant cousins for a few months. He'd treated her exceptionally well, even though they both knew it would never go beyond casual fun together.

Sure, there were some casters Cala would have loved to watch fight for their lives. Like the asshole pit master, for one, who made the new fighters spar in as little clothing as possible. She would offer to help with his trial if the chance ever arose.

"So, that's the famous Maybrie Hawkins," Ryun said, interrupting her thoughts.

She'd been so caught up in her own head that Cala didn't realize they'd turned the wrong way out of the little room where she'd met with Brie. At least, it was the wrong way to return to her dorm.

"Yep, that's Brie," Cala agreed. She slowed and took in her surroundings. They were in a sparse hallway with lots of closed doors, including a tall set at the opposite end. She would've been nervous if not for the wonderful scent of baking bread coming from behind those very doors.

"Are you going to make me work in the kitchen as payment for the phone call? I should really warn you, I'm an awful cook."

He barely hid a grin. "I just thought you might be hungry. You haven't eaten much since you arrived. Lucky for you, I'm an excellent cook."

Tilting her head to one side, she peered up at him. Was he messing with her? Ryun had that gruff sort of charm that was like a drug to her, making it hard for Cala to see past his good looks. Still, she knew better than to trust him.

"You've been watching me."

It wasn't a question, but Ryun offered an explanation anyway. "Everyone's watching you. You're an unknown. This is sort of a family-run organization, where only trusted people are invited to the inner circle. You're sort of a special case."

Ryun pushed open the double doors and gestured her inside the industrial kitchen. Loaves of fresh bread were stacked on cooling racks. Cala's mouth watered. Back in Hawaii, all her meals were takeout from restaurants. Being inside of a kitchen with homecooked food was a rarity that Cala hadn't experienced since she's left the Freelands. Memories surfaced, painful reminders that she hadn't let herself dwell upon.

A buzzer dinged over the oven. Ryun pulled on a mitt and withdrew a hot pan from inside the oven, placing it on the countertop. Cala watched wordlessly as he moved to the refrigerator and retrieved butter, a block of cheese, and two apples.

"Do you want some help?" she asked as he selected a

knife from a wooden block and began chopping the fruit.

He chuckled. "There's no way I'm giving you a weapon."

"What?" Cala wasn't sure exactly what he was suggesting, but she didn't like it.

Ryun looked up from his task. "You can't possibly be surprised that I don't trust you. You don't trust me either, I get it."

"I trust you," she said automatically.

He laughed. "You're a horrible liar. How did you last so long beneath a dome?"

Hands on her hips, Cala glared at the hybrid indignantly. "What's that supposed to mean?"

"Kissing caster ass takes a good poker face."

"I don't kiss caster ass," she shot back.

Ryun quirked an eyebrow and resumed prepping the meal. "If you say so."

"I don't. It's not...you don't get it. You don't understand what it's like."

Why was she defending the casters? They had taken her from her home, from her family. They'd forced her to fight for their enjoyment. They'd also given her a warm place to sleep and put food in her belly. Before the dome, Cala had never known what it felt like to be full. Or truly safe. Yeah, a lot about life beneath the dome sucked, and she understood why fae like Everly craved their old lives. Maybe if Cala had been made to share magic with the casters, she would feel differently.

"Tell me then. What's it like to live in a domed city?"

She couldn't decide if Ryun was genuinely curious or just screwing with her. Nonetheless, she gave him the truth. A version of it, anyway. He listened quietly as she talked about her life on the island, about the friends she'd made and the fun they'd had together.

"And you're okay with the way the casters monitor you. The way they treat you like you're beneath them?" he asked when she paused for breath. There was only mild accusation in his tone, though he tried to hide it.

"Look, there are parts of my life that are pretty shitty," Cala admitted. "Or, I don't know, there used to be. The past few years, fighting has just been like any other job for me. And I'm rewarded for it."

He slid a plate of sliced apples, cheese cubes, and buttered bread her way. "And you've had other jobs to compare it to, ones outside the dome?"

"No, smart ass." Cala bit into an apple slice. The crisp, sweet taste filled her mouth. "But I get paid. A lot. I also get invited to parties and go on dates. I don't worry if I'm going to freeze to death in my sleep or starve so my kid sisters and grandparents get enough to eat."

"Not everyone has it like that," Ryun replied.

"No, they don't." She met his eyes. "Have you ever lived beneath a dome?"

Ryun shook his head and popped a cheese cube between his lips.

"Don't knock until you try it," she said.

"As long as you remember that, too."

"What's that supposed to mean?" Cala demanded.

"I'm not stupid, Cala. Your friend Everly is genuinely glad to be here. And I'm sure you're happy to have a dome between you and the elements. But you don't want to be a part of what we're doing. You think the citizenship trials are cruel. I know Brie didn't kill Queen Lilli. I also know you've spent time with the new king and his sister."

She dropped the piece of bread in her hand without taking a bite. "So?"

"So, let's just be honest with one another."

"Honest?" She scoffed. "You think if you bat your lashes, I'll just spill all my secrets? Okay, sure. You go first."

"Fine. Your presence here is very precarious. The family seems to think they can control Brie as long as they have you." He shrugged noncommittally. "But you already know all that. Let me tell you something you don't know. All the fae and shifters who are deemed too friendly with casters will eventually face the citizenship trial or exile. If you aren't careful, even Brie won't be able to save you."

Her blood ran cold. None of what he said came as a surprise, she just hadn't expected Ryun to be so blunt. Cala refused to give him the satisfaction of seeing her squirm.

"From what I've seen, I'd do just fine in your trials," she said flippantly.

"Likely," he agreed. Oddly, his tone suggested that might not be a good thing. "But you don't know the stakes. Just because you'd pass the tests and complete the trial, that doesn't mean you'd come away unscathed. There are still consequences, a price that must be paid."

The doors burst open and Nya marched in, looking way too put together for the time of night. Her ear to ear grin gave Cala chills.

"We've taken the Carolinas. Queen Maxine's own

guards handed her right over," Nya announced gleefully. "She goes before the cameras at dawn."

The woman's dark eyes flashed as they landed on Cala. "Next we take L.A. We'll find out how good a friend Maybrie Hawkins really is."

CHAPTER THIRTEEN

DOMED CITY OF LOS ANGELES, KINGDOM OF THE AMERICAS

Kai

AT FIRST, KAI thought his mind was playing tricks on him; the spot of golden light didn't seem real. Then he felt the familiar rush he always experienced in the presence of fae magic. The dot of light grew bigger and brighter. Kai glanced at Kenoa beside him in the living room of the penthouse suite. His best friend's jaw was set in a grim line, muscles taught like he was ready for a fight.

The light gave way to a black hole. A portal, Kai realized. He watched with fascination as a tall, gangly form grew bigger, as though walking down a long tunnel. Kenoa stepped in front him, blocking Kai's view of the visitor.

There was a scuffling noise, and then a young, male voice spoke. "Oops. Sorry, I'm still getting the hang of this."

Kai peered around his best friend at a boy with a mop of dark hair and toothy smile. It was the eyes that got him, though. He would've recognized that keen, inquisitive gaze anywhere. That and the dark hair were about the only similarities between Brie and her younger brother, however.

"Illion?" Kai asked just to be certain.

"Your Majesty." Illion bowed awkwardly. "Is that right? Or should I call you King Kai? Or just king? Sorry, man. We don't have royalty where I'm from."

Kai couldn't help but smile. "Just Kai is fine. And this is—"

"Kenoa," Illion interrupted. "Yeah, I know. I'm a huge fan. Last year, I traded with a were-monkey at the fair for old fight tapes. I've seen a bunch of your matches. You're a legend, dude."

Kai chuckled, but the water fae didn't crack a smile. "And you're a dimensional fae," Kenoa responded flatly.

Dimensional fae were rare. Prior to Tanner Woods, Kai had believed they were just a myth. He still wasn't convinced they were a category unto themselves. Fae magic came from the elements, but what element allowed someone like Illion to manipulate time and space?

"Ah, so you've met others. That's awesome." Illion flashed a grin. It was so like the one his sister wore when she was truly happy that Kai's heart ached for Brie.

"Why did you want to talk to us?" Kenoa pressed, seemingly immune to the kid's charm.

"Not that I'm not totally geeking out right now because you're here, but I really came to get the caster king. I'm sure Dad will be cool if you want to come, too."

"We aren't going anywhere." Kenoa crossed his arms over his massive chest and gave Illion a glare that had brought older men to their knees.

Brie's brother wrinkled his nose. "I'm afraid you are. And we should probably go sooner rather than later. Magic of this magnitude won't go undetected forever."

The portal was still open, just one continuous dark tunnel to nowhere from Kai's vantage. Following the young fae into that void was probably stupid, yet Kai didn't hesitate. Kenoa grabbed the king's arm.

"This is very risky, you do get that, right? He's taking you outside the dome," the water fae hissed.

"To Fae Canyon, I assume," Kai replied, calmly peeling his best friend's fingers loose from the sleeve of his parka.

"Yep. Fae Canyon," Illion called over his shoulder. "My dad and the other elders are waiting."

Kai stepped into the portal, Kenoa on his heels. Brie's brother walked ahead of them, whistling a catchy tune that would likely be stuck in Kai's head for weeks to come. The air grew steadily colder the deeper they went. Kai knew the instant they crossed outside the dome. It wasn't any great light display like when he crossed in an airship, but a feeling in his stomach let him know. Well, that and the plunging temperature.

"You do realize that you might be marching to your death," Kenoa muttered. Not that there was a point to keeping his voice down; the tunnel was narrow, and all sound echoed within the confines.

"You do realize you're being dramatic," Kai countered. "This is Brie's family."

Kenoa sighed loudly. "Just because you rule a kingdom doesn't mean you know shit about the way stuff works in the Freelands."

The king rolled his eyes in the darkness as Illion's peel of laughter danced around the passage. "Just because you're fae doesn't mean you know shit about how stuff works in the Freelands," Kai countered.

Illion turned to face them but continued walking backward. "I'm pretty sure neither one of you knows shit about shit. The big man has a right to be nervous. Technically, we don't allow our people to date casters. Our elders could vote to kill you for messing with my sister."

Kai swallowed thickly. *This trip just became my most serious lapse in judgement to date,* he thought, unable to face Kenoa and the I-told-you-so expression his best friend was surely wearing. *Awesome.*

"Relax," the younger boy said. "That's not why Dad wants to see you. I mean, don't expect him to welcome you with open arms and call you son or whatever. But you're not in danger."

"Why does your father want to speak with me?" Kai asked.

The teen smirked. "Gaia, it must be really weird for you right now."

"How do you mean?" Kai's clothes suddenly felt too tight.

"You're a king, used to people doing whatever you want. Particularly fae." Illion tripped over his own large feet, laughing at his own clumsiness. "Now, I have all the answers, and you have only questions. That must really irk you."

Kenoa snorted. Kai frowned. "It might surprise you to know that I have grown accustomed to fae usurping my authority," he grumbled.

Illion turned back around and called over his shoulder. "Yeah, Brie's sort of stubborn. She's never been much for the rules."

The warmth that spread through Kai hearing the fondness in Illion's voice was short-lived.

"Dad says that's why she got caught."

They made the rest of the journey in silence.

Kai didn't know what he'd been expecting to find at the other end of the tunnel. Honestly, he hadn't given it a lot of thought. The homie log cabin with a fire roaring in the hearth was definitely not the first scene he would've pictured, though. An older fae with a full head of pure white hair sat in a rocking chair with a quilt spread over his legs.

At first glance, the fae appeared frail. But when a man who could've only been Brie's father turned to greet his guests, Kai felt the weight of his magic. In another life, this could've been his father-in-law. When he opened his mouth to greet the elder man, Kenoa clamped a hand down on his shoulder and shook his head in warning.

Brie's father appraised Kai openly, his shrewd gaze

making the king squirm.

"So, you are the mighty caster king who stole my daughter."

Kai shifted awkwardly from one foot to the other. "My name is Kai, sir."

"Elder Hawkins," Brie's father corrected. His wrinkled face turned to Kenoa. "You serve this warlock who kidnapped my Maybrie?"

"He doesn't serve me," Kai said quickly.

"I wasn't speaking to you," the old fae snapped. "Let the boy talk for himself. We allow that here."

Kai pursed his lips. The meeting was not off to a stellar start. It was obvious that Brie took after her father, which was probably why Kai liked the guy despite his prickly nature.

"I am employed by the royal family, Elder Hawkins," Kenoa replied, his tone firm but polite.

"In an advisory capacity," Kai felt the need to add. "He's one of my advisors." He knew before the words left his mouth that he would regret speaking up.

Elder Hawkins leveled him with a look that held more heat than one of Brie's fireballs. "And is my daughter *one* of your playthings?"

"Oh, Gaia. Come on, Dad. That's my sister you're talking about," Illion interjected, brushing past Kai and flopping down on a patchwork sofa in the small living room.

"I love Brie very much," Kai replied, refusing to take the bait.

The man's smile didn't reach his eyes. "And you believe my daughter loves you?"

"I know she does."

Elder Hawkins didn't so much as blink. "Then you are a fool. Caged animals do not love their captors."

Kenoa's hand was still on his shoulder, and the water fae gave him a warning squeeze. Kai pointedly ignored it. "I understand why you believe the worst of me. I deserve that. I have made a lot of mistakes, and I have let a lot of people around me treat others with disrespect. But I do love Brie. And I know for a fact she loves me."

The silence that followed was heavy with tension. Kai was convinced his little speech was yet another misstep. Kenoa was right, damn him. Fae communities like this one were led by proud elders with rules and customs that Kai could never fully appreciate. And still, he'd waltzed into this man's house and acted like the pompous king so many fae thought him to be.

Finally, the old man said, "How far are you willing to go to prove it?"

"Kai," Kenoa growled. "Be careful."

"I've already wagered my kingdom on her love for me, so I suppose you could say I am willing to go as far as it takes for her. For *us*."

Elder Hawkins offered him a genuine smile as Illion clapped his hands together like a child. "I had hoped you would say as much. The Council of Elders will grant you an audience at dawn. For tonight, you will stay here."

What did I just do? Kai wondered silently.

There were only two bedrooms in the Hawkins' house. One belonged to Brie's father, and the other was her brother's. Illion offered Kai and Kenoa his room, saying he preferred the couch anyway. Two twin beds were flush against opposite walls, several feet between them. Both beds were covered with handmade quilts and feather pillows. Illion's side of the room was covered in schoolbooks and drawing pads, while the other was tidy with only a few stuffed animals and a vase of fresh flowers.

Kai ran his fingertips over the bed where Brie had slept for most of her life. Tears stung his eyes but didn't fall down his cheeks. It wasn't the first time he'd felt like crying since Brie's arrest and subsequent escape, but it was the first time he blamed himself for her predicament. Not just for the arrest, either. This was the life his family had stolen from her. This was the house that had been her one true home. These were the people who'd been left to grieve for their lost child and sister. How long had they wondered what happened to her? How long had they known it was all his fault she was gone?

"You should get some sleep if you can," Kenoa said softly. He sat on Illion's bed, folding the many layers of clothes he'd shed while Kai beat himself up for all the pain he'd brought on this house.

Kai shrugged out of his parka and boots, then peeled off a sweater and collared shirt. He debated about the jeans. The Hawkins' house was warmer than he'd anticipated but still much colder than the palace. *You'll regret it tomorrow if you sleep in too many layers,* he told himself. Once down to his boxers and undershirt, Kai dove beneath the covers, pleasantly surprised to find the bed warm enough.

Kenoa extinguished the oil lamps, leaving only a wedge of hazy moonlight between the beds to illuminate the room. The water fae then climbed into Illion's bed and peered at Kai in the faint light.

"Don't," Kai said tiredly. "I'm really not in the mood for a lecture."

Kenoa propped himself up on one elbow. "I don't care. You need to listen to me, Kai. You don't understand what you've agreed to. Hell, I don't even completely understand. I'm just as much an outsider as you here. But I'm still fae, and I do know some of the customs. A declaration of love for the child of an elder is serious, particularly when it's followed by an invitation for an audience with the Council of Elders."

This was not news to Kai. "Serious how, precisely?"

"Children of elders are sort of like royalty. And by sort of, I mean they are. At least in places like this. Their suitors need to prove worthy. It's not uncommon for elders to betroth their children to one another, often to secure alliances with another community. You know, the same way that Sarah will marry a foreign prince."

Kai suddenly felt ill. "Brie has a fiancé?"

"That's your takeaway here?" Kenoa rolled his eyes. "My point is, you're meeting with the council so they can decide if you're worthy of Brie."

Oh, how the tables have turned, Kai thought, giggling a little under his breath.

Kenoa's brow creased. Starting the instant Kai had realized how he truly felt about Brie, he'd lived with the worry that his people wouldn't accept her as their queen. The fact she was fae was the least of it. Brie was opinionated and feisty, and not at all like Madame Noelani's girls, who were considered suitable spouses for influential casters. That was why he liked her so much.

Never once had it occurred to Kai that he would be the one deemed unworthy.

Wow, I really am an asshole, he thought.

"You need to get it together," Kenoa said as Kai laughed harder.

The king wiped his eyes with the back of his hand. "I'm fine, Ken. It's just, I don't know…funny, I guess. Everyone acts like she is lucky to share my bed, when this whole time I've been the fortunate one."

"We didn't need to come to Fae Canyon to figure that out. You need to take this seriously. I don't know how these things work, but I can't imagine it's going to be easy or pleasant for you."

That sobered Kai up quickly. What were the elders going to make him do? And was this really the best time for him to prove his worth? There was a war raging. The rebellion had taken a city and arrested casters. His little sister sat on his throne, ruling with her heart instead of her head.

"Since you are all knowing, why now? Why are you letting me go through with this—whatever this is—now, with everything else going on?" Not that Kai had given his friend a choice when he'd followed Brie's brother into a portal, but Kenoa could've kept him from taking the meeting at all.

Kenoa rolled onto his back. "Elder Hawkins knows things. Things we probably need to know, too. He isn't going to share those things with a caster king. But he might tell the man who's proven himself worthy of a woman who is considered a princess of the fae."

That night, for the first time in a long time, Kai went to sleep feeling like something other than a useless piece of crap. He didn't care what the fae elders put him through, just as long as it helped Brie. That thought and the sheets that smelled faintly of cinnamon, Brie's favorite flavor of tea, lulled him into a dreamless sleep.

Chapter Fourteen

REVIVAL, FORMERLY KNOWN AS THE DOMED CITY OF SANTA FE,
KINGDOM OF THE AMERICAS

Brie

"GET UP."

Something as cold and hard as my unwelcome guest's command poked me in the shoulder. Rolling onto my side, I groaned audibly and looked up into Delancey Dresden's dark eyes.

"What do you want?" At least, that was what I meant to say. Judging by her confused expression, the words came out garbled.

"We're meeting with the nomads for a prisoner exchange. You have ten minutes."

My head was still fuzzy from sleep, making it hard to process her words fully. "You want me to go with you? Why?"

Delancey's heels clicked on the floorboards. *Seriously, what does she have against sneakers?*

Botto's sister turned, one hand on the doorframe. "You lost him. You're going to help get him back." With those parting words, she marched from the bedroom.

I flopped onto my back and rubbed sleep from my eyes. The sky outside was a dark purplish-blue, sunrise still an hour or so away. I couldn't recall what time I'd gone to bed. After talking to Cala, I'd been too keyed up to sleep and wandered the palace halls to burn off the nervous energy.

"I wouldn't keep her waiting," Sienna advised, her voice muffled from beneath the covers of the bed beside mine.

She'd been asleep when I returned to the room the previous night, which was probably for the best since I hadn't felt like chatting. My eyelids drooped. Keeping them open was a struggle.

Five minutes. I'll just close my eyes for five more minutes.

"Brie," Sienna snapped, smacking her hands together loudly to get my attention.

"Yeah, yeah. I'm going."

"Do you want to get Botto back or not?"

The rhetorical question finally shocked me awake. As much as I hated to admit it, Sienna was right. I needed to move my ass. It was Botto we were talking about, and he was only with the nomad people because of me. He'd sacrificed himself to make sure I got away. So yeah, the least I could do was join his sister for this prisoner exchange.

Thanks to my procrastination, I only had about three minutes in the shower. It was barely enough time for the water to warm up to an acceptable temperature. If not for my fire magic, I would have spent the entire time shivering. After showering, I pulled on a heavy sweater with long underwear beneath cargo pants. I was just finishing lacing up my boots when Delancey banged on the door.

"Have fun." Sienna propped herself up on one elbow and smirked up at me.

Drying my hair with heated hands, I twisted the dark locks into a bun on the top of my head. "Why aren't you coming with us?" I asked suspiciously.

Sienna shrugged. "I wasn't invited." She flopped onto her stomach and pulled the covers back over her head.

Rolling my eyes, I grabbed my jacket and yanked the door open to find Delancey with her fist poised to knock again.

"Let's go." I marched past her and down the hall, having no clue if I was even walking in the right direction.

Four rebel soldiers, one female and three males, met us in front of the palace on snowmobiles. They still didn't trust me, because I didn't get my own vehicle for our trek. Instead, I rode with a were-bear named Cova who wore only a leather vest and jeans to ward off the cold.

Revival was quiet at dawn. The only people we saw were a few soldiers out patrolling the streets and bakery workers kneading dough in a storefront. It was no less weird to see the frozen city the second time around. If the Dresdens had their way, would this be the fate of all domed cities?

Guards waved us through the front gates, and our pack of snowmobiles charged into the snow-covered terrain beyond. I hadn't thought to ask where this prisoner exchange was taking place. More importantly, I hadn't asked where the prisoner was that we were exchanging for Botto. The farther we rode, the more I started to fear I might be that person. Not that I knew why the nomads would want me, but it seemed I was a hot commodity these days.

An hour later, my cheeks were windburned. Snow fell steadily from the gray sky above. I hugged Cova tighter around the middle to siphon some of his body heat, since the cold clearly had little effect on him. Delancey rode in front of us, and she made a hand gesture that was lost on me. The rebel soldiers understood, though, because the snowmobiles came to a stop in the middle of a large field covered in a thick blanket of snow. Cova swung his legs over the side and hopped off before offering me a hand. It stung my pride to accept his help, yet I was too cold and achy to refuse it.

"Where are we?" I asked through numb lips. Ice crunched beneath my boots as I shifted from one foot to the other to kickstart my circulation.

Hands on her hips, Delancey surveyed the barren landscape. What was she looking for?

"Neutral territory," Cova grunted, which seemed to be his primary mode of communication.

"Where are the nomads?" I pressed, mimicking Delancey's pose and following her gaze.

"They'll be here," she promised.

I wasn't sure I wanted to hear the answer, but I couldn't delay asking the question that plagued me any longer. "Are you trading me for Botto?"

The look she gave me was so like one her brother used when I complained about magic training that I would've smiled if my facial muscles could've managed the act. "If that was the plan, he wouldn't have sacrificed himself in the first place."

I felt the need to point out this wasn't really an answer but managed to hold my tongue. Several minutes of tense, cold silence passed. *Are we being stood up?* I wondered. Before I could voice my concern, a loud caw from above pierced the air. Along with the rest of our group, I looked to the sky. Three large birds swooped down toward us. One landed on two human feet, while the others remained in animal form. The first shifter nodded to Delancey, making me think they knew one another.

"Where's my brother, Ella?" Delancey demanded.

The woman replied in a language I recognized as old faerie. Unfortunately, I only knew a few ceremonial phrases, since it was a tongue that I'd only heard spoken by the elders in Fae Canyon. Delancey smiled coldly.

"Don't blame me. Your people asked for this," Delancey said.

The were-condor spoke again in old faerie, and this

time I actually picked up on a few words. One in particular sparked my interest: maeling. It meant mother, though it wasn't reserved exclusively for one's own mother. Female elders were also sometimes called maeling, and it wasn't uncommon for students to use it as a term of respect when referring to their magical mentor.

What I found curious, aside from the fact the shifter was using an ancient fae dialect, was that she'd used maeling in the same sentence as sangueling. Unless I was mistaken, the latter meant blood. Unfortunately, the only other words I recognized were broarie—brother—and archaeling, which didn't have a direct English translation. If memory served, it was a special, ceremonial meeting of the Council of Elders to rule on a major issue that affected the entire community.

"That was not the agreement," Delancey replied, crossing her arms over her chest. "Tell the hive priestess that she *will* honor the terms of the exchange." The "or else" was implied.

The shifter's gaze cut to me. She muttered something that sounded a lot like the faerie word for traitor. Technically, inlaling meant trespasser, but I understood her meaning. I met eyes that were more yellow than gold and tried to pull a customary fae greeting from my cache of childhood memories. The only phrases I could recall were too respectful for the bitchy bird before me.

"The priestess has asked no harm come to you," Ella finally said to me.

Before my mind could formulate a response, she turned and started walking away. Her transformation from a two-footed human to a two-winged bird of prey wasn't instantaneous, like many shifters I'd met. Instead, it was a relatively slow process that appeared more robotic than magical in nature.

Odd.

Joints popped and bones cracked as her thin arms turned to feathered wings. Her short auburn locks retreated into her scalp, and her nose elongated in stuttering bursts to form a beak. Next came the torso, followed by the feet. Tilting my head to the side, I watched with undisguised fascination as Ella's toes snapped together and then sprang apart, ten digits becoming six. Finally, the shifter took to the sky, her fellow were-condors close behind.

A lot of my friends were shifters, as were the majority of the opponents I'd faced in the fighting pits. I'd witnessed my fair share of transformations over the years. The process varied greatly depending on factors like species, experience, environment, and even gender. Some weres had so much control over the change, they could perform and maintain partial shifts. I'd gone up against a were-eagle that flew around the arena on wings while the rest of his body remained human enough to kick me with booted feet. One time, I fought a were-armadillo that shifted only his skin, creating a sturdy barrier that shielded his sensitive human body from my blows. A group of female were-panthers that frequented my group's favorite hangout on Oahu, Hideout, had mastered the art of transformation sampling, which was similar to a partial shift but more subtle. Instead of totally swapping individual body parts, sampling was more like freezing the desired feature mid-change. When done correctly, the shifter often took on an exotic, otherworldly appearance.

With all the different shifters, there had always been one constant in their transformations: magic. It was the spring from which a shifter's duality sprung. It was the thread that stitched human and animal souls together to form a single seamless fabric. It was the mediator that balanced a shifter's internal scales so that neither half could overpower the other entirely. It was the warm, gentle wave that washed over me every time I was in the vicinity of a transforming shifter.

Until today.

Somehow, someway Ella had managed to transform without the cloud of magic that surrounded all other shifters I'd met during the change. *It's not possible. Maybe she's a hybrid—half-caster and half-shifter.* If so, Ella could've used a concealing spell to hide her magic during the shift. Or maybe caster-shifter hybrids' magic was self-contained, like that of full-blooded casters. In that case, it wouldn't be felt during something like a transformation. Honestly, I had no idea how any of that worked.

Maybe she is a robot, I thought.

All I knew for certain was that any one of the crazy theories playing in my head was more probable than Ella changing into a bird sans magic.

"Brie!" Delancey snapped. Her irritated tone suggested this was not the first time she'd said my name.

I blinked away the snowflakes clinging to my eyelashes. *Is there a storm coming?* I wondered. Light snowfall was a daily occurrence outside the domes, that was normal. But in the short time we'd all been standing in the field, enough snow had accumulated to bury the tops of my boots. Overhead, dark clouds gathered.

"Are you coming?" Delancey shouted, revving the engine of her snowmobile. "Or should I leave you here to turn into a faesicle?"

When I trudged back to my ride, Cova held out his hand. Declining the offer, I climbed up behind him on the cold seat.

"Where are we going now?" I shouted in the rebel soldier's ear.

He gunned the snowmobile, and we shot forward. If not for my years of training and Gaia-given reflexes, I would've flown right off the back.

"We're following that bird." Cova spared a glance over his shoulder at me. "Hold on."

Thanks for the warning, asshole.

We sped out of the field as if trying to outrun the weather. To my dismay, we headed away from Revival, to some destination unknown. The field stretched for miles, like an endless white void. Ice pellets joined the snow falling from the sky, creating a slushy mix that seeped through my layers of clothes and chilled my core. Even Cova was shivering in the storm, his lips turning blue before my eyes.

Is there possibly a more embarrassing way for a fire fae to die than freezing to death? I wondered, calling my magic forth. Given the plummeting temperature, it shouldn't have come as a surprise that my skin took a few extra moments to heat than usual. Nonetheless, the niggling sensation in the back of mind served as a reminder that all I had was Sienna's word that she'd broken the curse on my magic. Would I become violently ill again with its use? Would I regret not conserving it for whatever was coming?

Calm down. You've been using it. It's been working fine.

Beneath my layers of clothes, I started to sweat. Keep my arms around Cova's midsection so I wouldn't fall off, I slid off one glove and pressed my palm to the were-bear's hairy chest. He flinched like I'd burned him. The acrid scent of burnt hair confirmed that I had.

"Sorry!" I said quickly. "Just trying to—ahhhh!"

It was like Gaia had flicked the sun right out of the sky, plunging us mere mortals into a literal dark age. Shock froze my mind. My body continued hurtling forward on the snowmobile, my arms locked around Cova's waist. The shifter's body tensed, and a low, guttural growl escaped his lips. That was when I realized my hand was still hot and pressed against Cova's chest. I reined in my magic and mumbled an apology in his ear.

My eyes began adjusting to the deeper darkness, shadowy amorphous blobs coming into sharper focus. We were in the woods, I realized. The sky above was the color of midnight, and quite a few stars were visible in the areas with less tree cover. But most notably, there was no snow on the ground. That fact registered when I started sweating beneath my heavy winter clothes.

What the hell?

It was like we'd entered a wormhole into a domed city. Adrenaline coursed through my veins as fight-or-flight instincts kicked in. I weighed my limited options in the space of a heartbeat. Every nerve in my body screamed at me to run. Or tuck and roll off the snowmobile and then run, in this situation. *Run where? You don't even know where you are. Is this a better-the-devil-you-do-know situation?*

Cova expertly navigated the snowmobile between trees and rocks, catching air at one point when the vehicle leapt a small stream. I could see Delancey's taillights up ahead and hear the other two snowmobiles as they tore through the forest on either side of us. A few moments later, we burst out of the woods. It was like someone had flipped a nightlight on again. Cova slammed the brakes. My chest pressed painfully into his back, and my head bounced off his shoulder like a rubber ball. The tires skidded on loose rocks and dirt. Cova fought to keep control of the handlebars. The vehicle spun dangerously close to the edge of a deep ravine before finally coming to a stop.

Guess running is off the table, I thought, groaning audibly. Peering over the bluff, I saw sapphire water twinkling below.

"You okay?" Cova asked as he climbed from the snowmobile.

Still disoriented from the bizarre and abrupt course of events, I slid from the snowmobile and surveyed the area. From where I stood, it looked like we were on the edge of a giant bowl. I counted seven bridges that connected various points on the bluffs to the center of the bowl. There, a large glass structure loomed larger than life on an island in the middle of the sapphire sea.

"Where are we?" I hated the hint of fear that leaked into my question.

Delancey and the rebel soldiers had dismounted their snowmobiles and were busy removing gloves and jackets to accommodate the warmer weather. Overhead, Ella and her fellow bird shifters circled twice before coming in for a landing.

"Where are we?" I repeated more firmly.

"Midnight," Delancey said simply. She produced a small mirror from the back pocket of her jeans and checked her reflection.

My hands balled into fists. Was she serious? Lipstick and eyeliner were her biggest concerns at the moment? I wanted to shake Botto's sister until her teeth rattled. The desire must've been plain on my face, because Cova stepped between us.

"The hive lives down there, in Crystal City," he explained.

Ella, once again in human form, crooked a finger. "The priestess is waiting," she croaked, speaking in English.

The others followed the shifter without question. I remained where I was, as though my boots had grown roots. Enough was enough. Before I took one more step, I needed answers.

"Where are we? What is this place?" I demanded to know.

With a heavy sigh that made her annoyance clear, Delancey stopped walking and turned to face me. I expected her to give some vague, noncommittal response like "Start moving and you'll see" or make a thinly veiled threat to Cala's life. Maybe it was my murderous expression that made her reevaluate the wisdom of doing so.

"The Dome of Midnight. It's the largest and oldest vampire hive in the Americas," she informed me.

The sweat that slicked my back froze instantly. A vampire hive? Delancey had taken me to a fucking vampire hive? Beneath a dome? That was a ridiculous waste of magic; vampires were even more resistant to the cold than shifters. They didn't need a protective barrier from the elements.

"I thought you said nomads had Botto," I said uneasily.

"They do," she agreed, not bothering to elaborate.

"So, he's here?" I pressed. "We came here to get him back?"

"Yes. And the sooner you shut up, the faster we can do that."

"What are we trading for him? You said this was a prisoner exchange."

Ella arched an eyebrow in Delancey's direction.

"It is. We're giving the high priestess something she wants in exchange for Botto's safe return."

"What are we giving her?"

Delancey rolled her eyes. "A meeting. With you. Now you know everything I know. Start walking."

I doubted I knew a fraction of what she did about all of this. Nonetheless, I shrugged out of my jacket and joined the others. Ella led us to the closest bridge, where a solitary vampire stood guard. The guy had been changed early in life and appeared no more thirteen or fourteen years old. It was something in his eyes that made me believe he was much, much older. The sparkling silver irises were ringed in crimson. For a minute, I felt like I was falling into their endless depths.

"Miss Delancey, a pleasure to see you again," the vamp said with a faint British accent. He sounded as young as he appeared, like he'd been turned before hitting puberty. His skin was the same milky white as most vampires I'd encountered, though the smattering of freckles across his cheekbones and neatly combed ginger hair suggested his complexion had been just as fair in life.

"Hello, Rhett," Delancey replied, her tone devoid of warmth.

Ella and Rhett exchanged a few words in old faerie, then the vampire moved aside and allowed us to pass. The other two condors changed into their human forms, making me wonder if Rhett would've permitted them on the bridge otherwise.

The trek across Crystal Bridge—the name Ella had used when talking to Rhett—only took about ten minutes, but it felt like ten hours. While not much scared me these days, and a fear of heights had never been among my phobias, the walkway terrified me. It was made of clear glass, or maybe actual crystal, and had no rails on either side despite the height. I'd thought the sea was beautiful from the safety of the bluffs. Once crossing above it, all I could think about was the fact enchanted creatures no doubt patrolled the waters below. The waves seemed more treacherous with the real possibility that I might plunge into them.

Finally, we reached the other side. I took several long, calming breaths and focused on steadying my racing heart. Delancey and Ella spoke to another vampire guard stationed on this side of the bridge. The woman appeared to have been turned in her thirties. Judging by her teased bangs and love of lemon-yellow eye shadow, that turn had occurred ages ago; her style had frozen along with her lifeline.

The female vamp showed us to what seemed to be a loading platform. Instead of tracks and connected cars, like a train, a single gondola hovered beside the platform. Our group piled inside, including the bird shifters. There was no steering wheel or other obvious controls, but the car began moving on its own once the door closed with all nine of inside. The jerky nature of the ride made me wonder if there were invisible tracks beneath us.

It's either that or magic, I thought. I couldn't dwell on the specifics, though, not when there was so much to see. Crystal City lived up to its name. Beautiful stained-glass spires topped narrow buildings designed by someone who had clearly prized aesthetics over practicality. Gardens of night blooming flowers were tucked between condo buildings. White sand shores ringed the small island city, and the two beach clubs I spotted were packed with moonbathers sipping crimson cocktails.

The gondola deposited us in a courtyard behind a private residence. Compared with the activity I'd seen from the gondola, it was quiet and still. A wooden gazebo with a sizable skylight was in middle, and Ella led us over to it. Soft, classical music floated on a gentle breeze. The song that played was oddly familiar, and I found myself humming along.

Delancey sat on the gazebo's wraparound bench, directly opposite a pile of embroidered pillows that I guessed the high priestess used while stargazing or whatever. Bright orange blossoms grew from the ivy vines twined around the wooden posts. They filled the air with a sweet fragrance that stirred up childhood memories of Goddess Day celebrations. Something about the whole scene was familiar, but it wasn't something I could put my finger on.

Weird.

Delancey patted the cushion beside her, but I was too amped to sit. We were in the center of a vampire hive; there was no way I was letting my guard down. The extra split second it would take me to leap to my feet could very well be the difference between life and death when vampire speed was in play.

"Don't be rude, Brie," Delancey snapped like I was a naughty child.

My hackles raised. Was this girl serious? Delancey was the queen of rude.

"Actually, Miss Dresden, it is customary to stand until the priestess takes her seat," a cool female voice said.

Dressed in a flowing, Grecian-style dress the same shade of orange as the flowers, the vampire high priestess of Crystal City swept across the courtyard. She had the grace of a ballerina and moved slowly, deliberately. It was almost as though she was trying to put us mortals at ease.

Delancey's cheeks flushed with anger and embarrassment at the vampire's rebuke. She wasn't stupid enough to snap back at the priestess on the vampire's home turf, but Botto's sister did refuse to stand. I had to admire her moxie.

The high priestess floated up the gazebo steps, offering us a serene smile that did nothing to warm her soulless eyes. That was when I got a good look at the woman's face.

"You!" I blurted, head whipping from side to side as I searched frantically for an exit.

Alarm registered on Delancey's pretty face, her gaze darting back and forth between the vampire and me.

"Do you know her?" she hissed to me.

I didn't *know* the vamp, but we had met. She and her cronies were the ones who'd ambushed us outside the first safe house. That same bloodsucker had agreed to trade Granite Dresden's son for a meeting with me?

That can't bode well.

"I mean you no harm, Maybrie." The priestess sat on her pile of pillows, still holding my gaze. "I only want to talk." She smiled sadly. "And we do have a lot to talk about, my child."

CHAPTER FIFTEEN

FAE CANYON, FREELANDS OF THE AMERICAS

Kai

BREAKFAST WITH BRIE'S family was the most awkward and uncomfortable meal of Kai's life. That title meant a great deal, considering he'd dined with the czar of St. Petersburg. That guy was the epitome of a narcissist and spent the entire dinner talking about his sexual escapades while his wife sat next to him. The meal with the fae elder was definitively worse, like he was actively trying to bring about discomfort and not simply unaware of social etiquette.

Brie's father stared at Kai with eyes that looked just like hers, but he said nothing. Illion at least tried to make conversation, asking a lot of questions about life beneath the dome.

"I heard you have oceans that you can swim in, true or false?" The younger fae shoveled a forkful of eggs into his mouth and grinned.

Kai sipped plum juice and then cleared his throat. "True."

"What about a throne? Do you have one?"

Kai shifted uncomfortably in his wooden chair. Brie's father squinted as if taking a deeper look inside the king's soul. Kai and Kenoa exchanged looks.

"Yes, I have an actual throne," he said at last.

Illion's eyes went wide. "Will my sister have a throne, too?"

Elder Hawkins shifted his gaze to his son. "You sister, my eldest child, will not marry an unworthy partner." They were the first words he'd spoken, and Kai cringed at them.

Silence descended over the small cottage. Kai didn't know where to look. His gaze landed on the fire in the hearth, where bright orange flames danced the tango. The king's lips quirked into a smile. Memories of watching Brie fight with her fire magic filled his head.

Gaia, please keep her safe, he prayed silently.

Kenoa scraped his fork across his plate and ate the last bite of cheesy grits. Kai looked down at his own meal and frowned. The impending meeting had his stomach in knots. Nonetheless, he knew better than to ignore the food; it was poor form to refuse hospitality. So, he forced himself to eat the runny eggs and strips of unidentifiable meat.

Brie's father gave him a knowing look, like he was aware that Kai was struggling to be polite. With a satisfied sigh, Illion placed his fork and knife across his empty plate and pushed back from the small, square table.

"Man, I can't remember the last time we had a breakfast like this." He arched his back and patted his stomach. "We should entertain royalty more often."

Kai fought the automatic instinct to offer financial help to the Hawkins family. In their short acquaintance, one thing was very obvious: Elder Hawkins was a proud man. *Just like Brie.* Offering him money would be taken as an offense. Guilt made Kai's stomach turn, though. His fist clutched the fork with a white-knuckle grip.

"Thank you for breakfast, Elder Hawkins," Kenoa said, head slightly bowed out of respect.

"It is my pleasure," the old fae said.

"Yes, thank you. I apologize for taking so long to eat." Kai shrugged sheepishly. "I must admit, I have a case of the nerves."

The admission softened Elder Hawkins' frosty expression. He used his fork and knife to scoop the last bite of rice grits from his plate, his eyes focused on Kai. Somewhere in the distance, a bell rang three times. Kai's stomach dropped. This was it, his turn to face a council of fae elders and prove he was worthy of Brie.

Elder Hawkins finished his tea and stood. Kai and Kenoa followed the old man's lead.

"Only the king," he said gruffly to Kenoa.

The water fae started to protest, but Kai cut him off.

"It's okay, Ken. I'll be fine."

"The king is here at my behest, as my guest," the Elder assured. "He will not be harmed."

"You can hang with me," Illion offered. "I'll take you on a tour of the canyon. You've never been to a real fae community, right?"

Kenoa pursed his lips. "No, I suppose I haven't."

Elder Hawkins gave Kai long underwear, a pair of snow pants, a thick sweater, and a parka that was made to keep the wearer safe in sub-zero temperatures. The boots he borrowed from Illion came up to Kai's knees and were a bit snug with the three pairs of socks underneath.

Elder Hawkins didn't wear nearly as many layers, reminding Kai that fae were much better equipped for the cold. And they were used to it.

Kai followed Brie's father out of the warmth of the cottage and into the blistering cold. Icy snow crunched beneath his feet, though the sun shone brightly in the blue-gray sky. It wasn't the first time Kai had been outside of a dome. This experience was very different, though. In Fae Canyon, Kai wasn't a mighty caster king. He was the enemy. He was the man responsible for the loss of an elder's child.

Why did I come? he wondered miserably. The answer was obvious; he would do anything for Brie. Apparently, that included walking willingly into this situation. She was the sole reason he was putting himself at the mercy of fae who hated him, with good reason.

The Council of Elders met in the Temple of Gaia, which was a place of worship for the fae. Elemental symbols were carved in the stone archway. Kai's body vibrated from the fae magic infused in the walls. There were also statues for fire, water, air, and earth. They were awe-inspiring and full of powerful, ancient elemental magic.

Four fae sat on a dais at the front of the room around a long wooden table. The fifth chair in the center was clearly reserved for Elder Hawkins. Brie's father took his seat, leaving Kai alone to face the entire council. Straightening to his full height, Kai's gaze went down the row and met the eyes of each elder of Fae Canyon.

Elder Hawkins tapped a gavel and called the session to order. The fae cleared his throat and narrowed his gaze. "Today, this man comes before us to prove he is worthy of my daughter, Maybrie Hawkins."

All eyes were on Kai, like he was supposed to give a certain response. He shifted from one foot to the other as a shiver ran down his spine. Unlike the Hawkins' house, the temple didn't have fires burning to ward off the cold.

"Yes, sir," Kai said finally. "I love Maybrie Hawkins. I am eager to prove that I am worthy."

Elder Hawkins offered a small, genuine smile. The woman next him stood. "You are the caster king of Hawaii?" she asked. Her long white hair was fixed in an intricate braid, and she wore a long wool cape.

Kai nodded uneasily. "Yes, ma'am."

The woman frowned. "Elder Stanton," she corrected.

Kai felt his cheeks redden. Before arriving at Brie's old house, it had been a long time since he'd been chastised. This woman was the second to do so. His mouth went dry, and his fists clenched.

"Yes, Elder Stanton. I am the reigning king of Hawaii."
You're doing this for Brie. You owe this to her, he told himself.

"Are you aware that no caster has ever come before us to seek approval?" asked Elder Stanton.

Kai nodded again. "Elder Hawkins informed me of that fact."

"Are you aware that no caster has ever married the child of one of our elders?" she continued.

"Yes, Elder Stanton." Kai tried to sound deferential but wasn't sure he pulled it off.

When she slowly sat, a male fae with neatly groomed facial hair stood. He was much younger than the other elders, probably somewhere in his thirties. The royal tutors had instructed Kai on fae and shifter customs, so he knew being an elder was a hereditary position and not age-based like it sounded. The five in front of him came from ancient fae lines that likely dated back to the age of humans. The younger man must've inherited his spot upon the death of a parent.

This was Brie's destiny, Kai realized. Had she not been taken and relocated to Hawaii, she would be training to take her father's spot one day. *Why didn't she tell me?*

"My name is Elder Jenson," the man said, bringing Kai's attention back to the situation at hand. "You were the crowned prince of Hawaii when Maybrie was kidnapped?"

It wasn't really a question but rather an accusation. Kai tilted his chin defiantly. He'd known this would happen and was prepared for the line of questioning.

"That is correct, Elder Jenson."

"And now, as king, you still employ vampires for

stealing fae to power your dome?"

Again, it wasn't really a question. "I have passed a decree outlawing the practice," he answered evenly. "However, I do still employ hunters who offer fae and shifters in unfortunate situations a place within our society."

He thought he saw Brie's father smile, but the expression was gone as quickly as it had come.

"You were the crowned prince for the five years Maybrie Hawkins was forced to fight in the pits?" Elder Jenson continued.

Kai took a deep breath. They wanted him to confess his sins before Gaia. So, he did. "Yes, Elder Jenson."

"Even after you started courting Maybrie, without the approval of this council, you did not free her from forced servitude."

It was a tricky question. Brie liked fighting, and she was good at it. No, she was the best. She had been excited to compete in the Interkingdom Championship, proud of her abilities. Kai wasn't sure how to explain that to the council. Technically, Brie was still under contract to fight.

Elder Jenson arched an eyebrow. "What do you have to say for yourself?

"You are correct that Brie is still under contract with my kingdom," Kai began, choosing his words carefully. "You may not believe me, but Brie enjoys the matches. She is an amazing fighter, truly." An image of Brie in the arena, her expression fierce, flashed in his mind. "Elder Hawkins, your daughter is a warrior. I will not stand here and make excuses for my family. The practice of relocating fae and shifters in the past was wrong. Now, as king, I will make amends for the inexcusable treatment of fae and shifters." He paused to catch his breath. "Truthfully, I never considered terminating Brie's contract. Had she asked, I would have done it in a heartbeat."

Shame made Kai bow his head. Why hadn't he cancelled her contract? *Because she would've refused to quit the matches.* Still, standing in front of the elders, he felt like a piece of shit.

Elder Jenson sat. Brie's father was the next to speak, though he didn't stand. Kai couldn't decide whether this was a sign of disrespect or just customary for the senior-most fae. Either way, Kai tensed in preparation for the severe words that he knew were coming.

"I lost my wife when my children were faelings," Elder Hawkins began. "Our caravan was attacked on the way to the fair. By vampires." His expression hardened further. "They killed half our people and took the rest. My Julia was among those taken. Then my fifteen-year-old child was taken as well. By vampires. Your mother wanted a fire fae, or so my sources tell me. She asked them to find one. I did not even know my daughter's whereabouts, whether she was alive or dead, for five very long years. It was only once she entered a relationship with you that I learned her location."

Kai's eyes widened in surprise. Brie had never said what happened to her mother, only that she'd died when Brie was very young. She'd never spoken of vampire involvement or told him anything further.

And you never asked, Kai thought miserably.

"I was not privy to my mother's directives at that time," Kai said stiffly. Then, remembering his manners, he added, "Elder Hawkins."

"Do you truly love Maybrie?" the elder asked.

The question was clearly for the council's benefit; Kai had told him many times already.

"I do, Elder Hawkins." Kai met the fae's gaze. "Very much so."

"Do you intend to make her your wife?"

Kai hesitated for a beat. He loved Brie, and their relationship was very serious. But things were complicated now that Brie had been named as a member of the rebellion and accused of regicide. Even if he was able to clear her name, his subjects were not likely to accept her as their queen.

Screw them, Kai thought. He was a king. His word was law. Unless, of course, his advisory council invoked their right to challenge his authority and permanently replaced him with his sister.

In a calm, clear voice, he said the words he felt deep in his soul. "I wish to marry Brie. I wish her to be my wife. No matter the consequence."

My kingdom for the love of an incredible woman. It's an easy choice.

Elder Hawkins nodded, leading Kai to believe that he'd given the right answer. He breathed a premature sigh of relief. The fragile peace wasn't meant to last.

"You have completed the first phase," Brie's dad said. "You have answered for your sins. Marriage can only work if both parties enter the union with honest hearts." Elder Hawkins paused for dramatic effect. "Now it is time for you to pay tribute to the elements."

What does that mean?

Elder Stanton rose and retrieved a metal box from a pedestal at the back of the dais. She handed it to Brie's father, who winced as if in pain when he opened the lid. Reaching inside, he produced four stones.

Kai's breath caught. Element stones were a myth among casters in his kingdom. They were said to hold the power of ten thousand fae. The rush of energy that filled the room told Kai the legends were real.

Elder Hawkins held up a ruby between his thumb and forefinger. Kai stared at the jewel curiously. It had clearly been cut, which meant someone else had a piece of the stone.

"This ruby represents fire." He held out the jewel.

Tentatively, Kai walked forward and took the magical object. Its power washed over him. The feeling was glorious, like an infusion of magic from hundreds of fae all at once. In that moment, Kai was so full of power that he felt like he could take on the entire rebel army. His fingers closed around the ruby. The stone grew warmer by the second, burning his palm. Kai fought against the pain and refused to let go.

Is this the test? he wondered.

Flames burst from between Kai's fingers. He gritted his teeth against the agony and looked down at the fire that engulfed his hand. It spread up his arm, bringing more anguish than Kai had ever felt. Somehow, his skin remained unblemished by the flames.

Kai looked up at Brie's father, his jaw set in a hard line.

"May luck be on your side," the elder fae said.

Flames overtook the king's body. The pain peaked, and Kai fought the urge to scream. Then, when he wasn't sure he could stand it for another moment, the blaze subsided. Kai blinked and looked around. He was no longer in the temple, and the fae council was nowhere in sight. Fire flickered in the distance, creating bizarre shadows in the void where Kai found himself.

With a deep breath, Kai walked forward. *What have I gotten myself into?* he wondered. The flames twisted and turned like they had a mind of their own. Kai looked to the left and right, seeing nothing but empty space. When he refocused on the fire, a gasp escaped him. The inferno had taken the shape of a man.

Shit.

The fire monster growled and lumbered toward him. Kai threw his gloves to the ground and raised his hand, muttering an incantation. A wave of power shot toward the monster. The creature stumbled but kept coming. Fear lanced through Kai's chest. The spell was hugely powerful and should've sent the monster flying backward.

Think. Brie's dad said I must pay tribute to the elements.

But what did that mean? Then, it clicked. He had to fight fire with fire.

The monster shot blazing streaks at Kai. He dove to the side, fire singeing his coat. The creature kept advancing. Kai summoned his magic. He felt the familiar swell of power in his gut. White-hot balls of flame shot from his palm, striking the monster's face. The fire creature clawed at his cheeks, which were sizzling from Kai's attack.

Kai sent another stream of power, this time aiming for the creature's torso. The fire monster squealed as parts of his chest and stomach turned black before dissolving. Unfortunately, the monster kept moving forward despite the damage to his body.

Scrambling to his feet just as the fire creature reached for him, Kai released another round of fireballs. His aim was off, and only one of the projectiles skimmed the monster's shoulder. Kai's breath was coming in short gasps. The many layers of clothing hindered his movements and sweat made his undershirt stick to his back.

Is this my punishment for Brie's time in the fighting pits? Was this desperation what she'd felt when entering the arena?

If that was the case, he definitely deserved it.

Thoughts of Brie gave him a second wind. For years, he'd watched her take on opponent after opponent. No matter the odds, she'd never given up. Kai channeled that determination, trying to emulate his fierce love. This fight was for her, after all.

The monster lunged. One of his fiery hands clamped down on Kai's shoulder, burning a hole through his parka and the layers beneath. A guttural cry burst from Kai. He screamed the first incantation that came to mind. Cold washed over his hands as more blue flames erupted from his fingers. Kai thrust his palms against the monster's chest, his efforts rewarded with a howl. Hands still engulfed in icy flames, Kai grabbed either side of the monster's face and pressed as hard as he could. For good measure, he sent an extra wave of pure energy into the creature's skull.

With a piecing cry, the monster shattered before his eyes. Panting heavily, Kai sank to his knees. It has been a long time since he'd used so much magic, if ever. Since he'd started dating Brie, he hadn't been visiting the palace fae to replenish his magic. Just her presence had been more than enough to sustain him. Or so he'd thought. This fight had cost him, and he still had three more elements to go.

In the blink of an eye, Kai found himself back in the temple facing the Council of Elders. The ruby was clutched in one of his hands. Brie's father looked down at Kai, still on his knees, and smiled.

"You have paid tribute to the fire god." He removed another stone from the box, this one a large sapphire. "Your next element is water."

Kai struggled to his feet, a little surprised to find that his jacket was still smoking where the fire monster had touched him. He'd assumed the injuries and effects of the fight would stay in the void along with the shattered remains of the beast.

He handed the ruby to Elder Hawkins. The fae appraised him with a critical eye. Kai didn't know what the elder saw, but whatever it was made Brie's father hesitate. "Are you sure you want to continue?" he asked.

Kai squared his shoulders. "I would go to hell and back for your daughter, Elder Hawkins."

The old fae gave him the sapphire. "Careful want you wish for, king."

CHAPTER SIXTEEN

DOME OF MIDNIGHT

Brie

THE HIGH PRIESTESS invited Delancey and the others for tea in the inside parlor; an unsubtle way of requesting to be alone with me. "Your brother is waiting for you," she told my snotty companion.

To a degree, I understood why Delancey had a chip on her shoulder. Botto's sister was used to getting her way, that much was evident. Even though a break from her should've been nice, I didn't want her to leave. I didn't want to be alone with the all-powerful vampire priestess;

just the thought of it made my stomach turn. Delancey was reluctant to leave, though I suspected she was more interested in the impending conversation than my safety.

The priestess fixed Delancey with golden-brown eyes that had only a touch of crimson at the edges. "I am sure you're eager to make sure your brother is unharmed," she said in a syrupy sweet voice.

The compulsion was subtle, which was all that Delancey needed; she was oddly susceptible to whatever brand of vampiric persuasion the priestess was using. Compulsion resistance did vary from person to person, but most fae and shifters in the Freelands took precautions. Growing up, my father had added an herbal elixir to my and Illion's nightly tea. That same elixir had a lot of practical applications, including giving the drinker shiny hair, so it was easy to acquire on Oahu. Of course, I also didn't have the same need for such an elixir beneath the dome and had been sloppy about keeping up with it.

Delancey stood and followed Ella across the courtyard. They passed through the backdoor of the priestess' residence, leaving me alone with the vampire.

The woman's hypnotic eyes appraised me. Her perfect mouth curved into a small smile that looked like a strain on her facial muscles. I stared back with the neutral expression I'd perfected for royal meetings and political functions. Even with my hatred of vampires, I had to admit the priestess was beautiful. No, she was gorgeous.

All vampires gave off universal pheromones that very few could resist, making them seem more physically attractive than they really were. And yet, that wasn't the case with the priestess. She was truly a gorgeous woman without even turning her charm on me.

"You have grown into a beautiful woman," the priestess said, finally breaking the silence between us.

The words made my insides freeze like I was outside a dome. "Thank you, I guess," I said uneasily.

Five feet separated us, and the gazebo was open. Nonetheless, the space felt too small for the intimacy she was projecting. Claustrophobic, even.

"I understand you are an incredible fighter," the priestess said hopefully, like she was desperate to find a topic that might draw me out.

I shrugged. "I'm not bad. I get lucky." I wasn't being modest; I just didn't want to make small talk. The sooner we got to the point of her summons, the sooner I could leave the oddly beautiful vampire hive. Though the Dresdens' hospitality did leave something to be desired. At least the vampire was making a pretense of friendliness.

"I wouldn't say that." The priestess' silky-smooth voice broke into my thoughts. "You have been through a great many trials in your relatively short life, it is admirable."

Where is she going with this? I wondered.

"I am told you were kidnapped from Fae Canyon as a teenager?" she tried when I remained silent. Since it was posed as a question, I felt obligated to answer.

I nodded in confirmation.

"And your boyfriend—Tanner Woods, I believe?—died a few years ago?"

Again, I nodded. Were the conversation taking place anywhere else, this would've been the point where I demanded to know what I was doing there. If my companion weren't a vamp, I would not have indulged any small talk at all. In my current situation, I didn't have the luxury of directness. I might've been a great pit fighter, but I was no match for a vampire priestess if it came to hand-to-hand combat.

Those arrows had sure slowed her down, I thought wryly. Then again, she bore no signs of our run-in. Conversely, I still ached from the events of the day. And I'd even drank more of Samira's healing tonic to get on top of the damage. *Damn vamp healing.*

"You did lose your mother at a very young age," the priestess said carefully, watching me closely as if to gauge my reaction.

Woah. What the actual fuck?

Dating Kai had thrust me into the public eye, making my life a hot topic for gossip sites and news outlets alike. Until our ill-fated trip to Los Angeles, I hadn't really understood the global interest in my relationship. People the world over knew my name, and many thought they knew *me* just because they'd read every article some idiot wrote about my life.

Because of that, I wasn't surprised the priestess knew when and where I'd been kidnapped—that was a common fact that many so-called journalists used as an introduction in their write-ups. Of course, they usually spun the story so it sounded more like a rags-to-riches fairytale than the reality of the situation. The stuff about Tanner was no secret either. As Cala always said, it made me sound even more tragic that my last boyfriend had died suddenly at a young age.

Even with all that information floating around in the world, my fae family in the Freelands was rarely mentioned. When they were, the details were vague and scant. Regardless of the ambiguous stories and speculation, my mother was *never* mentioned. Hell, I never mentioned my mother. It wasn't so much that talking about her was too painful or whatever. Really, I was just so young when she died that I couldn't even remember what she looked like. All my memories were hazy and seen through the lens of a naïve child.

"It was a vampire attack that took her, is that right?" the priestess pressed, arching one perfect brow.

"What do you want?" I asked. My voice was so cold, I sounded like a vampire who'd been on this earth too long.

The priestess didn't seem offended. In fact, if not for knowing that she had vampire hearing, I might've thought she didn't catch my question. She kept talking as though I hadn't spoken.

"Do you know what happened during the attack?" the priestess asked.

"What. Do. You. Want?" I bit off each word, no longer caring about the consequences.

The priestess pursed her lips. "I think I've made myself very clear, Maybrie." She sounded like a parent chastising a child. "I want to talk with you, that is all. That is what I offered Granite Dresden in exchange for his son. Before he leaves, I will get my due."

This was what I expected from a vampire—coldness and detachment, just like the soulless creatures themselves. Even still, I couldn't help but flinch at the harsh tone. It was devoid of emotion in a way I couldn't comprehend, like Botto's freedom was merely something to grant or deny without thought to the fact it was a life in her hands. Seeing my reaction, the priestess closed her eyes and took a deep breath.

"Indulge me, Maybrie," she said in much softer tone.

My short bark of laughter was humorless. "You're asking personal and prying questions on a subject that I rarely talk about. No, one I *never* speak about. So, you'll have to forgive me if I'm not feeling particularly chatty. This isn't something I'm willing to discuss, it's that simple."

The priestess folded her hands in her lap. "Fine. How about this, why don't I tell you about me?"

I don't care about your vampiric warlord ways, I thought.

Of course, that wasn't what I said aloud. "Sure, if that'll help me keep Granite's end of the bargain. A deal, by the way, that he made without consulting me. But anything for Botto."

The priestess gave a wry smile, but her expression sobered when she began speaking. "I was a fae before joining the ranks of the immortal. An earth fae." While her gaze drifted to the sliver of moon above, I had a feeling she was seeing her past life instead of the glowing orb. "I had a husband. We'd been blessed with two beautiful faelings. My life wasn't perfect, of course. No one's is, that's simply the reality of life. But it was close. I was happy, extremely happy. Cold sometimes, yes, but happy."

The priestess paused to take a breath she didn't need, and then continued. "The story of my turning isn't unique. It's rather typical, actually. I was in the wrong place at the wrong time. Or maybe the right place at the right time, depending how you view vampirism."

Not favorably, I thought but didn't say.

"Cessius, my sire, gave me a choice: be sold to the kingdoms and used for their purposes, or become a vampire," she continued.

"Not much of a choice." The words popped out before I could stop them. Had I been offered the same deal, would I have taken the alternative?

Never. I knew that for certain. I could never have become one of the creatures who'd ruined my life.

Her lips curved upward, while her gaze remained on the sky. "That is exactly what I told him. I said I'd rather die than be undead. Cessius informed me that wasn't an option. He said if I didn't choose, he would choose for me. Then, he gave me three days alone in a cold, dark cell to think it over." She finally looked at me again. "Sadly, you can see what I decided in the end."

"Why? If you had the happy family like you claim, why would you choose this existence?" Despite myself, I'd become invested in her story somewhere along the way.

"There were so many others to think about." The priestess met my gaze squarely. "As a vampire, I could keep my family safe. I could keep my entire village safe. As a magic feeder…." She shook her head, her tone taking on a bitter note. "I wouldn't have been able to keep myself safe, let alone the people I cared about."

"Did you?" I asked, genuinely curious. "Did you keep them safe?"

Sadness filled her eyes, something I found surprising

since I didn't think vampires were capable of true emotion. "At first. Cessius, my sire, was an ancient. His power was unparalleled, as was the deference the other vampires paid him."

Although I noticed her use of past tense when talking about Cessius, I didn't comment on that fact. Regardless of my feelings for the bloodsucker, I already found her story sympathetic. There was a wistfulness in her voice that appealed to something deep within me. It was almost like a lost piece of me felt the emotions and echoed them.

"He told me that my family's village would be off-limits if I went willingly," she insisted, almost like she couldn't believe she'd taken the older vampire at his word. "The others respected his wishes without question, so it seemed like the smartest thing to do for the people I cared about. Since my magic survived the change, I was also able to cross the wards to visit my husband and children."

Again, her tone made my heart tug. The melancholy nature of her niggled at the edges of my brain, feeling familiar. It was likely because I knew what it felt like to be ripped from my family; I could barely stomach the thought of it. The experience was painful beyond compare, and no one deserved to go through anything like that. Did her kids ever find out what had happened to her? Then her words registered, and something equally as shocking occurred to me.

"They didn't care you were a vamp? Your family didn't mind?" I asked. Most fae were on the same page when it came to bloodsuckers, even when the vampire was someone they'd known before the change.

For the first time in our brief acquaintance, the vampire's perfect composure faltered. "They didn't know," she admitted.

"The fangs weren't a giveaway?" I was dubious that it had been as easy as popping in on occasion to be a mother and wife.

Then again, compulsion could make someone forget what they saw. It could also alter the way a person remembered the encounter. It couldn't create a complete disguise, though…could it? Honestly, I knew very little about the vampiric world.

"They didn't see the fangs," the priestess replied. "For that matter, they didn't see me. I visited at night, after they were asleep. My husband is a proud fae elder. He never would have accepted my transformation. He wouldn't have understood the choice I made. Where we come from, vampires are hated. Reviled, really. My husband would have preferred me to take my own life than become an eternal."

Again, I experienced a pang of sympathy for the bloodsucker across from me. *Gaia, the world really is upside down right now.*

"You can't know that," I said.

She smiled sadly. "Sweet of you to say, darling. But I do know he feels that way. He told me as much."

"He caught you sneaking around the house?" I guessed.

She nodded. "He forbade me to enter his home ever again." Anger flashed in her eyes. "He said if I ever came back, he would happily watch me burn. They were tragically hard words to hear from a man I once loved more than life. He was the father of my children, and he acted as though I were already dead. I was irredeemable in his eyes despite the fact it clearly wasn't something I'd willingly chosen. My life wasn't something I would've traded for anything."

I couldn't blame the guy. If one of my family members turned vamp, I wouldn't have let them anywhere near the rest of us.

"I wouldn't have chosen this," she reiterated. "Ever."

"And you just accepted that? I mean, you are a vampire. Few fae can hold their own against one of you." I reconsidered, recalling her burning comment. "I guess fire fae do have better odds. Still, couldn't you have challenged him?"

"I respected his wishes," the priestess said stiffly. "In return, he promised that he wouldn't tell my children what I'd become." A single, bloody tear rolled from the corner of her eye and down her cheek, leaving a vivid crimson trail on her alabaster skin.

"Cessius died," she continued. The frank admission was both startling and not, and I had to bite back the instinct to ask what had happened. "At that point, my family's safety was no longer assured. So, I went to see my husband again. Despite his threats, I *had* to warn him that things had changed."

"What happened?" It was like listening to a soap opera; I really wanted to hear the next episode.

"There is a potion that protects against compulsion, as I'm sure you know," she replied, ignoring my question for the time being. "What you probably don't know is that a tattoo can protect a person permanently."

What? I wondered. Why the hell hadn't my father told me about that? Still, I wasn't surprised. Charmed tattoos weren't uncommon, for that matter. Rumors, or maybe urban legends, said that some kingdoms tattooed fae and shifters using ink infused with spells. Those were purportedly used for loyalty and compliance. One fae friend of Everly's who'd attended Madame Noelani's had tattooed herself with a love spell before her wedding to a wealthy caster. Supposedly the guy was very nice and treated her well, but there was zero physical attraction on her end.

Is it better to be happy and in manufactured love, or miserable and depressed but know your feelings are real? It was a question I'd wondered a lot since hearing the story.

"They aren't common because the main ingredient is hard to obtain," the priestess was saying when I tuned back in.

"Vampire blood," I guessed.

She looked pleasantly surprised. "Yes, exactly. Good for you for knowing. That night, I gave my husband a vial of my blood. He knew what to do with it." She swallowed thickly. "But I wanted to do more. I *needed* to do more. I never wanted my children to face the same choice I had. That is when I began my rise to power. I wasn't going to ever allow my people to deal with the things that had ruined my own life."

The priestess made a gesture meant to encompass the entire hive.

"I took over Cessius' empire," she continued. "Of all those who were loyal to him, some of them stayed with me. Only about half, though. The others went with another of Cessius' progeny, my vampiric brother. I'll spare you the details of the bloody turf war that followed. In the end, I came away with one-third of my sire's business holdings and one-third of his followers. From there, I scraped fang and nail to rebuild. What you see here is my crowning achievement. Cessius started Crystal City, but I am the one who made it what you see today."

Kudos, I thought dryly. She raised an eyebrow but pressed on with the story.

"Nevertheless, being High Priestess of a hive wasn't enough for me. I still longed for my children. I wanted to see them, to touch them and know they were okay. With my rise in status, I was narcissistic enough to believe I had the right to do just that. And I was naïve enough to believe my brother and I had truly made peace after the turf war. That proved to be an egregious error.

"His people tailed me every time I left this dome. They followed me when I went to see my family. I didn't know it at the time, of course." She paused, and her jaw tightened. Pain flashed in her eyes as her gaze fixed on me. The priestess cleared her throat. "I only found out about my pursuers when I learned a caravan of cowboys took two girls and a boy from my village, from Fae Canyon."

My vision swam as the world spun faster and faster. Then, the truth of her words hit me fully. *This woman is from Fae Canyon? A fae from my home was turned vampire? How had I never heard about that? When was it? What poor family had lost their matriarch?*

"H-h-how long ago was that?" I asked uncertainly.

"Just a few years," she said simply. The priestess watched my face as expressions ranging from anger to disbelief flitted across it. The kids who'd been taken by the vampires because of her return...me and my friends. It was her fault I'd been taken. The priestess's vampire brother had sent the thugs who'd kidnapped us, and he'd done so as petty revenge on her.

Accusations rose in my throat, but I never had a chance to voice the thoughts.

"One of those girls was my daughter," the priestess finished.

My mouth dropped open. The spinning scenery picked up speed until I rested my hand against one of the gazebo's railings to steady myself. I knew Sienna's mother. This wasn't Sienna's mother. And yet....

I shook my head and squeezed my eyes shut like a petulant child. It couldn't be true. It just wasn't possible. I would know if I was sitting in a gazebo with my own mother.

"Maybrie, look at me, sweetheart."

My eyes popped open. "My mother is dead," I hissed. "She died when your kind attacked her convoy. The vamps killed everyone."

"No, sweetheart."

"Stop calling me that!" I leapt to my feet. "I am not your daughter!"

The priestess was calm in the face of my anger. Her guards, however, weren't as convinced that I wouldn't do something stupid. A dozen vampires swept silently into the courtyard. The guards held guns, which seemed silly given all their supernatural abilities. The priestess smiled serenely in their direction and waved them off.

"Sit down, Maybrie." She snapped her fingers like I was a dog.

Incredulity made my eyes go wide and my mouth gape for a second time. "I don't care who you are. You do not order me around like a pet." Though I didn't scream this time, my voice was still louder than normal.

The priestess chuckled as if there was anything amusing about this whole situation. "You always were a stubborn child. Will you please sit down, so we may speak like adults?" she asked. The politeness was there but seemed almost feigned.

Anger and confusion mixed inside of me to form one very volatile fae. My hands warmed as flames waited just below the surface. Though I knew better than to allow the fire to come, I wanted to hold the priestess above an inferno until she took back her words. I wanted to have never made the trip to Crystal City. Surely Delancey could've traded something else for her brother. I wanted to know how I could've been so stupid and not realized where her story was going from the start. I wanted to never hear another word from the priestess' mouth. Instead of voicing any of the wishes flowing through me, I stared at the vampires still waiting on the periphery of the courtyard. It would almost be easier if they'd killed me before ever making it to the meeting with the priestess. My life would've been at least ended without this painful truth permeating my soul.

"Do you believe that Granite Dresden is being completely honest with you?" she asked. "You don't, do you?"

That got my attention. I still didn't sit, but I did meet her eyes.

"That fae peddles half-truths and pretty lies," she continued, not waiting for an answer. "That's what makes him such a good recruiter for the rebels. Young, impressionable fae and shifters climb over one another to fall at his feet and join his cause." She narrowed her gaze, studying my reaction. "Let me guess, you were taken to meet with him as soon as you arrived? And you probably thought him a kindly old fae?"

"Not exactly." I sighed loudly. "What's your point? Do you even have one? Or is this just a ploy to get me talking about something so you can bring this all back around to your fan fiction story of my life?"

"I'll admit, I am trying to get you to stay so we can speak more," she agreed without a trace of shame. "But I do have point. Granite Dresden is not trustworthy. Whatever he has told you about his intentions isn't the whole story. This current rebel uprising is not what it seems."

"I'm well aware," I shot back. "You could've saved your breath."

She chuckled humorlessly. "I don't breathe, dear. Long-winded speeches cost me nothing. Do you want to know Granite Dresden's grand plan or not?"

Of course I did. She *knew* I did. The old cow just wanted me to say it aloud, to ask her for something. I hesitated for another moment. The priestess waited patiently.

Finally, I crossed my arms over my chest and spoke.

"I'm just supposed to take it on faith that you'll tell me the whole truth. Do I look stupid?"

"I haven't lied to you yet."

"Debatable," I interjected.

"I can't lie to you. My blood runs in your veins. In more ways than one."

"Now I know you're lying." I jabbed an accusatory finger in her direction. "I don't have a compulsion protecting tattoo."

"No, but you do have a mole on your left heel. There's a lot more to that story, too. If you'd like to hear it—"

"No." I held up my hand. "I want to hear Granite Dresden's plans."

She smiled and gestured to the cushioned bench behind me. "All you have to do is sit."

I wanted to pull my hair out. The prideful part of me didn't want to comply with her directive; it was akin to forfeiting, and I never forfeited a fight. Not that long ago, I might have walked away from the priestess, even if she was the only person who had the information I sought. But I'd learned a thing or two about negotiating and power balance in my time by Kai's side.

Sitting on the bench, I sat and leaned back against the gazebo again. "Happy? Your turn. Tell me what's really going on."

"I will, darling. First, let's have tea, shall we?"

CHAPTER SEVENTEEN

FAE CANYON, FREELANDS OF THE AMERICAS

Kai

AS FAR AS Kai could tell, the water test was a challenge of heart meant to tell the council what type of man he was at his core. Within it, the only demons he faced were those from his own past.

With the stone clutched in his hand, he was once again transported from the Temple of Gaia to a void. This one was full of water, like he'd been dropped in the center of the ocean without a single thing to use as a flotation device. He had to tread water to keep his head above the waves, and it was so much more difficult with all the layered clothing. The garments soaked through and pulled like weights. Nothing else happened for a full minute, so Kai picked a direction and started swimming.

He was in decent shape thanks to Kenoa's insistence that there was no better stress relief than a tough workout. Still, swimming in snow boots was next to impossible. Before long, his legs burned from exertion. He would have kicked them off then and there but knew whatever happened in this void would carry over to the real world. Arriving back in Fae Canyon sans snow boots wasn't an option.

An island materialized in the distance, and relief washed over him. Kai doubled his efforts, kicking his legs with all his might and fighting against the water with every stroke of his arms. Twenty minutes later, Kai was no closer to reaching land. Having grown up on a domed island, he was familiar with the difficulty of determining distance on the open water. Still, he felt there was more to it in this case. This was a test, after all.

What am I missing? he thought, desperation starting to take over.

He didn't know the answer to that question, but it was beyond time to ditch the boots. As soon as he did, the island grew closer. *Oh, for Gaia's sake.* Feeling much lighter, Kai started swimming again. It didn't take him nearly as long this time to realize what he needed to do.

With each item of clothing he sacrificed to the water gods, he was transported closer to the island. By the time he reached the sandy shores, Kai was only wearing his boxer briefs. Getting back to Fae Canyon in the lack of clothing would be brutal, but it was obviously what the water gods were asking of him. Kai's legs were rubber, so he crawled up the beach past where the break lapped the sand and flopped down. For several minutes, he lay beneath the beating sun and tried to catch his breath.

Brie's face filled his mind's eye. Her dark hair fanned across the pillows as a lazy smile spread across her face. She reached up and touched his cheek. "I love you," she breathed. He sank into her touch, kissing the edge of her palm closest to his mouth. Then, he leaned down and brought his lips to hers. Before their mouths met, Brie whispered something so softly that it took a moment to register in his mind.

"If you love me, you will get your ass up off the beach."

Kai's eyes popped open. He scrambled to his feet as if the vision had burned his brain. Or had it been a dream? Maybe exhaustion was making him hallucinate.

After his heart returned to a normal rhythm, Kai looked up and down the beach for a sign that would show him his next move. From a distance, the island had appeared very small. Once he was there, the beach seemed endless. With no better idea of how to proceed, Kai picked a direction and started walking.

That direction was forward, toward the center of the island. The sand became rougher beneath his bare feet as he descended into a forest of palm trees. Kai was on high alert, jumping at the slightest noise or shift of the wind. At any second, someone or something was bound to jump out and attack him. He just knew it.

A peel of laughter filled the air, and Kai froze. The

sound of pounding feet came next. More laughter rang out, this time from more than one person. It sounded like a boy and a girl. Kai looked around, searching for a place to hide. When he saw nothing but thin trees that looked like they might snap in a windstorm, he summoned his magic and prepared to fight. Kai caught sight of his would-be attackers. They were children. They weren't enemies to be fought…right?

Well, not quite children. Teenagers. One boy and one girl, and they appeared to be on a date. No, they *were* on a date; Kai knew this for a fact, because he was the boy. The girl was named Maria, and she worked in the palace kitchens. She was also a fae.

The duo ran past him, wearing nothing more than bathing suits and flip flops. He followed them, forcing his tired legs into a run. The couple dodged and weaved through the trees, laughing and giggling like they were high on love.

They were, he thought. To this day, the lone date with Maria was seared into his memory for many reasons.

Kai followed his younger self and the beautiful water fae, not worrying about being quiet or sneaky. He was nearly positive they couldn't see or hear him. The teens came to a stop at the edge of the tree line. Kai slowed and came to a stop a short distance from where they stood. He knew what was about to happen, and he wasn't sure he wanted to relive the experience. Kai also knew he had no choice but to do just that.

Teenage Kai turned to Maria, a smile that he'd thought at the time was seductive on his face. Maria bit her bottom lip nervously. Strands of rich auburn hair clung to her slightly sweaty cheeks. His younger self brushed back the hair and leaned closer.

"You're so beautiful," he murmured softly.

Kai cringed. It wasn't the words themselves that bothered him but the cheesy way he'd said them.

Maria giggled, and teenage Kai brought his lips to hers. The twosome kissed for several minutes. Kai wanted to look away, but he forced himself to watch as his younger self reached around Maria's back and untied her bathing suit top. It slid down her slim body, and she pressed her hips to his. There was a lot more kissing, and a lot of clumsy touching. Then, they finally broke apart, both panting like they'd run a marathon.

"How about a skinny dip?" teenage Kai asked breathily.

Maria smiled. "Okay."

Kai knew there was a cliff with a warm pool beneath and a waterfall on the other side beyond the tree line. If this played out now as it had before, the duo would jump next.

That was exactly what they did. Hands joined, they ran and leapt over the edge. Maria screamed, and teenaged Kai let out a whoop of excitement. Present-day Kai walked slowly to the edge, dreading what would come next.

The two teens plunged into the pool, making small splashes. Their heads broke the surface. Both laughed, eyes sparkling from the adrenaline rush. His younger self reached for Maria and folded her into his arms. He spoke too softly for present-day Kai to hear, but that didn't matter. The king knew the words.

"I am falling in love with you," teenaged Kai said.

Because a fourteen-year-old knows anything about love, Kai thought dryly.

Maria blushed. "I love you, too, Kai."

And that was when Kai lost his virginity. Maria had lost hers on the same night. The act itself was painful to watch, mostly because neither he nor Maria knew what they were doing. It was over in minutes, but the two remained in the water.

Again, their voices were too soft for Kai to hear up on the cliff, but this was a conversation he would never forget.

"That was amazing," teenaged Kai breathed.

Maria eyes were so bright, they were almost luminescent. Her arms were wrapped around his neck, and she giggled. "It was."

Only with the added benefit of hindsight, Kai knew that Maria was lying. He'd lied, too. The sex had been super awkward and uncomfortable. For them both, apparently.

"You know what else would be amazing?" teenage Kai asked his fae companion.

"What?" She offered him a huge grin.

This was the face of girl who'd thought she was on the verge of becoming a princess.

"If we shared magic while we did it," teenage Kai said.

That was not what Maria had expected him to say. Nonetheless, the young fae girl put on a big smile. "Okay, let's try it."

On the cliff, Kai cringed. The teenagers went for a second round. This time, Maria shared her water magic with him. He remembered the sensation like it was something that had happened yesterday. The cool wave of power that flooded his vein made him feel like a god. Maria wasn't particularly powerful, not like Brie. Still, the water around them made her magic so intense.

When it was over, the two teens swam to the shore, emerging from the water as naked as the day they were born. There was a blanket laid out on the grass shore. A picnic basket and vase of tulips were in one corner.

Teenage Kai and Maria flopped on the blanket, side-by-side. He wore a satisfied smile, his eyes slightly unfocused. The boy was on a magical high. The girl was drunk on love.

Maria turned toward teenage Kai and curled up like a cat by his side. She rested her head on his bare chest. He stroked her wet hair lazily. They stayed like that for several minutes, neither of them saying a word.

It was Maria who broke the silence. "How do you think your mother is going to react?"

Teenage Kai looked confused. "What do you mean?"

"Is she going to be upset you have a fae girlfriend?"

His hand fell, as did his corny smile. He propped himself up on his elbow and looked down at her.

"Maria," he began, knowing the rest of his sentence would be painful to them both. "This has to be between us. Just us. You can't tell anybody."

She blanched. "You said you were falling in love with me."

"I am," he assured her.

"So, I am your girlfriend?" she pressed.

Teenage Kai hesitated. "My secret girlfriend."

On the cliff, Kai wanted the ground to open and swallow him whole. Despite the fact he'd genuinely liked Maria a lot, he'd been such an asshole to her. She was pretty and fun to talk to, but he'd told her he was falling in love because he wanted to sleep with her. He'd also really wanted to share magic while doing it; one of his friends had told him the experience was like nothing else. Being the crown prince, Kai couldn't stand the idea that any of his classmates was more worldly than his own experiences.

Gaia, I am horrible person.

Maria took the blow in stride. "Okay. What do you say we secretly meet up tonight? I could come to your suite. Or you could come to the servants' quarters? That might be better, there's less security."

"I can't," he'd told her, the moment perfectly reenacted in front of present-day Kai. "I have a function tonight."

Her hopeful smile faltered. "What sort of function?"

"It's debutante ball for caster girls, sort of," he'd said matter-of-factly. "I don't know, it's boring stuff."

Maria frowned. "Are you escorting one of these girls?"

Teenage Kai averted his eyes and chewed the inside of his cheek. He blew out a long breath. "Yeah. It's tradition."

She pursed her lips and narrowed her eyes. "Who is she?"

This was the moment that teenage Kai had delivered the real blow. On the cliff, in the real-time, Kai sank to his knees. He'd been unnecessarily cruel to the girl, never taking into account the ramifications of what he'd told her.

"I'm taking Lana, my girlfriend."

Maria pulled back, clearly stunned. "Your girlfriend?" she stammered.

Teenage Kai never got the chance to offer her an explanation, not that there was anything he could've said that would've made the situation better.

Lincoln, one of his bodyguards, burst into the clearing. Maria scrambled to cover herself with the blanket.

"What are you doing?" Lincoln demanded, anger flashing in his eyes. He was big for a caster, with broad shoulders and a trim waist. "You know better than to go out without protection." His gaze landed on Maria. "And you, what the hell were you thinking? This will cost you your position. Get dressed. Then, you will go back to the palace and collect your things."

"Come on, Linc," teenage Kai said, also using part of the blanket to cover the royal goods. "That's not necessary."

"Yes, Your Highness, it is. A servant getting involved with a member of the royal family is strictly forbidden. Maria knows that." Lincoln's hard gaze once again shifted to Maria. "You were told the rules when you came to the palace."

Maria began to cry. "What's going to happen me?"

"You will be relocated."

"Where will I go?" she sniffed.

Lincoln's jaw tightened. "You will become a house fae. That shouldn't be a problem for you, since you are so willing to share your magic."

Maria choked on her tears. "Kai, do something."

Teenage Kai was still high on her magic and embarrassed that his bodyguard had just seen him naked. "I'm sorry," he said simply.

To his surprise, Maria drew her arm back and punched him in the face. Then, with no regard for the consequences, she started beating his chest with her fists. Lincoln was there in a flash to subdue the fae. He pulled Maria, and by extension the blanket, off the prince and dragged her away. She screamed obscenities at Kai, calling him horrible names that he now knew he deserved.

That was the last time Kai had ever seen her.

Why didn't I do something? I was the fucking prince for Gaia's sake. I could've insisted she was treated differently. I could've saved her from whatever fate she'd faced.

Up on the cliff, present-day Kai shed tears for Maria. What had become of her? Was she okay? He vowed to track her down once he returned to Hawaii. He would break her contract and give her a hefty stipend. It wouldn't make up for his treatment of her, he knew that, but maybe he could finally apologize for his actions after all these years.

This day will always be my greatest mistake, he thought, the mortification weighing on him until he could barely stand it. *She didn't deserve the disgrace she'd found simply for being with me.*

With that thought, Kai found himself back in the temple, on his knees and shivering terribly. Elder Hawkins looked down at him and nodded slowly.

"You know shame and humility. Next you will pay

tribute to the air gods."

"Did I pass?" Kai asked through chattering teeth. He hugged himself to try and conserve body heat. Without all the clothing he'd shed during the swim, the cold was bitter and brutal.

The answer came from Elder Stanton. "Yes. Which means I have lost my bet."

For a minute, Kai didn't feel the bone-rattling cold. He'd passed two of the four tests; he was halfway there. Never before had he been filled with such a sense of accomplishment. Kai was nearly worthy of Brie. Or half-worthy, anyhow. He could do this.

Instead of offering Kai the next stone, Brie's father produced a stack of clothing from beneath the council table. The king had never been so happy to see a jacket in his life. Ice ran through his veins, making every one of the five steps to the dais a chore. Elder Hawkins wore a blank expression as he watched Kai struggle.

Taking the clothes, Kai dressed as quickly as possible. Then, Brie's father summoned him closer with the crook of a finger. The elder fae placed his hands on either side of Kai's head, and warm air washed over him like a pleasant breeze. Within seconds, Kai's dark hair was dry.

"Thank you, Elder Hawkins," Kai said politely. Regardless of the tests, he hadn't forgotten his manners after all.

Brie's father nodded but didn't seem to be doing a kindness. "I don't want you at a disadvantage in the next test," he said, the words as cold as the air surrounding them.

He handed Kai a yellow stone that, like the ruby, has

clearly been cut. Kai wasn't an expert in gemstones, but his family did have Crown Jewels and a lot of them were diamonds. So, he was pretty positive the stone was a yellow diamond.

As before, once his fingers closed around the jewel, Kai was transported to a void. More specifically, this one was a wind tunnel that churned with strong moving air. Kai covered his eyes with a forearm and took a deep breath. It turned out to be a critical mistake. Air rushed down his throat and flooded his lungs with a suffocating pressure. He gasped, which only made it worse. Dots danced before his eyes. He was going to lose consciousness; it was inevitable.

No. This can't be happening, I won't allow it, Kai thought. But the elements didn't care that he was a king. There, in that void, he was not top dog. He was nobody.

Darkness crept in. With the last of his strength, Kai summoned his magic. He'd survived two of these tests. There was no way he was giving up now. Elder Hawkins had asked how far he'd go to prove his love for Brie. Even after the fire monster, the terrifying depths of water, and being confronted with his greatest shame, Kai had yet to walk through brimstone. It might be time for the ultimate test. In fact, he knew it was.

CHAPTER EIGHTEEN

DOME OF MIDNIGHT

Brie

THE PRIESTESS SIPPED her cinnamon tea from a gold-rimmed china cup with black roses painted on the sides. A tray of little cucumber-and-cheese finger sandwiches sat on a table that had been set up between us in the gazebo. The priestess nibbled on one between sips of tea. There was also a tray of frosted cookies: ham rollups on crackers, a tower of bite-sized pastries, and a basket of biscuits with honey butter.

A maid had poured me a cup of the tea, which sat

untouched in front of me on the table. There was no way I was eating or drinking anything in a vampire hive; I didn't have a death wish that would allow me to die among a bunch of bloodsuckers.

"So, you chose a caster king," the priestess said finally.

"It's complicated," I replied stiffly.

The priestess shrugged. "I like complicated. Tell me the story?"

"Tell me about Granite Dresden and his plans for the rebellion," I countered through gritted teeth.

She waved away my demand. "After tea, dear. I prefer to not mix business with pleasure. So, tell me about this king of yours."

"Fine," I huffed. "Kai is not *my* king. I just spied on him for the rebellion." That was the story Granite was peddling, and I thought it best to play along for the time being. Besides, I was in no mood to have a heart-to-heart with a vampire.

The priestess gave me a knowing smile. "That doesn't sound particularly complicated to me. There must be more to the story."

I licked my lips. "Yeah, well, I was there when the rebellion killed his mother." While I was willing to perpetuate some of Granite's half-truths, I wouldn't bring myself to say I had a hand in killing Queen Lilli. Still, the statement I'd made said as much.

She set her teacup and saucer on the table. "Yes, I know, dear. You were there when my brother and his cohorts killed the caster queen. I know you didn't play a role, though. That was him, the same jerk who tried to steal my kingdom from me."

"So?" It took a minute for the me to grasp the entirety of her words. "Wait…that was your brother?" There was so much to absorb in that moment that I couldn't begin to comprehend it. She waited out my hesitation while my brain caught up.

"Mat is your brother?" I finally asked, praying that the only real deduction to make was wrong.

My real mother had been an only child. I didn't have aunts and uncles on her side. She couldn't be saying what I thought she was saying.

"Yes, Mat," she confirmed. Wind blew in my ears as if to drown out the reality of her admission. "We share a sire. Cessius had many children over the years."

Every muscle in my body tensed. "Mat is the brother that you had the turf war with? The one who came to Fae Canyon?" Though it was phrased like a question, it wasn't an actual query. All the pieces clicked into place. Suddenly, I was seeing my past in a very different light.

The priestess nodded. "Yes. And Alyssa is his child. I believe you met her briefly."

Yes, I'd met Alyssa. I'd met her when my former friend, Christina, brought her vampire girlfriend to the palace for the annual luau. They were the other two people responsible for Queen Lilli's death. The vampires that I'd been unable to stop from killing my boyfriend's mother.

"I know you tried to ruin their efforts," the priestess continued. "And I know, at some point, you fell in love with the caster king you were sent to spy on."

I squared my shoulders. Was this woman serious? She didn't know she shit about me.

"You're not my mother," I shot back. "You're not Julia Hawkins. Don't pretend otherwise." My voice was as cold as the chill in the air in Fae Canyon.

"You're right," she said, a concession that I didn't expect. "I am not Julia Hawkins any longer. The moment I turned, I left her in the past." She pinned me with a pointed gaze. "But that doesn't mean I can't read body language. I have seen footage of you with the caster king—that is how I know you two are in love."

My heart was racing. What if she told Granite her suspicions? On the one hand, I doubted he would care. But it was the fallout that worried me. The rebellion was already holding Cala, Everly, and Rocko over my head...I didn't want them going after Kai, too.

"Don't look so scared, dear. Granite Dresden doesn't care about the truth. He spins facts to suit his purposes. In this case, I am very sure he already knows that you were not involved in the caster queen's murder. It makes a better story for his followers if you had killed the witch, though," the priestess said. Her words made me feel as though she'd read my mind. "I'm not interested in all that. I want to know about this king. He is nice, but does he treat you well?"

I was at my wits end. There was a war going on outside the hive dome. A second kingdom had already fallen, and I was having tea with a freaking vampire. Unfortunately, the vampire had home field advantage. We were playing by her rules, and I had no say in it whatsoever. If I didn't answer the questions about my personal life, it was unlikely she'd tell me about Granite's plans.

"Kai," I said softly. "His name is Kai. He's very sweet.

He's done a lot for me." I swallowed thickly. Thinking about the risks Kai had taken for me recently made me a little queasy. He had so much to lose, yet he'd never once hesitated when it came time to help with the escape. If he'd been able to stop the Los Angeles enforcers from arresting me, there was no doubt in my mind that he would've done so. Kai would've done anything possible to save me from Sarah's arrest warrant, I knew that. If I'd thought otherwise for a moment, I wouldn't have let them take me so easily.

The priestess smiled almost kindly, her sharp white fangs poking out over her bottom lip briefly. "I hear he is a very powerful caster."

I shrugged. "I mean, yeah. I guess. Kai doesn't use his magic much around me."

Where is she going with this? I didn't know, but I didn't like the direction her question was steering us.

"And this Kai knows the truth about his mother's murder, I assume?"

I nodded stiffly. "His sister, Princess Sarah, signed the warrant herself once she thought she knew what'd happened."

The priestess drained her tea and went to pour herself another cup. I'd thought teatime was nearly over, so the refill annoyed me. That was the last straw; realizing she intended on dragging out this bizarre faux mother-daughter reunion as long as possible—a fact I should have picked up on immediately.

Flames shot from my fingertips as I slammed my hand on the table. "Enough," I snapped. "You aren't my mother. Maybe once upon a time you were Julia Hawkins.

I doubt that entirely but, even if you were, that's over. You didn't raise me. You weren't there went I first discovered my element. You didn't teach me to control my magic. You didn't hold me after my first heartbreak. You weren't there the night I was taken. You weren't there when I needed a mother. You've *never* been a mother to me, whoever you are."

Even with my anger at a breaking point, I had control over the flames. Though the sudden and sharp increase in temperature was another matter. When I was the one wielding the fire, the heat didn't really affect me. The priestess, however, began to sweat as the temperature warmed with my restrained powers.

Even though it seemed to annoy her, the priestess fanned herself nonchalantly with one pale hand. I thought I saw a flicker of fear in her eyes when they landed on the flames, but she did her best to mask the discomfort she might have felt.

"You are far too old for temper tantrums, dear," she said mildly, a subtle rebuke in her words.

"Yeah, well, I didn't grow up with a mother." My cold tone chilled us both.

Are you really thinking she's your mother? I questioned myself. I was certainly acting like it, even if my head hadn't caught up with the same facts my soul was believing.

All pretense vanished. "Put out the flames, Maybrie. Now."

She didn't use compulsion on me. Whether that was because she truly couldn't, as she claimed, or because she wasn't quite ready to sink to that level, I honestly didn't know. I didn't care, either. Nonetheless, I recalled the magic threatening to burst from my skin. The scorch mark on the table gave me a childish satisfaction that I hid adeptly. I still wasn't convinced this vampire was telling the truth—that she had once been Julia Hawkins. And yet, something about her brought out the rebellious teenager in me. If she wanted to claim to be my mother, I was going to treat her like a mother: infuriatingly contrary.

The priestess poured her tea and calmly sat back on her pile of cushions. Despite my determination to be obstinate, her next words doused the fiery coil of anger still burning inside of me.

"You have met Delancey Dresden. You also, of course, know Botto Dresden. You have spent time in Revival. I am sure you have noticed that Granite Dresden has an unusually high number of offspring."

Yes, it was something I'd noticed. It was sort of hard to not notice when every other person I met had the same last name.

To the priestess, I simply nodded. "Yeah, I noticed."

"Do you know why that is?"

Because he's narcissistic old man who wants to pass on his seed? I mentally countered. To me, it was a foregone conclusion that didn't bear discussion.

"A lot has been going on. I haven't really thought about it much," I told the priestess evenly. My true thoughts wouldn't help me get out of the vampire hive alive, so I bit them back. I just wanted to leave. Really, I wanted Kai. Unfortunately, that wasn't an option. Still, I would've preferred to be anywhere besides the gazebo with my purported mother.

Despite my desire to leave, we were finally circling a topic I wanted to discuss. Instead of biting back with all the things I wanted to say, I tried to play nice. As much as I was confused by the direction of our conversation, I didn't want her to switch back to my relationship with Kai.

"Do you find it odd that so many of his children are hybrids?" she continued, sipping her tea despite the obvious steam swirling from the cup.

Once she mentioned it, I did realize it weird that so many Dresdens were hybrids. Regardless, I shrugged. "I guess it's sort of strange, but hybrids often get the best traits of both their parents' races. Maybe he thought it would be a strategic advantage?"

The priestess smiled. "Exactly. Fae-shifter hybrids have better resistance to the elements, and they can wield magic. Fae-caster hybrids don't typically need magic infusions. Their fae genes allow them to pull magic from the outside world, which replenishes any magic their caster side pulls from within. They are also able to live outside domes. Caster-shifter hybrids are able to turn, to tap into their animal natures, so they can survive outside a dome as well. Those fare better than fae-caster hybrids."

Thanks for the genetics lesson, I thought.

"So?" I asked aloud. "Is there a point to your lesson about inheritances?"

The priestess set down her teacup and leaned forward. "My point is this: Granite Dresden has spent three decades trying to make the perfect hybrid. He wants to create a race that is utterly free of weakness. He's been using his own DNA to do so, and he'll continue to attempt it until he's found the exact progeny he's been seeking."

It felt like someone had poured a bucket of ice water over my head. To be honest, the biggest shock was that I hadn't picked up on the signs on Granite's master plan. When I looked back on my short time in Revival and all my conversations with Delancey and Granite, there were a lot of clues that I'd dismissed as regular rebel ranting.

"That is not the only experiment Granite Dresden has been performing," continued the priestess, seemingly oblivious to my inner musings. "I am sure you also learned that magic rarely survives the transition to vampirism."

She paused long and waited for me to give some sign of confirmation. What she'd said was something fae were taught in our Races of the World lessons, so I nodded. A horrible, slimy feeling bubbled up in my gut. The priestess was prone to abrupt subject changes, but I had an inkling that her previous line of questioning was related to this new topic.

"It is common knowledge that very strong fae and casters sometimes retain their abilities if turned to vampires," the priestess continued, once she was satisfied that I was hanging on her every word. I was, much to my own chagrin. "Granite Dresden wanted to know why this was not universal. Why can't all powerful casters survive the change, let alone retain their magic?"

Having no answer, I said nothing. When her eyes bored into me, I shrugged. It was enough to make her continue.

"Why do some relatively weak, magically speaking, fae retain their abilities when turned? Along with gaining immortality?"

Again, I had no answer. I hadn't known this phenomenon was possible, but I was staring at proof that it was.

If she is who she says she is..., I reminded myself.

With fae, two powerful parents didn't necessarily guarantee that their children would also be powerful. Likewise, two magically weak parents could produce a powerful kid. Hell, I'd known fae who came from that exact situation. In my case, my father was a powerful air elemental, exceptionally so. As an elder, he even had some proficiency in the other three elements. Illion had been too young when I was taken for me to know his power level, but I wouldn't have been surprised to know that he was remarkably adept with his abilities. He was an earth elemental, that much I did know.

From Dad's stories, I knew that Julia Hawkins had been sort of average. I found that hard to believe of the woman in front of me—if she was even who she said she was—but I knew it of my mother. She'd been run-of-the-mill in every sense, as far as I knew. Neither of her parents were elders, which was only relevant because my dad came from a long line of fae elders. In Fae Canyon, it was a big deal when a prized son of the community chose to marry the daughter of commoners. But he'd married for love.

Sort of like it's a big deal that a caster king wants to marry a lowly fighter fae, I thought wryly.

The priestess's expectant stare told me that she expected an answer.

"I don't know. I mean, we're talking about magic. Fae and casters wield it, but there is a lot we still don't know about magical phenomenon," I said finally. "We could sit here for days coming up with possible explanations, and we'd probably never land on the right one."

In rare show of humanity, the priestess snorted. An odd scratching sensation clawed at the back of my skull, like a memory I couldn't quite access.

"Try decades," she said.

Out of nowhere, a petite middle-aged woman appeared. Her name was Daisy, and she served the vampire priestess like a courtier would serve a queen. We'd met briefly when the tea and food was delivered, though she'd hung back and observed as the maids set up the table and arranged the plates. At the time, I'd been too annoyed to give Daisy much thought. Belatedly, I realized that had been a mistake.

The small woman was a caster. I sensed her magic, faint as it was. My expression must've betrayed my surprise, because the priestess gave me a smug smile.

"Are you not hungry?" Daisy asked me. She sounded worried that it wasn't a matter of my appetite so much as her baking.

It took some effort, but I managed to look up at her with my arena smile in place. "I ate before we came," I lied, then fumbled for something nice to say. "Everything looks great, though. Those little orange sugar puffs look particularly good," I rambled.

"I will wrap up a care package for you to take home."

Well, shit. As long as you don't expect me to eat vamp food in front of you, I'll take it.

"Thank you," I told Daisy.

She gave me a polite smile and small head bob, and then Daisy turned her attention to the priestess. Bowing her head, both her gaze and her words were directed at her feet. "May I clear the table for you, ma'am?"

"No need for the formality today, Daisy. Our guest is my daughter."

I opened my mouth to protest, then decided it wasn't worth it. The priestess would use any excuse to prolong this meeting, and I just wanted to keep the focus on Granite.

Daisy's head swiveled back to me so fast I thought she would suffer whiplash. Her jade green eyes were wide with a light that hadn't been there before, as if seeing me for the first time. She didn't say anything, just nodded again and turned back to her employer.

"We're fine for now, Daisy. How are our other guests?"

Daisy hesitated, and then chose her words carefully. "Mr. Botto is anxious to see Miss Maybrie. And Miss Delancey is anxious to return home to her father. They have taken tea, as well, and that has soothed their worries."

Something about the way she said that last part made me think maybe Daisy had spiked the tea. Thank Gaia I'd refused to consume anything on that table.

"Thank you, Daisy."

The woman knew a dismissal when she heard one and hightailed it out of the gazebo.

"You want to know how I have a caster in my employ," the priestess said once the other woman was gone.

I was dying to know how that situation had come about, and the priestess clearly knew it. *No detours,* I lectured myself. Crossing my arms over my chest, I met the priestess' knowing grin.

"No, I want to know Granite's plans. So far, all you've told me is that the man fancies himself a geneticist. Unless I'm missing something, his little experiment has nothing to do with the current war."

The priestess' expression hardened. "Oh, Maybrie, dear. Granite Dresden's 'little' experiment has everything to do with the current war." She sighed heavily, a little of the oomph going out of her.

This is it, I realized, literally on the edge of my seat.

The priestess rose, and my hope blew away on the light breeze.

"Let us take a walk, dear. I find light exercise helps the digestion." She motioned for me to join her.

"You're dead," I retorted. "I think digestion is the least of your worries. Besides, you didn't even really eat." Despite my antagonistic words, I did follow her lead.

The priestess laughed. "That sharp tongue comes from me, you know?"

We descended the gazebo steps and started down a stone path. While the guards didn't follow us on the walk, I knew they were watching.

"Actually…," I began. We strolled past a bush of black roses that could've only survived the eternal night via magic. "My sharp tongue is learned. Beneath the dome, you have to learn to fight with words. That's the only weapon they allow us. Besides using magic in the pits, of course."

The priestess led me through lush gardens full of flowers that most certainly would never occur in nature. Some were iridescent and beautiful in the scant moonlight. Some glowed like fireflies in summer months, the blossoms in every color of the rainbow. Then there were the orchids with impossibly long stems. Their scents curled around me like a warm blanket.

As I took in the sights and sounds and smells, the priestess watched me curiously. It was different than I'd imagined a vampire hive would be. Where were the coffins? And the well-muscled vampires openly feeding on beautiful women? At the very least, I would've excepted the priestess to drink blood from a crystal chalice instead of serving tea like this was the royal age of humans. Of course, I'd never considered that a hive might exist beneath a dome. I assumed vampire lived in dark caves or something equally as primitive. Instead, this was a city. A vampire city.

The thought made me shudder.

We exited the gardens through an iron gate, which put us out on the street behind the priestess' house. She led the way up the sidewalk, smiling and waving politely to those we passed. Most were vampires, though I did spot a shifter and fae carrying bags of groceries. There was a girl who looked about my age, maybe slightly younger, that nearly dropped her bloody latte when she laid eyes on the priestess.

"Jane, how are you, dear?" my guide asked her.

The girl stopped walking but kept her gaze fixed on

the ground. "I am well, Priestess. Thank you for asking." Her tone was polite albeit robotic, as if repeating a programmed response.

"This is Maybrie, Jane."

The girl's head shot up, revealing hazel eyes with only the slightest hint of red. Pale skin stretched over pronounced cheekbones. All vampires had dark circles unless they covered them with makeup, but there was no amount of concealer that could've hidden the ones beneath Jane's eyes. I didn't know what she'd been before the change, but she was pure vampire now. And newly turned, by the look of it.

I extended my hand. "It's nice to meet you, Jane."

Her cool palm slid against mine, and I willed myself not to flinch. Friendliness toward vamps was not part of my typical day. Nevertheless, there was something so tragic about Jane that I sort of wanted to hug her.

"You're Maybrie Hawkins." When Jane smiled, her whole face lit up. In that expression, I saw some of the girl that must've been there before she turned. "I'm a huge fan."

"Thank you, I really appreciate it." Though I'd become accustomed to that sort of attention from casters, shifters, and fellow fae, I didn't know what to say to a vampire who evidently watched my matches.

Luckily the priestess spoke up. "Have you been watching the caster queen's citizenship trial, dear?"

Jane's focused turned back to the priestess, a different sort of worship in her gaze. "A little, ma'am. They thought it might help me." Her eyes shifted to her feet. "I am embarrassed to admit it has not. I guess I'm not progressing as much as they'd like."

"No, Jane. All it means that your heart has remained good despite all the evil you have known." The priestess smiled at the girl. "Go on, now. Enjoy your day."

"Thank you, Priestess." Jane glanced back at me. "And thank you, Brie. The rebellion is lucky to have you."

That was when I realized she wasn't a fan of my fighting so much as my supposed murdering. I didn't correct her false assumption. Not because I cared about how I factored into Granite's plan, though. For Jane, I was clearly a symbol of hope. Of change. And the girl had been through a lot. Someone like her needed that hope to go on.

The priestess and I continued on our way, passing cute shops in a downtown area that I wouldn't have thought necessary for vampires. There were two grocery stores within as many blocks, which seemed like overkill. Vamps could eat, sure, but as far as I knew they didn't need to consume food to live. Or not live? Whatever. I didn't know the correct terminology, and I didn't care enough to ask. There was also an astounding number of nail salons.

We came to a stop in front of a bar called Fang 'N Talon.

"Now you want to get drunk?" I asked, confused. "Wait. Can vamps even get drunk?"

The priestess frowned. "It really isn't polite to call us 'vamps', dear. We prefer vampire. Or eternal. And yes, *vampires* can get drunk. But that's not why we're here. There is someone I'd like you to meet." She gestured me inside.

The establishment was the diviest of dive bars. The

stools were lopsided, and there were cracks along the surfaces of most tables. An unfortunate perfume of stale beer, cheap liquor, and even cheaper wine wafted up from the wooden floorboards. The ground also had more bloodstains than a murder scene. None of that, however, affected the patronage. The place was packed, without an empty barstool in sight.

The priestess wove through the crowd, her long dress sweeping the dirty floor. Not that she seemed to care. I followed, noticing more than a few curious looks from the vampires in the bar. I mirrored the expression back to the fae and shifters in the room.

Why would a fae or shifter choose to live in a vampire hive?

People stood four-deep in front of the bar, all vying for the bartenders' attention. The crowd parted for the priestess. By extension, they created a walkway for me as well. One of the bartenders, a water fae, gave her a big, cheesy grin.

"What'll it be, Jules?" he called.

I couldn't hide my surprise. He'd called her Jules. *Jules.* Like they were friends. It was the same thing my father had called my mother. Everyone else we'd encountered had been respectful and deferential. Not this guy; he acted as though they played poker every week.

"A moment of your time?" the priestess replied in a voice that shouldn't have been audible over the music and chatter.

"You've got it." The bartender put down his shaker without pouring and serving the drink he was making. Grabbing three pint glasses, he filled them from the beer taps and hurried around the bar.

There weren't any empty tables in the room until the priestess fixed her gaze on the occupants of a high-top table nearby. All four vampires scurried away from the booth, leaving us a small alcove of space for our meet and greet.

"I'm guessing this is more business than pleasure," said the fae bartender as he sat down our drinks. He handed the priestess a mug of reddish-brown liquid. "Oh-Neg Special Brew. Keep it around just for you, Jules. No one else can afford it."

The priestess smiled affectionately. The look was off-putting; I wasn't aware vampires could feel affection. "You know me so well. I do love a rare vintage." She cut her eyes to me. "It's O-Negative caster blood. Very hard to come by." Her expression softened again when she glanced back to the bartender. "Actually, it's a little bit of both. Business and pleasure. Hern, this is Maybrie Hawkins. Maybrie, I'd like for you to meet Hern. He is also from Fae Canyon."

Hern and I stared at each other with wide eyes. "You're from Fae Canyon?" I asked at the same time he said, "You're Jules' daughter?" We both laughed, though I sounded awkward and uncomfortable. Which I was.

"Hern was with me when the caravan was attacked," the priestess explained.

"But he's not a vampire?" I asked. The question seemed abrupt and maybe rude, but I had to be sure I wasn't missing something.

The guy was on the paler side, but his complexion looked more like he needed sun than blood. There wasn't even the slightest hint of red in his eyes. And I definitely sensed magic in him. Like a lot of magic. More than even Kenoa had, and he was the strongest water fae I'd ever met.

"No, I'm not," Hern answered. He slid a mug over to me. "Silver Ale. I think you'll like it."

Yeah, there was no way I was drinking alcohol there. My stomach was too upset anyway.

"Hern was sold to King Joaquin's predecessor, Queen Joanne," continued the priestess. "She was a horrid woman, who kept a revolving stable of men at her disposal once her husband had died. She didn't discriminate between the races. She had many fae lovers, many caster lovers, many shifter lovers, and one very awful vampire lover."

Hern pulled down the collar of his shirt so I could see his neck, which was covered in scars. I gasped, my hand flying to cover my mouth and nearly knocking over my mug.

"She let a vampire feed on you?" I asked, horrified.

"I was a magical feeder for the caster queen." Hern spoke matter-of-factly, making eye contact with me the whole time. "She loved to use her magic for tiny things, for big things, for everything. She needed frequent infusions, sometimes as often as five times a day."

Five times sounded like a lot to me, but I didn't actually know what was normal. Kai was careful not to mention when he had infusions. He sheltered me from that facet of his life.

Hern sipped his beer. "I was her favorite." He laughed humorlessly. "If you can imagine an old fae like me when I was your age. Well, I wasn't hard to look at. That had something to do with it."

There was no way I was going to delve into that last comment. This story was sad enough.

"I'm guessing your incredible power also had something to do with it," I said to fill the silence.

He shrugged. "Yes, it likely did." Averting his eyes, Hern drained his beer, clearly hoping the alcohol would give him courage to finish the tale.

Honestly, I sort of wanted alcohol before he finished the tale. I eyed my beer but didn't touch the mug. *He's not as over what happened as he pretends,* I thought. *Don't test his allegiance.*

"The caster queen liked to be full up before…." He trailed off, searching for a delicate way to say it.

"Before she banged one of her concubines?" I offered helpfully.

Hern smiled. The priestess frowned. "Maybrie, must you be so crass?" she chastised.

I ignored her. Maybe she had been Julia Hawkins, but that gave her no right to give me shit.

A server appeared out of nowhere with a fresh beer for Hern. He thanked the woman and waited for her to leave before continuing.

"When her vampire was the man of the night…well, he liked to be full up, too," Hern said. He touched his neck, in the spot where the scars were the worst. My heart went out to him. I had only been bitten once, and it was an experience I would never forget.

Hern cleared his throat. "Your mother and other rebels, they freed me. And when Jules became High Priestess and really got this hive up and running, she offered me a place. A home. Hell, this bar."

"You own this place?" I asked.

"I do."

The priestess reached out and placed a pale hand over one of Hern's, which were both wrapped around his beer mug. "Thank you, for sharing your story with Maybrie."

He smiled. "Anything for you, Jules."

The way they looked at one another was not okay. There was more than affection in their eyes. If I wasn't mistaken, and I prayed I was, they were…lovers. Because I wasn't already on the verge of puking.

Why do you care? She isn't your mother.

Why did I care?

"We should be going. There are more people I'd like for Maybrie to meet."

I said goodbye to Hern and thanked him, just as the priestess had done. We left with a somber cloud around us. I wasn't stupid, I knew what the priestess was doing. She was introducing me to people who'd suffered greatly at the hands of casters, showing me why an uprising was necessary. What I still didn't understand was her motive. I mean, she didn't support Granite's plan. Or did she? Maybe she just didn't like his methods?

"Hern is the strongest fae here," the priestess said softly as we resumed our tour of the town. She reconsidered her statement. "Present company excluded, of course. He is also one of the few not turned vampire. Granite has used everything but compulsion to persuade him, and I have refused an unwanted turning in Hern's case, given his past."

What was I supposed to say to that? Granite had told

me that working with vampires was a necessary evil. He made it sound like they were foot soldiers in his war. But the priestess made it sound like their relationship went much deeper. Since I didn't trust either of them, I had no idea what to believe.

"The girl you met, Jane," continued the priestess, her voice still low.

We passed a café with outdoor seating. Vampires sat in clusters drinking bloody coffees and munching on cakes and cookies.

"Yeah, what about her?" I asked uneasily. The answer was not going to help my nausea.

"She too is an escapee from the Domed City of Austin. Their monarch is one of the worst offenders in the Americas. They employ torture for the smallest offenses. King Joaquin enjoys public humiliation so much that he sentences fae to magic feedings in Royal Square. The insufferable Queen Katherine casts stasis spells on shifters who look at her the wrong way. Reportedly, a were-tiger was forced to remain in his human form for over a year. The pain was crippling. He said it was like the tiger was trying to claw his way to the surface."

Bile burned my throat. The previous night, I'd actually felt sorry for Queen Katherine. I'd rooted for her to complete the citizenship trial and show the rebel leaders in Austin what's up. Gaia, I felt stupid.

"The caster queen has two panthers that follow her everywhere. Their loyalty is unquestionable." The priestess waited a beat to see whether I had yet to understand where this was going.

Unfortunately, I did know. Those panthers were shifters that Katherine kept in animal form. She assured their obedience with a magical tether.

"Every so often, she switches them out. She kept one of them in panther form for so long, the poor girl went delirious when she was finally free to change back. They had to put her in a special facility. The rebellion freed her only a few months ago. I had her turned to save what was left of her sanity. What you saw today is a far cry from the filthy, rambling shifter Granite's people brought me. Remember Jane?"

We turned down a street with brick townhouses. Vampires sat out on their balconies enjoying cocktails. I saw a fae couple tending to their garden. The hive was a very strange place, I decided. It was nothing like I'd expected.

And that was when it happened.

The attack came out of nowhere. Two vampires latched onto my arms, their fangs bared and aimed for neck. One even managed to slice my throat, though he didn't bite down. The ground rumbled beneath my feet as flames burst from my hands. They spread up my arms so fast that one of the vampires didn't have time to let go. His hands turned to ash before his crimson eyes. Then his entire body went up in flames. I pivoted, muscles tensed and spoiling for a fight.

A fight I didn't get.

The priestess had conjured a lasso out of a tree limb and had the vampire around the waist. Her guards surrounded us, their guns pointed at my attacker. He was no one I recognized.

"Why would you dare attack a guest of the High Priestess?" demanded the priestess in a voice so cold my flames almost went out.

"The girl has a bounty on her head. Dead or alive," he sneered, his fangs poking out. "All I need is her corpse."

The priestess tightened the lasso, causing my attacker to cry out in pain. "By the laws of the Hive, attacking a guest of the High Priestess is punishable by death."

"She's a pointy-eared caster-loving—"

I threw a fireball at his feet. He danced away from the flames.

"What hive do you belong to?" asked the priestess in that same icy tone.

He simply sneered in response.

"Maybrie's next fireball will light you up. And I know a few spells that can prolong your agony in the flames." She gestured to the pile of ash behind us. "It won't be quick like your friend. Or, you can tell me your hive."

"You're going to kill me either way," he spat.

I threw another fireball. This one landed in front of him, and then spread slowly in a circle with him at the center. The flames stretched higher and higher, until they were at his chest. They were far enough away that he wasn't in danger of catching fire, but close enough that he was sweating sheets.

"It's a simple question," the priestess said calmly.

"The Moon Hive," he shouted. "Mat is my Hive King."

The name made me freeze, icicles in my chest as the identity of the guy's sire sunk in.

"Oh, how unfortunate for you to belong to my

brother." The priestess' smile was as cold as her beauty. "For that offense alone, I sentence you to die." She turned to me. "Would you like to do the honors?"

I blinked. Her watching eyes made me realize that she expected an answer to her offer, like it was an honor.

"What? You want me to kill him?"

She shrugged. "If you like. You were the one he attacked, it's your right."

It felt like one of those crossroad moments. I'd killed a vampire before. Apparently, I'd just killed another one with my fire magic, and I hadn't even meant to. Still, this felt different. This kill wouldn't be self-defense. This wasn't the fighting pit. If I killed him, it would be in cold blood. I wasn't prepared for that.

I shook my head. "I don't want him dead." Meeting the vampire's snarly gaze over the flames, I spoke directly to him. "You go tell the masters you serve to screw themselves. Tell them, if they want me, they're going to have to do better than two weak-ass bloodsuckers. Tell Mat, he and I have unfinished business. Remind him that I am not a child any longer."

If the priestess found my use of "bloodsuckers" offensive, she didn't let on.

"You will tell your masters that Maybrie Hawkins is under the protection of the Midnight Hive. Should you come for her again, I will destroy your hive and everyone in it. I will personally drain the person offering the reward, and I will revel in the experience." Her gaze narrowed. "You will tell the casters you work for my name. I am Julia, High Priestess of the Midnight Hive. If they don't know who I am, they had better learn."

I extinguished the fire, and the guards rushed in. They had him in silver cuffs, which were toxic to vampires. Now I understood why Hern had brought me Silver Ale.

The priestess reached for my neck, and I flinched at her cold touch. Her fingers came away smeared with my blood. The adrenaline rush was fading fast, and I was feeling queasy again. For a second, I saw two priestesses. I blinked, and my vision sort of righted itself. I only saw one-and-half priestesses.

"Maybrie?" she said my name like she cared. "Maybrie, darling. Say something. What's wrong?"

"I think…," I mumbled.

The bile rose so fast that I vomited all over the priestess' pretty dress. My knees gave out. I should've hit the ground, but she caught me. She turned my head to the side as I spewed more sickness. Stroking my hair, she murmured soft, soothing words.

Just before the world went black, and I passed out in the middle of the street inside a freaking vampire hive, I looked up into my mother's eyes.

"I'm still poisoned," I muttered. And then the darkness consumed me.

CHAPTER NINETEEN

FAE CANYON

Kai

AFTER A ROCKY start to the air test, Kai found it easier than the first two. Mostly because he knew to expect the unexpected. Plus, it was neither as physically demanding as the fire test nor as emotionally draining as the water one. The scavenger-hunt-like aspect meant his brain did most of the work, which was familiar territory for him. He'd spent most of his days thinking up ways to keep his kingdom from crumbling to ash around him, and this felt uncomfortably similar. One could say, it was a breeze.

Conversely, as soon as he entered the void for his final test, Kai knew this one—the earth test—would be the hardest of the four. Like before, the instant his fingers had closed around the stone, Kai was transported. This time, he found himself standing in a jungle. A very hot, very humid, jungle. Having learned something from his earlier tests, he began removing layers of clothing, leaving only the loose pants between his long underwear and snow pants, and no shirt whatsoever. And, of course, the boots. Then, he picked a direction and started walking.

There was no path, just overgrown bushes and trees with small, dark purple berries. They weren't like any he'd ever seen before, but he had the feeling they were poisonous. For someone who'd grown up in the Freelands, edible versus toxic plants and fruits was common knowledge. For a royal caster who'd never been made to cut his own meat let alone forage for food, Kai was just happy that he even considered not eating the berries.

He heard the hiss in his ear an instant before pain shot through his neck. Kai reached for his attacker, but his hands slid right down the creature's long, cylindrical body. Gasping for air as the pain spread through his chest and down his arms, he managed to angle his head just enough to see the great black snake dangling lazily from a thick tree branch overhead.

Think. What do you know about snakes?

But all he knew was that they could wrap around their prey and suffocate them to death.

Not helpful.

The snake drank from him like a vampire, while simultaneously pumping a venom into his veins that made Kai feel funny. Not a good funny, like the illegal substances he'd tried as a teen, but more like the world was about to be upside-down funny. He tried pulling the snake off himself again, but the reptile had latched on and only an act of Gaia would get it to let go.

Or, you know...an act of magic, he thought, feeling foolish.

Kai wheezed out an incantation. The snake jerked violently. Its tail uncoiled, and it fell to the ground with a heavy thud. And yet, the snake's teeth were still firmly wedged on the side of his neck, and the creature was still drinking his blood. What was worse, since the snake had been attached to him when he cast the spell, the bolt of electricity he'd passed to the snake had also hit him.

For a minute he thought the earth was spinning around them, like he and snake were at the center of a wheel. Then Kai's knees struck the hard ground. At some point along the line, the snake's bite had stopped hurting, but the force of the impact from his short fall sent fresh waves of pain shooting up Kai's legs. Just as it had on the beach, an image of Brie filled his mind. He didn't need her to tell him to get his ass up, Kai had figured out that much on his own. But seeing her did give him an idea. Summoning his magic, he focused it all into his hands. They began to glow red. This time, when he yanked on the snake, the reptile released him. Kai threw the heavy creature as far as he could in his weakened state, which wasn't far.

Adrenaline gave him the ability to leap to his feet. He

started running deeper into the jungle. Over the sound of his own labored breathing, Kai didn't hear the wet, slithering sound that followed him. It wasn't until he risked a glance over his shoulder that he saw the snake in pursuit.

"You've got to be kidding me," he panted.

He had no clue how fast snakes in the real world, particularly ones so big, moved. Nevertheless, this one seemed to have preternatural speed. And possibly feet. That might've just been the venom talking, though. Kai honestly wasn't sure.

Outrun it. You've got to outrun it. Even as the thought popped into his head, Kai tripped over a tree root buried beneath lush, green foliage. Managing to stay on his feet, he swore loudly. The snake lunged, sharp fangs slicing through his clothes and nicking his flesh for a second time.

So, outrunning it is probably not going to work. And since the reptile could climb and slither up trees, that wasn't an option either. *Stand and fight.*

With reflexes he didn't know he had, Kai stopped, spun, and fired off the first spell that came to mind. The snake halted, coiled into itself, and then started chasing its own tail like a dog. Admittedly, it wasn't the most elegant solution, but it had worked. Using the snake's distraction, Kai summoned flames to his hands just as he'd seen Brie do. He launched one fireball after another at the creature until it finally disintegrated into ash.

"Take that you piece of shit!" he cried triumphantly, thrusting a fiery fist into the air.

The elation didn't last long. Spots invaded his vision,

causing him to reach for the nearest tree to steady himself. He felt the twin puncture wounds on his neck. Blood poured freely down his throat and stained the collar of his shirt. He was on the verge of summoning more magic to heal himself, when he realized that was part of his problem. Kai was low on magic and probably had been for a while.

It had been a long time since he'd known this feeling of extreme exhaustion. As crowned prince, he'd been able to replenish his magic as often as he needed. Or wanted. Ever since his ill-fated trip outside the dome with Kenoa, Kai had been a lot more cognizant of just how dependent casters were on fae for survival. He'd stopped using his magic for everyday tasks, only casting spells for very special reasons or when necessary. Until recently, with Brie being at risk in L.A., no situation had ever fallen into the latter category.

In this void, there were no fae to give him magic. The snake was likely only the first of many obstacles he'd face in the jungle. If he kept using his magic, how long before he was depleted? Yet if he didn't use magic, how long before one of these creatures killed him? His vision swam again, and he leaned more heavily against the tree. Gloom rushed in, and Kai fought it back with willpower alone.

No. This is not over. Just think. These tests are designed for you personally. They're meant to be hard, not deadly.

Or were they? Had the elders put him through all of this not to prove he was worthy of Brie but to torture him before his inevitable death? With his mind fuzzy from the venom and loss of blood and magic, he almost believed that might be true. Except, Kenoa had known about these worthiness trials before they came to Fae Canyon. The Council of Elders had not just invented them. Besides, Kai believed Elder Hawkins an honorable man. Had he brought Kai to Fae Canyon to answer for kidnapping Brie, there would have been no subterfuge. And fae weren't devious like vampires; it wasn't in their nature.

"Which means there is a way for me to get through this," he mumbled to himself.

The berries.

Kai blinked until his vision came into focus. A string of the dark purple berries grew on the tree beside his head. He snatched a handful and shoved them in his mouth. Suddenly, his legs felt sturdier, strong enough to hold him up. The fog inside his head cleared. He flexed his fingers and summoned enough magic to heal the wounds on his neck. That was when he realized the truth: the berries hadn't replenished his magic, they'd just counteracted the venom. He still had magical reserves, but he was low. Extremely low, considering the number of tasks that were likely still ahead of him.

As he started walking again, Kai kept his eyes peeled for something else that might contain magic. Ordinarily, he would've tapped into his sixth sense. Unfortunately, everything in the void was imbued with magic, so he was forced to rely on a human's mere five senses. Somewhere along the way, he picked up a walking stick Brie would've brandished as an effective weapon.

"I can still use it as *a* weapon," he muttered to himself with a small smile.

Kai liked that Brie was tough. It was part of what drew him to her. Too many of the girls he'd dated looked to him to be their knight in shining armor. But he wasn't a knight. He didn't want or need a damsel in distress. He was a king, and he needed a queen. A true equal to rule beside him, not cower behind him. He wanted a partner.

No, I want Brie to be my partner, he corrected himself.

But these tests had made him realize that maybe she was his knight in shining armor. He'd always known she could kick his ass, but she wasn't just physically stronger than him. While he was mistreating fae teens beneath the dome, Brie was helping to raise her younger brother. When he wrecked his first speed boat drag racing with Kenoa, Brie had been stolen from her home. While he played with the beautiful yet vapid female population of the city his family ruled, Brie fought for her life inside the pits. When his family had pushed Tanner to his breaking point, she was left to pick up the pieces. Through it all, Brie never broke.

Yes, there was no question which one of them was stronger. In some ways, she always would be. Kai couldn't picture himself spending the hours in the gym per day required to learn hand-to-hand combat on Brie's level. Regardless, he would spend decades learning to be a better caster, if it meant they would be real partners and true equals. Until then, he would be the king to her queen, not the other way around.

Lost in thought, Kai hadn't noticed the subtle darkening of his surroundings until he couldn't see more than a few feet in either direction. Panic started to set in, but all the time he'd spent thinking about Brie gave him an idea. He summoned a small flame and held it to one end of his walking stick. It took a minute for the branch to catch fire. Once it did, Kai relaxed and kept moving.

Two yellow dots appeared ahead of him in the distance. He swung his torch to the right and left. In both directions, identical spots appeared. Then, he chanced a look behind him. Those yellow dots were much larger. They were also attached to a large shadow that was in the shape of a panther. The animal leapt toward him, snarling and snapping at the air. He didn't think twice about his short magical supply when he sent a wave of energy at the cat's soft underbelly. The panther yelped in pain, falling to the jungle floor in a heap of tangled limbs.

Had it not been for the other three cats, Kai might've tried running again. That wasn't an option. So, he prepared to fight. He lit the other end of the walking sticking, two flames now burning brightly in the dark night. The hurt panther was on its feet again, advancing along with the other three. He lunged at Kai again. This time, he swung the stick like a club and struck the side of the cat's head. Blood dripping from its ear, the cat retreated, only to lunge again immediately.

You're going to need more than a flaming bat, Kai told himself.

But he was still reticent to use much magic. Still, he needed to do something. Brie fought and defeated shifters without using magic all the time. This situation wasn't all that different.

She's a lot more skilled.

That was true. Skill had gotten her far in fights. But she was almost always smaller than her opponents, and sometimes size really did matter. Brie won because she played smarter not harder. That was what Kai needed to do now, he decided. Instead of using magic to fight the panthers directly, he infused the stick with power—a one-time shot that cost him way less than if he'd continued to blast the animals.

Holding the flaming stick like he was about to hit a grand slam, Kai was ready when the panther lunged a fourth time. When the bat connected with the cat's shoulder, the animal exploded into a million tiny particles of light. *No, not light,* he realized when they landed on his face. *Magic.*

Two more panthers attacked in concert. He smashed his magical bat into one's chest, even as another's jaws closed around his wrist. In a move he would applaud himself for later, Kai took the bat in his good hand and drew back. With one whip of his arm, he slammed one fiery end against the panther's ribcage. It burst apart on impact. With the magical rain falling all around him, he faced off with the final animal. This one was larger than the other three and foamed at the mouth as though rabid. Saliva dripped from the cat's jaws, making white, bubbling holes in the moss covering the ground. There was no way Kai could let that animal get anywhere close to him.

The panther's yellow eyes bore into his as Kai shifted the bat above his shoulder and the cat pawed the ground. Kai steadied his breathing. He only had one shot at this, he needed to be patient. Seconds stretched into minutes, with the two fighters staring at one another. Kai's arm ached from holding the large stick, and his wrist was bleeding freely.

Wait for it. Be patient.

The panther leapt. Kai threw the stick like a javelin, putting every ounce of strength he had behind that throw. One flaming end of the spear sank into the cat's black fur. And then, just like the others, the animal evaporated. If this had been a video game, the last panther would've been worth way more kill points than the other three. Even in this game of sorts, the final animal brought not more points but a ton of magic. Dripping sweat and panting, Kai turned his face up toward the falling specs of dust-like magic and smiled.

Deciphering rhyme or reason out of these tests was hard enough, anticipating when and where his next attack would come from was even harder. Ample time for him to recoup and recharge had passed between the snake and the panthers but killing the snake hadn't recharged his magic. All that really meant to Kai was that he needed to remain vigilant. He tore a strip of fabric from the bottom of his shirt and wrapped around the bite on his wrist. No reason to use unnecessary magic, after all.

Not long after he'd procured another walking stick, which he once again turned into a torch for visibility sake, he spotted a wasp's nest cradled in the space where a large tree trunk had split to form two offshoots. The insects didn't immediately swarm him, but Kai wasn't taking any chances. Still several yards away, he lined up the flaming end of his walking stick with the nest and fired three fireballs. All three hit their mark, engulfing the next in flames.

Busy patting himself on the back for his quick thinking,

Kai didn't notice that his boots were sinking deeper into the softer terrain than moments before. In fact, the thick brown mud was around his ankles before Kai thought to look down. He yanked one foot up, which caused the other to sink even deeper.

Don't panic. Just think.

Fire couldn't help him this time. Neither would a magically charged stick. He shouted the first incantation that came to mind, a freezing spell. It worked. The mud around his boot hardened instantly, leaving Kai with another problem he hadn't anticipated. Now his foot was stuck. He tried thawing the mud, but his leg sunk until the mud was halfway up his calf before he was able to refreeze it.

I still have one foot free, he thought and attempted pulling his trapped leg up using his other foot as leverage. All that achieved was strain on his nerves. He started slamming the walking stick against the ground and felt the icy mud loosen around his calf. After a few good blows, only his foot was still trapped. Kai bent and started clearing away the chunks of frozen mud with his hands, clawing at the impacted ice encasing his foot with stubby nails. Several minutes later, all he had were bleeding fingers to go with his bloody arm.

Now what?

Each test so far had required some sort of magic use, he reasoned. Thawing the mud hadn't worked. Manually breaking the ice with the stick had to an extent. What if he tried using magic to crack the lower layers of ice? Placing both palms on the ground, Kai sent out a short, controlled burst of power. The earth right around him shuddered, creating more fissures in the frozen mud, enough that he felt confident attempting to pull his foot free again. This time his boot came loose, but his foot was at an odd angle and twisted painfully in the process.

Still, he'd gone through another hurdle and for that he couldn't be too upset.

The walking stick became more of a crutch after that. He dealt with other small inconveniences along the way to what he knew would be his final battle. He didn't know what the council had in store—whether it would be magical or physical or emotional—but he knew it would require all he had left to give.

Kai couldn't have said how long he traipsed through that jungle, every nerve ending on hyperdrive. Finally, there was a light at the end of the tunnel. Or, more accurately, behind a thick cluster of trees. Leaning heavily on his walking stick, he half jogged, half limped toward the light, only realizing too late that maybe he shouldn't have been so quick to meet his final challenge. He hobbled out from the jungle and into an arena. Just like the one where he'd watched Brie fight so many times.

No, it is the arena, he corrected himself.

The stands were packed to bursting with fae and shifter faces. He found the royal box, where Kai had so often sat to watch the fights. That was where he found her—Brie. She sat on a wooden throne, wearing a platinum crown atop her dark hair with a large ruby in the center. The jewel caught the sunlight, making it appear more orange than red. Her hands were folded neatly in her lap. Bodyguards in ceremonial black dress stood behind her with their hands behind their backs, and their eyes searching for the slightest sign of threat.

People cheered and jeered in equal measure as Kai shielded his eyes and gazed up at Brie. *She's so fierce, so beautiful,* he thought, his chest swelling with pride.

An enormous roar engulfed the arena. In the stands, people were on their feet, clapping and whooping. But for the first time in his life, the excitement had nothing to do with him. His opponent—that was who the crowd was cheering for. When Kai turned to face the newcomer, his stomach dropped to his feet. His final test, and he knew without a doubt this was his final test, was Brie. She was his opponent.

The fire fae smiled coolly as she waved to her fans. When she turned to face Kai, there was no love or light in her eyes, only cold, hard determination. This fight wasn't personal for this version of Brie the way it was for him. No recognition shown in her gaze.

She doesn't know me.

That thought was harder for him to swallow than the knowledge that his defeat was a certainty.

Some announcer introduced both Brie and Kai respectively, drawing more cheers and more boos from the stands. Then, somewhere, a referee blew their whistle. The first fireball whizzed so close to his head that felt the heat on his cheek, and then he smelled burnt hair. This version of his girlfriend played to win, just like the real one.

For the first few minutes, Kai simply played defense, dodging Brie's flames with the evasive maneuvers that his security detail had taught him in case of attack. His ankle throbbed but adrenaline masked most of the pain.

Finally, one of Brie's fireballs hit his leg, catching his pants on fire. Kai produced a spout of water from his fingertip and doused the flames. The smug smile she gave him suggested that there was nothing wrong with her aim, she'd been playing with him the entire time.

A little shaky from the close call, Kai flipped through his mental catalogue of spells. After a beat, he decided on a power move similar to one he'd seen earth fae use in the pits. Magic gathered at his core. He held his arms out to the sides, palms down, and two bolts of electricity shot from his hands to the ground below. The entire stadium quaked with his power. Brie's steps faltered as she tried to steady herself. Beneath her feet, the ground split apart, and it was all she could do to dive out of the way lest she fall into the small chasm.

Brie rolled to her feet, eyes alert as the searched the arena for him. She must've scraped her head in fall, because there was a smear of blood near her hairline. Kai chanced a glance up at the royal box, where a very different version of Brie sat on the edge of her throne.

"Come on, caster. Show me what you got!" taunted the Brie in the arena. She rushed toward him, leaping over the cracks in the earth to reach him.

Kai didn't have a fighter's instincts, so it didn't occur to him until after Brie had knocked him to the ground that he should have fired off another spell. Her fist struck him around on the chin. It was the first time in his life that Kai had been hit in the face, and he was too dazed to react. Another few hard blows from Brie, and Kai's fight or flight finally kicked in. One problem persisted—Kai didn't actually know how to fight. Not with his hands, anyhow. He called the magic and sent a powerful wave of energy toward the fire fae on top of him.

Brie flew backward, somersaulting through the air but landing on her feet. She grinned and crooked a finger as if daring him to attack again. He hesitated, which proved a misstep. Flames streaked from Brie's hands, forming a ring of fire around where he stood. An invisible fist struck him hard and low in the gut. Kai doubled over, and that same fist hit him so hard in the face that his head snapped back. Iron filled his mouth, and he spat blood that sizzled on the fire around him.

I can't beat her, he thought, not for the first time. And yet, he had to. This was all for Brie. If he lost this fight, her father and the other elders would decide he wasn't worthy. *Think. This isn't the real Brie. This isn't your Brie.* This woman wasn't the one who'd spent the last five years in the fighting pits. This was a version of Brie, an idea of her that the elders had conceived. He smiled to himself, even as another of those invisible blows struck his side.

Summoning more magic than he had in a very long time, maybe ever, Kai straightened to his full height and muttered an incantation. He knew he was a powerful caster, but he'd never actually put that notion to the test. Unconsciously, he held his breath as a thin layer of ice coated his skin and he walked through the flames. Brie hurdled one fireball after another at him. Each one sizzled on contact. Kai's hand shot out as he advanced on the woman who, now that he looked closer, didn't even look that much like his Brie. Icicles flew from his fingertips, striking her in the stomach. Her eyes went wide, and she stumbled. Kai pressed his advantage, sending another earthshaking bolt of power into the ground.

This time, Brie wasn't fast enough to leap out of the way of the chasm that developed between her feet. She teetered precariously before slipping between the parted earth.

"No!" Kai sprinted the last few yards that separated them.

This might not have been his Brie, but the woman still had incredible reflexes. Her fingertips were curled around loose chunks of earth, slipping another millimeter with each passing breath. Kai reached for her just as she lost her grip. Kai didn't think twice. He reached for her with his magic, calling her back before she could disappear into the gaping black hole he'd created. He was injured and extremely low on magic, but none of that mattered. Sweaty and panting, Kai pulled an unconscious Brie out of the hole and onto the ground beside. Her chest wasn't moving.

"No. No. No," he muttered.

The logical part of him knew this wasn't his Brie, and yet he still couldn't let this woman die. With the last of his magic, Kai placed a hand on her chest and delivered a shock that made her whole body spasm. Brie's eyelids fluttered open as Kai's drooped. He fell to the ground beside her, his magic so low that his body was shutting down. He didn't care. He would've done it again. He would always choose Brie, even a pale comparison of her.

The words sounded like they were inside his head. "Congratulations, king."

CHAPTER TWENTY

DOME OF MIDNIGHT

Brie

IT HAD BEEN a long time since I'd remembered my dreams after waking. I also couldn't recall anything from the periods of unconsciousness during previous bouts of magic poisoning, but I was certain this time was different. Between fits of nausea that left me vomiting over the side of a very soft bed and crippling body pain like I'd never experienced, the sandman kept pulling me into dreamland. More specifically, he pulled me into the same dreamscape each time. It may have had something to do with my desire to return to that particular scene, though.

Kai.

He was the star player in a dream where the world had been inverted. I sat on a throne with ancient fae fire symbols carved into the wood, looking down on the arena where I'd fought so many matches since arriving in the Hawaiian Kingdom. I was alone in the Royal Box, save the squad of bodyguards that stood behind me silently; Kai wasn't beside me in his usual place. It was like I was queen in my own right, just as Kai's mother had been. The stands weren't full of wealthy casters looking to gamble away their money on a blood sport. Instead, fae and shifters made up the majority of the faces in the crowd. The most startling aspect of all was that Kai was one of the fighters in the pit. Oddly, his opponent looked like a cross between the vampire priestess and…me. The whole event was odd and made me feel uneasy.

Even stranger, the last thing I remembered before a familiar voice dragged me back to reality was Kai looking like he was about defeat the pseudo-me.

"Good, you're awake," a female voice said when my eyelids fluttered opened.

I blinked several times and groaned. Even my eyelashes hurt. Sienna's pretty face came into focus. Despite her annoyed tone, like my illness was a major inconvenience for her personally, my former friend had two deep worry lines between her brows. She was pale, as if she'd been the one who'd vomited for hours. Or was it days? Time had ceased to mean anything since my arrival in the dome of perpetual night.

"What are you doing here?" I demanded in a croaky voice, my body protesting as I tried to sit up.

"Don't push yourself." Sienna crossed her arms over her chest and frowned down at me. "You're still sick."

"No shit." I attempted a glare that lacked any heat due to my sore facial muscles. "Thanks for that, by the way."

She took a step back from the bed, her frown deepening. "I did the spell right. I cured you before we left L.A."

My throat was scratchy, and I looked around for water. Regardless of my own rule about not eating or drinking anything while in the vampire hive, I desperately needed hydration. My tongue felt thick and fuzzy, and my lips were cracking. Wait. Was I even still in the hive? The room I awoke in was simple yet elegant. The sheets were gold and green silk with a matching bedspread. There was a landscape painting on the wall behind Sienna's head that, if I wasn't mistaken, was an aerial view of Fae Canyon.

"Here. Go slow." Sienna handed me a cup of clear liquid, which I sniffed. She rolled her eyes. "It's water. I promise."

"You also promised you cured me," I grumbled. Despite my protest, I dared a small sip of the odorless, colorless drink. It tasted like water, the kind that came straight from the source in the Freelands. Living under a dome, I'd forgotten how different the filtered, nutrient-enriched water was from the real deal.

"You *are* cured," Sienna insisted, then reconsidered. "Well, you were. If you don't believe me, I don't give a damn. Regardless of what you think, I kept my end of the bargain." The blasé tone was at odds with her pinched expression.

Since the water didn't make me sick immediately, I drank more. "Then what's wrong with me? Is it possible you messed up?"

Even though I wasn't trying to be bitchy, my questions sounded more like accusations. I couldn't really blame Sienna for being so defensive.

Exhaling loudly, she ran a hand down her long, blonde ponytail.

"I don't know," she snapped. "I mean, you have magic poisoning. Again. Not still, you haven't had it the whole time. But again. Like maybe you were re-infected."

I finished the water and stared down into the empty glass clutched between my hands. If this had happened right after leaving L.A., I might have thought she was just saying that to cover her ass. That maybe Sienna had screwed up the spell and just didn't want to admit it. After all, we'd only agreed to smuggle her out of the dome with us because she swore that she could perform the counter curse. Had our roles been reversed, I would've made the same promise even if I wasn't positive that I could manage the requisite magic.

But too much time had passed since had Sienna supposedly uncursed me. I'd used my magic on several occasions without being affected by the poison in my blood. Her claims that I had been re-infected at some point actually made sense. Unfortunately, it also meant there was a traitor in our midst. Someone who was following everywhere I went.

"Is there a chance that's not what's wrong with me?" I

asked softly.

"Um, no." She averted her eyes and shifted awkwardly from one foot to the other. "You definitely have magic poisoning. Julia confirmed it."

I am still at the hive. Good to know.

"Confirmed it how?" There was no doubt in my mind that I wasn't going to like the answer. Then something even more alarming occurred to me. "When you say 'Julia', do you mean the priestess? Do you know her?"

Sienna narrowed her gaze. "Yeah, so do you. Didn't she tell you?"

It was my turn to look away. "She told me. I just didn't want to believe her."

The corners of Sienna's mouth curved downward. "I should've told you," she said quietly. "I should've warned you."

The words themselves surprised me just as much as her apologetic tone. Sienna wasn't contrite enough to say she was sorry, but it was at least something. With a loud sigh, she sat on the edge of the bed. I scooted toward the middle to give her more room.

"She reached out to me…maybe two years ago?" Sienna shrugged and shook her head. "I can't remember exactly. She has a lot of contacts in L.A., and I guess she saw me on a broadcast. Julia had one of them get word to me. She wanted to know if I knew where you were. While she knew you'd been taken, no one would tell her where you'd ended up. The Hawaiian factions of the rebellion don't much contact with the mainland by design, so that was a dead end. It wasn't until you started dating the caster king that we all learned your whereabouts."

That was in line with what the priestess had told me, so I nodded and let Sienna continue without interruption.

"I'd known since we were younger that your mother had become a vampire. I overheard my mom and dad talking about it one night. I should've told you." She scratched at a nonexistent spot on the bedspread with a ragged nail. "At the time, I thought it was better for you to believe Julia was dead. It seemed easier for everyone."

"And now?" I asked. The way she'd said my mother's name suggested a familiarity that I didn't have with the vampire.

Sienna met my gaze. "Julia has helped a lot of people. Not all fae who live beneath the domes meet a prince and live happily ever after."

There was only a trace of bitterness in her tone. I almost asked if she thought running for my life in a frozen and tenuous world really constituted happily ever after, but I held my tongue. My body didn't contain enough energy to argue the point simply for the sake of it.

"Some fae are in really bad shape by the time the rebels get them out," Sienna continued. "Shifters, too. Their minds are so screwed up, and they can't really go on. You know?" She didn't wait for an answer. "Julia takes those people in. She turns some of them. In most cases, that repairs both the physical and mental damage inflicted by the casters."

"Yeah, I met one. A shifter," I said absently, recalling my brief meeting with Jane. "So, Julia and Granite work together?" It was still a point that I was unclear on. The way the priestess talked about Granite made it sound like she wasn't his biggest fan. She'd also taken Botto as hostage to force the Dresdens to bring me to her. But there had to be some sort of truce or cooperation; they wouldn't be able to co-exist in the Freelands otherwise.

"They're both rebel leaders. Sort of. Julia is more interested in helping those who've been hurt by the casters. Granite is more interested in taking revenge on the casters. They're just working in different ways."

"That's putting it mildly," a deep voice interrupted from the doorway.

"Botto!" I exclaimed. Forgetting my achy body, I started to get out of bed to hug him.

My trainer waved a hand. "Stay put. Don't hurt yourself." He came over and wrapped his arms around me. "Glad you're okay," he whispered.

"You, too." I squeezed him hard, a little surprised to find tears in my eyes.

"I'm going to let Julia know you're awake," Sienna muttered, making a hasty exit.

Botto took her spot on the bed. I looked him up and down, noting his clean jeans and crisp t-shirt. They definitely weren't the clothes he'd been wearing the last time I'd seen him. His face and arms bore no signs of a fight, meaning someone had healed his injuries. *Interesting.* Botto had been well taken care of, a fact that made me feel slightly better about getting him kidnapped by vampires. After all, they never would've been after us if Julia wasn't…..

"So, you met my father," he said with a frown, nostrils flaring as though he'd smelled something rotten. Depending on how long I'd been in that bed, it could've been me.

"Thanks for the heads up about him," I replied, only half joking.

Botto offered me a wry smile. "My relationship with Granite is complicated. My mom raised me away from the Dresdens to prevent me from ending up beneath a dome." He laughed humorlessly. "Guess fate had other plans, huh?"

"Guess so." I swallowed thickly. "Did, um, Julia treat you well? You look good."

"Your mother has been very hospitable," he assured.

The words made me cringe.

"She told you."

Botto nodded, a sheepish expression crossing his handsome features. "The whole ransom thing was sort of my idea."

"What do you mean?"

He plucked the glass out of my hands and refilled it from a pitcher on a side table. I smiled my thanks when he handed the water back, but I wasn't letting him off the hook.

"Granite isn't a bad man," Botto began to explain, reclaiming his seat on the bed. "He's not a good man, either. If I'd known that was the plan when we left L.A., to take you to Revival.... I don't know what else I would've done, but I would've done *something* differently. Once I became aware of our destination, I couldn't exactly refuse without a backup. I knew he would take you in, at least. And I knew he would keep you safe, if only because he needed you." He laughed bitterly. "Those are the only kinds of people Granite protects:

the ones he needs. It's how I knew he would agree to exchange a meeting between you and the priestess for my safe return."

I didn't understand the correlation but kept quiet, sensing that Botto needed to get this off his chest.

"I'd only met Granite once or twice when I was very young," he continued. "It was long before the extent of my power and abilities became clear. I knew he wouldn't be able to resist the urge to meet me now, even if it meant risking the loss of you."

With my thumb and forefinger, I rubbed my temples. My head was pounding as I tried to connect all the bits of information everyone kept throwing at me. Maybe the poison was affecting my logical reasoning abilities, because I couldn't seem to make sense of the random knowledge. I couldn't put the puzzle pieces together without at least a peek of the final product, and no one had shared that yet.

"We can talk about this later. You should rest." He stood, but I grabbed his wrist.

"No. I want to know what's going on. Everything. Please, Botto. Nobody is telling me anything. They're not telling me *enough*. The priestess promised to tell me Granite's big plan, but then…." I trailed off, shaking my head. "Please, Botto."

My trainer had never looked so uncomfortable around me. "I think you should let your mom explain." He held up his free hand to halt my protests. "She knows a lot more than I do. Like I said, I don't really know Granite Dresden. I've never been an active part of the rebellion, just helped out here and there. I've done some favors for

Delancey, and she's done some for me. But I'm nowhere near the top of this thing. I'm barely in it at all."

"Fine. Take me to her." I threw the covers back, aghast to find that someone had dressed me in silk pajamas. *Gaia, I must be out of it,* I thought, not sure how it had just occurred me that I wasn't wearing the same clothes from our trip.

When I tried to stand, a wave of dizziness overtook me. Botto grabbed me around the waist and supported my weight against his forearm.

"I'm fine. I'm fine," I said, more for my benefit than his. "Just find me some clothes, will you?"

My trainer gently guided me back to the bed and went in search of suitable attire. He returned minutes later with a pair of lightweight linen pants and a soft cotton t-shirt. I changed while Botto waited in the hallway. Sienna had joined him by the time I exited the bedroom. They walked on either side of me, supporting me just as much as leading me to the priestess. On that short trek, I learned that Botto had given me a massive magical transfusion to flush the poison out of my system before Sienna arrived from Revival Palace. She'd attempted the counter-curse again, but it hadn't taken.

"What happens to me now?" I asked as we turned down a long hallway with floor-to-ceiling windows on both sides.

"Julia will find someone else. Someone better equipped," Sienna told me.

"Better equipped?" For some reason, that was funny to me. I laughed, wondering if mania was another symptom of the poisoning.

Sienna's answer halted the giggle immediately. "The dark magic that poisoned you was recent. *Very* recent. And potent. I'm not strong enough to reverse it."

"What you need is a dark practitioner," Botto added. "Julia knows a few."

Of course she did. Because my mother was a vampire. A blood-drinking, power-hungry vampire. Sienna's words came back to me: *Julia has helped a lot of people.* My feelings were still conflicted where my former friend was concerned, and I didn't entirely trust her judgment. Nevertheless, I'd already met several of the people Julia had helped, so there was likely some truth to it.

She isn't all bad, I told myself. Sort of like how Botto said Granite wasn't a bad man or a good man. That was how I felt about Julia, I decided.

We found the priestess in what I could only describe as a modern-day drawing room. It had the same old world feel of the more formal areas of Iolani Palace but with modern furniture. There was also a crystal pitcher of blood on a side table, which wasn't something I'd ever seen. The priestess had changed into a loose silk jumpsuit that looked like a cross between something worn to a dinner party and something worn to bed. A white, gauzy shawl was draped around her shoulders, purely for the fashion since vampires rarely got cold.

"Oh, thank Gaia. Maybrie, darling, how are you feeling?" she fussed, hurrying to fold me in her arms.

It was such a motherly thing to do, my body stiffened instinctively. So far, she'd refrained from physical contact. I quickly realized why; her cool embrace was a stark reminder of what she was. For a moment, I let her hold me. At first, I refused to hug her back. Finally, I cracked and gave Julia a quick squeeze.

"Don't vampires have another goddess they pray to? Someone besides Gaia?" I asked awkwardly, taking the opportunity to step back from her.

The priestess frowned but didn't dignify the question with a response. With cold fingers, she took my arm and led me to a low white couch that was clearly only for aesthetics. I perched on the edge, afraid I might never get up if I tried to lean back. Julia joined me, while Botto and Sienna sat in chairs that were equally impractical.

"What did you ingest before coming here?" the priestess demanded. She gestured to a woman standing in the corner of the room, who brought me a glass of water.

"Thank you," I said to her before meeting the priestess' narrowed gaze. "No. We aren't having this conversation right now."

The lines between Julia's brows deepened. "You've been poisoned, darling. This is precisely—"

"No," I snapped, feeling woozy again as blood rushed to my face. "No. First, you are going to tell me what is really going on." Turning my glare on Botto and Sienna, I directed my demand to them as well. "One of you is going to tell me the truth. Now."

The priestess sighed heavily and reached for a glass of blood on the end table. My nose wrinkled in disgust.

"Fine," Julia said after several moments of tense silence. Clutching the blood between her palms, she looked down into the dark crimson liquid. Her eyes went slightly unfocused, and I wondered what she was really seeing.

Resigned, the priestess sighed. "Granite Dresden has

seen the worst of caster society. His children have gone through hell at the hands of witches and warlocks. He's jaded, rightfully so."

Get to the point, I thought, tapping my foot impatiently.

"You've experienced life beneath the dome, you know what I'm talking about," she reasoned. "The poor treatment of fae and shifters is flagrant and unchecked. You've been forced to fight for their enjoyment, an exceedingly barbaric practice. You must harbor resentment, at the very least."

It wasn't a question, so I didn't feel the need to answer.

"By all reports, the Hawaiian Kingdom is paradise compared to the others," she continued, nodding as if making excuses for me. "The ruling casters are—or should I say, *were*—progressive enough to consider a fae queen. So that's something, I suppose."

Before I could stop myself, I grumbled, "Not everyone in the kingdom is so 'progressive'."

Julia's small smile was the only clue that she even heard me. "Do you know what Granite's biggest grievance is? The thing that bothers him most of all?" Though the question was rhetorical, my head shook automatically.

My eyes shifted to Botto. His expression was annoyingly blank, I had no idea what he was possibly thinking. Was this revelation something that he already knew?

"He hates that casters rule the world when they are so weak," the priestess answered. "Fae built the domes for them. Fae power the domes, too. We give them magic so they can survive. We cater to their every whim. Why? They need us, not the other way around. So why should we perpetuate their ridiculously unbalanced society?" Her use of "us" didn't escape my notice; something inside of her felt that the plight of fae was still her own.

There was a part of me that agreed with her, bringing feeling of guilt. I also hated the part of me that wanted to defend the casters.

Defend them all? Or just one? Even Sarah had betrayed me.

"It is time the for the casters to fall," Julia continued. "On this, Granite and I agree. I believe we should overthrow them. Without us, their race will have to learn to adapt."

Learn to adapt?

"Without us, they'll die," I said. I knew she really meant fae, since vampires didn't give magic to casters. "That's a little harsh, don't you think?"

"Living is harsh, darling. Dying is easy." She patted my arm absently. "Don't worry. Magic users have been around for millennia. Casters aren't going anywhere, they just need to take a step back." She paused and met my gaze. "Unless Granite Dresden has his way."

"He wants to kill the casters?" I asked, my eyebrows drawing together. It felt very anticlimactic. The hostile takeovers, the citizenship trials—it was obvious that Granite wanted to kill all the casters. Why didn't someone just say that earlier?

"He does plan to kill the weak, either through execution or his ridiculous trials," Julia said quietly. "Those who pass the trials, though…the casters who prove their strength…. They will become vampires."

CHAPTER TWENTY-ONE

FAE CANYON

Kai

ONLY ONCE IN his privileged life had Kai been in real danger of depletion. That experience was one he would remember until the day he died.

That might be today, he thought, the realization bouncing through his fuzzy thoughts. He wasn't cold. He was too numb to be cold. Voices screamed around him, but it was like being underwater; the words sounded garbled to his ears. Someone placed a blanket over his body, which was curled in the fetal position on hard ground. His mind was hazy, like he had a high fever or had ingested too much of a bad drug. The only thing that seemed clear was Brie.

She wasn't there—in the temple in Fae Canyon, if he had to guess his own location—but rather in his head. When he closed his eyes, Kai saw her beautiful, enraged face staring back at him.

"Why so angry?" he mumbled. His lips moved, even though the words were meant for the vision in his mind.

Brie didn't answer. It was like she couldn't hear him, though he had no problem hearing her. His gorgeous girlfriend appeared pale and weak. Well, weak for Brie. Despite her pallor, she stomped around a strange sitting room that looked like something his sister might've chosen if she ever became queen.

"You should have told me earlier!" Brie hollered inside his head.

A warm sensation washed over Kai, followed closely by cold that penetrated to his core.

"I won't allow this to happen!" Brie screamed at a woman that Kai thought he recognized. Or maybe she just looked like someone he knew. It was hard to tell.

Kai began to shake. Spasms contorted his body as he writhed on the hard floor. Without warning, heat poured over him like he'd been tossed on a bonfire.

"Your king is strong, darling," said the woman taking the brunt of Brie's rage.

Sweat soaked his hair and back. The cold came again, but this time it wasn't as biting. Some of his strength returned. He blinked and stared up into familiar dark eyes.

"Kenoa," he breathed.

"Yeah, I'm here. Think you can stand if I help you?"

With every breath, Kai felt more lucid. It was a shame, since he wanted to be back with Brie, wherever she was.

"Yeah. I can," Kai decided.

Kenoa looped an arm beneath the king's shoulders and helped him to his feet. The fae temple came into focus, while the images of Brie faded like a distant dream. Illion was there, too. Brie's little brother rushed to Kai's other side and helped Kenoa support the weight. Elder Hawkins still sat on the dais with the rest of the fae council.

"You are strong, King," Brie's father said.

The words were so close to what the woman had told Brie in his head, but Kai was still too out of it to think clearly. "That's what she said," he muttered.

"What who said?" Kenoa asked, scowling up at the Council of Elders.

"Huh?" Kai shook his head. "Sorry. I'm not feeling well. I'm babbling."

His best friend seemed to accept the answer, but Brie's father smiled knowingly. "You saw her," he said simply.

Some of the faces on the council registered surprise. On Kai's right, Illion grinned and nodded approvingly. On his left, Kenoa just looked confused. That made two of them.

"You saw Maybrie," Elder Hawkins clarified.

Kai nodded slowly. His body still throbbed, and he was in desperate need of some warm clothes. Otherwise, his condition was rapidly improving.

"Then you truly are worthy," Elder Hawkins continued. He stood slowly, and the rest of the council followed suit. "I will explain everything once you have had time to recover. For now, I will only say this: it will be my honor to one day call you son."

Pride swelled in Kai's chest. For the first time in his life, he'd earned something on his own. *Really* earned it. Elder Hawkins wasn't honored to have him in the family simply because he was a king or a caster. In fact, Kai was certain Elder Hawkins was honored in spite of those things. Because Kai had walked through the fires—some of them literal—and come out the other side a stronger man. He was better for it.

"I will speak with you soon," Elder Hawkins said. Kai nodded, and Kenoa and llhelm helped him from the temple.

"Please wipe that stupid look off your face immediately," his best friend growled as they plodded through the village and up to the Hawkins' cottage.

Fae men, women, and children stopped to stare at as the trio passed. Many wore dubious expressions, mostly the adults. The kids were more in awe. One went so far as to clap, which set off a chain reaction among the faelings. Kai straightened and shrugged away from Kenoa and Illion. Walking slowly on his own, he waved to the children cheering for him.

"Gaia," Kenoa muttered. "You were born to be king, yet this is the proudest I've ever seen you."

"Guess he really does belong here," Illion replied.

The impromptu victory parade had given Kai an adrenaline rush that quickly faded once he was inside the Hawkins' home. After taking a long, hot shower in the tiny bathroom, he dressed in the layers of clothes that

Illion had left for him. When he emerged from the teenager's bedroom, the cabin was filled with delicious food scents and more people. Covered dishes littered the countertops, and half a dozen fae were busy finding plates and silverware.

Kai sought out a familiar face, landing first on Illion. "What's going on?"

"It's tradition." Brie's brother shrugged. "It's rare for anyone to undergo the tests, let alone complete them successfully. It's sort of like a big deal around here. Plus, you formed the connection. That like *never* happens anymore."

"I prepared this especially for the caster king," an elderly fae woman told Kenoa as she unveiled her dish. "I am told you eat a lot of fish in Hawaii. I hope I prepared it correctly."

Kenoa bit back a smirk as he looked down at the salmon and pineapple concoction.

"It looks wonderful," Kai interjected, moving away from Illion to greet the guests.

"King, my name is Bea." The old woman grinned to reveal a gap-toothed smile. "I have known Maybrie since the day she was born. I am so happy for you both."

"Thank you, Bea."

"Normally we hold this feast outdoors, but we are all very happy to accommodate your more delicate nature," she continued without a trace of maliciousness.

Kenoa didn't bother hiding his laughter.

Bea patted Kai's arm affectionately. "You've done so well, King. You should be very proud."

Kai smiled at the old woman. "I am, ma'am. Very

proud, indeed."

For the next several hours, Kai and Kenoa mingled with the never-ending stream of guests. It seemed everyone in Fae Canyon wanted to express some sentiment or another to the king. Like Bea, nearly all of the fae called Kai "King", as though it was his name. A few said it with enough derision that Kai knew he would never win them over, no matter how many trips he and Brie made to Fae Canyon in the future. Those were the people he was kindest to, the ones who'd apparently just shown up to scoff at him.

Will there be more trips? he wondered. Kai thought about it over a plate of fried bison nuggets that, so far, were his favorite dish. It was a question he couldn't answer. Kai didn't even know whether he would see Brie again.

No, you simply don't know when *you'll see Brie again.* Maybe it was naïve of him to hope, but he wasn't ready to accept that their current positions were the new normal. The world where he was something of an exile and the woman he wanted to share his life with was running for her life couldn't be the end.

Normally reserved at public functions, Kenoa seemed embarrassed to find himself at the center of so much attention. In the Hawaiian Kingdom, the water fae had always been an oddity. Not because he worked for casters, though his role as bodyguard to a prince and now advisor to a king was unusual for a fae. What most found so strange was that Kenoa liked his work and considered Kai a friend. His best friend, really. The king felt the same way, making Kai as much of an oddity as Kenoa.

Outside of the dome, the fae found the duo's

friendship fascinating. There were a few who clearly looked down on Kenoa and his chosen path. Most just wanted to know why, given the choice, Kenoa stayed by his king's side. For the first time Kai could recall, Kenoa was put in situation of publicly defending their friendship. It was a complete role-reversal.

The faelings bombarded the men with questions about life beneath a dome. They wanted to know all about the palace and parties. Kai fielded questions about Brie and her time in the fighting pits, which came as a surprise to those who'd known his girlfriend as a child. Once upon a time, Brie had been a mild-mannered faeling without an aggressive bone in her body. Talking about her brought a smile to his lips, but the revelation about Brie's nature made him feel hollow inside. He was the reason she'd become a warrior. She'd had to become one. He was the reason she fought viciously in the arena, and the reason she'd been taken away from her people.

"Don't be hard on yourself, King," Elder Hawkins said softly. He'd spent most of the evening in his rocking chair by the fire, observing the festivities.

Kai looked down. "Excuse me, sir?"

"You are only responsible for your own choices. If you think my daughter didn't always have a fighter's spirit, you don't know her as well as you believe."

Can he read my mind? Kai wondered, not for the first time. It was like Brie's father had a sixth sense.

"I know it is about time you returned to L.A.," he continued. "We need to speak privately before that happens."

"Of course, Elder Hawkins," Kai replied.

He'd known he needed to go back. Outside of the fae's idyllic enclave, a war raged. His kingdom was in jeopardy. The American royals were in chaos mode. Kai needed to take his rightful role, the one he was born into, and be a leader. And yet, he wasn't ready to leave. He wanted to spend more time getting to know this part of Brie's life, to meet those who'd called her a friend before she was taken. It didn't matter that a lot of Fae Canyon hated him, he didn't care that many were only being civil because of what Brie represented to them. In a weird way, Kai liked the new perspective. These people didn't gush about how great he was to his face, only to turn around and question his every decision to the first person they encountered. The people of Fae Canyon made their feelings very clear to his face.

Elder Hawkins stood. A younger fae rushed over to give Kai a heavy coat, warm scarf, and gloves. He donned the additional layers, then followed Brie's father outside to a small winter garden not far from the cottage. Illion and Kenoa were busy entertaining the guests, which Kai thought was the reason Brie's father had chosen this moment to draw him away. Whatever Elder Hawkins wanted to talk about, it was for Kai alone to hear.

The two men sat on a bench among the icy blossoms and stared at the white fish swimming below the surface of a small icy pond. They weren't far from the house, but either magic or the sheltered nature of the garden prevented the music and voices from drifting to the serene spot.

"My wife loves to garden," Elder Hawkins said, finally breaking the silence.

Kai didn't miss the use of present tense. "Brie told me her mother passed when she was very young. I am so sorry for your loss." It was the sort of thing people usually said for lack of anything else to say. Kai had heard those words from so many mouths after his mother was killed. They didn't help but were nice to hear all the same.

"I did lose my Julia when Maybrie was young," Elder Hawkins replied, his weathered face carefully composed. "But it is not quite as you think."

From there, Brie's father launched into a tragic story that Kai had not expected. Julia Hawkins, Brie's mother, was a vampire. A prominent and powerful vampire, according to Elder Hawkins. Even more surprising, the two had kept in touch. From the sound of it, their relationship had been strained since she'd turned, even more so after Brie's abduction. Finally, with time, they seemed to have settled into a tentative peace in the recent past.

"Fae Canyon is under Julia's protection." The old man smiled wryly. "That is not common knowledge, King. Only the council knows that we accept aid from vampires."

"What about Brie...does she know about Julia?" Kai was certain he knew the answer. He'd seen the pain in Brie's eyes when she talked about her limited memories of her mother. There was no way she knew that Julia still walked the frozen earth.

"I would imagine Maybrie knows all I am telling you." The elder met and held Kai's gaze. "They are together right now."

"What?" Kai jumped up from the bench. His eyes

searched the garden as though he might find the mother and daughter together having a similar discussion.

Elder Hawkins motioned for Kai to reclaim his seat. "I don't know much about Julia's hive, including the whereabouts. For safety, we both thought that best. I do know that Maybrie is there now, though. I spoke with Julia last night."

Kai ran a gloved hand over his hair. "So, Brie is safe?" he hardly dared to believe it. "That's wonderful news."

Remembering the woman in his vision with Brie, he realized it must have been Julia herself. She looked enough like Brie that the resemblance should've tipped him off.

"Maybrie is safe at the moment," Elder Hawkins agreed. Kai sensed there was more coming, and he wasn't disappointed. "She is sick, though." Brie's dad held up a hand to halt Kai's reaction. "Before you get any notion of running off to find her, let me assure you that Julia is working to get her healthy again. I simply wanted to tell you before you saw it for yourself."

Kai narrowed his gaze. What did Brie's father mean, exactly? He'd mentioned a connection between Brie and Kai earlier. Was that how Elder Hawkins thought Kai might "see" that Brie was sick?

"Fae, like many shifter cultures, believe in true mates, particularly among elder families," Elder Hawkins continued, once again seeming to read Kai's concerns right out of his head. "Fate, and destiny play no part in our beliefs. I am merely talking about two people suited for one another in a way that allows them to understand each other on the deepest level. Love is not always enough. Being a worthy match is not always enough, either. Do you understand what I am saying?"

Honestly, Kai was having a very hard time wrapping his head around the elder's meaning. He was reluctant to admit just how ignorant he was when it came to fae culture, though. Particularly after he'd just gone through one of their most sacred customs to prove his worth and marry into that culture.

"Sometimes two people are truly right for one another," Elder Hawkins explained. "Not meant for one another, but *right* for each other."

The difference was subtle, yet Kai thought he understood.

"In those instances, a connection may form once the tests are completed. This is not to say that you will always be able to see into Maybrie's head or vice-versa. But when you need the connection, truly need it, it will be there. Do not shy away from it. That bond could save both your lives one day."

Kai swallowed thickly. "I am not sure we have quite the connection you're talking about. I did see Brie, but I was not inside her head. It was more like being a bystander and watching her, if that makes sense?"

Elder Hawkins took a few minutes to consider Kai's words before finally answering the question. "I suppose I am not surprised. This type of connection is normally between two fae. Being a caster, your magic is different. That must affect the bond," he mused thoughtfully. "Time will tell, of course."

Unsure how to respond, Kai switched gears. "You said Brie is ill. Do you know what's wrong with her?" The idea that she wasn't in peak physical condition, even if she did have her mother taking care of her, made him feel queasy. He suddenly wished he hadn't eaten so much of Bea's salmon pineapple dish.

"Julia says it's magic poisoning." Elder Hawkins' tone was even, but his gaze never left Kai's face. "Do you know anything about that?"

"I do, actually," Kai admitted, unsure if the news was a relief or even more concerning. "She was poisoned in L.A. My understanding was that Sienna had performed the requisite counter-curse, however. I thought it was dealt with."

Elder Hawkins nodded in agreement. "She has. Twice. From what Sienna told Julia, the current theory is that Maybrie was re-poisoned after her escape. How well do you know Botto Dresden?"

Kai blinked in surprise. "Botto? I can't say I know him well. He was an incredible fighter and is reputed to be an even better trainer. If Brie is any indication, then that is true. I know she trusts him implicitly. Personally, I don't think he would ever hurt her."

"And what of Sienna?"

That was a tougher question. Despite her rough demeanor, Kai sort of liked the brusque air fae. He didn't blame her for the chip on her shoulder. Like so many fae and shifters, she'd clearly suffered at the hands of the casters.

"I think she is very angry," Kai said finally, choosing his words with care. "She yelled a lot of not very nice things at Brie when the two first saw each other in Los Angeles. I don't know if they will ever rebuild the friendship they once had."

"Do you think she would harm my daughter?"

Hesitating only briefly, Kai shook his head. "I don't." He was a little surprised to realize he meant it.

"Me neither," Elder Hawkins agreed. "More importantly, neither does Julia. She believes Sienna really did cure Maybrie and has nothing to do with our daughter falling sick a second time." Elder Hawkins sighed heavily, clearly exhausted from the day's events. "I don't believe this is a coincidence, however. Do you happen to know if they brought tonics with them when they escaped? I would imagine the trainer had a supply that he brought from Hawaii. Possibly one of the tonics was tainted?"

"I wouldn't know," Kai admitted. He gave an embarrassed laugh. "I don't know much about how that all…." A thought had occurred to him and he trailed off midsentence. "Samira gave her a healing tonic right before we got on the airship. It was in the bag Brie took with her on the escape. I really don't think Samira would hurt Brie, though. She is very fond of your daughter. Much more so than she is of me."

"Is this Samira woman a caster?"

"Yes, but like I said—"

"You say she gave the tonic to Maybrie just before you both left Hawaii?"

Kai's stomach sank. Brie had been taking that tonic to recover from her injuries sustained during the matches. And she'd packed it in her go-bag for a reason before the arrest, when she'd known she would likely run. The Freelands were dangerous. Chances were good that Brie would had been hurt at some point and taken the tonic to repair her body. Still, he just couldn't believe Samira would poison Brie.

"Did Samira act strangely or say anything weird?" Elder Hawkins pressed.

Kai tried to recall. Samira was a quirky old witch; everything about her was sort of strange. "Not particularly," he replied at last. "Samira is married to a fae, though. She is a big proponent of fae rights, I just cannot fathom her harming Brie."

"Maybe she wasn't the one to add the poison. We may never know, but I will let Julia know to ask Maybrie about the witch's healing tonic." Elder Hawkins stood, a clear sign the conversation was over.

"Can I talk to Brie?" Kai asked before he lost his chance.

Elder Hawkins looked at him sadly. "I am afraid not. It would be too dangerous. You must return to Los Angeles before your absence is noted."

That's already happened, no question about it. But that wasn't worth bringing up. Instead, Kai pressed on the other issue.

"Forgive me, Elder Hawkins," he began with all the respect he could muster. "But if you are in contact with your wife, and Brie is with your wife, I don't see the problem."

The old fae smiled. "Julia and I are true mates. We don't need any outside magic to speak. Our bond survived her transition to vampire. Now, let's find Illion and get you back to where you belong."

Resigned, Kai sighed. It was time to focus on the

turmoil he was returning to. At the very least, his advisors would have noticed that he wasn't in his hotel room. King Ronald had likely sent for him at some point, only to be told no one could find the Hawaiian monarch. How would Kai explain his time away?

You could not go back. Not right away, at least, he thought. He could ask Illion to take him to Brie and Julia, so he could be with his sick girlfriend. That was what Kai wanted more than anything, to be by Brie's side. But he'd been born to rule a kingdom, and he'd allowed his sister to make decisions on his behalf for too long. He needed to get back to Los Angeles so he could return to Hawaii. Reclaiming his throne was the only way to clear Brie's name. Then she could return home, too.

Another thought occurred to him on the short walk back to the cottage. *Wouldn't it be better to ask Illion to take him straight back to Hawaii?* Kai didn't need to explain himself to his advisors, not really. He was the king. He'd deferred to their judgment too often in his short tenure, contributing unintentionally to Brie's predicament.

The cottage was still full of guests when the two men returned. Kai sought out Kenoa to ask him about the possibility of bypassing Los Angeles in favor of a direct shot to Hawaii. The water fae was the only one of his advisors that Kai cared to take advice from anyway.

"I thought you would ask him to take you to Brie," Kenoa said when Kai finished telling him his idea.

"I want to, but I know my responsibilities. The best help I can give Brie is to nullify her arrest warrant and expose what really happened the night my mother was killed," he replied with more conviction than he felt.

Kenoa studied him long and hard, then nodded tightly. "It is the right decision, Kai. Brie needs your help right now. She has plenty of people with her to look after her health and safety, but only you can erase the target on her head."

These were all truths that Kai knew deep down. Nonetheless, having his best friend say them aloud gave Kai the strength to trust his own mind.

"Your people need you," Kenoa continued. "But they don't need me. Let me go to Brie, to protect her."

The offer wasn't one that Kai had anticipated, and he felt conflicted about how to respond. A part of him wanted to tell Kenoa that he needed his best friend by his side. That Kai needed the support of the one person who had never broken his trust. Kai also knew that Kenoa wasn't making the offer for Brie's sake, not entirely. It was for Kai, so he wouldn't worry so much about Brie's safety while he found a way to save her life.

"Are you sure? Botto is with her," Kai said.

"Botto is fine. He cares about her," Kenoa agreed. "He's also a member of a notorious rebel family, or I've been hearing. We have no idea how deep those ties truly run."

"She's also with her mother," Kai reasoned. "Though I don't know whether to feel better or worse because of that. All things considered."

Kenoa narrowed his eyes. "Brie's mom is dead."

Kai looked around to make sure Illion wasn't close enough to overhear the conversation. He spotted the teenager talking to girl around his own age. They looked very into whatever they were discussing, but Kai lowered his voice to be safe.

"Technically, Julia Hawkins is undead. A vampire. Which Brie apparently just learned, and Illion does not yet know."

Kenoa scratched his chin thoughtfully. "Unexpected, but okay. That makes me think I should definitely be with her. Let's talk to Illion."

Brie's brother was happy to oblige both requests. Kai and Kenoa said their goodbyes and thanked Elder Hawkins for his hospitality. He agreed that their plan was the best way forward, which made Kai feel a little better about his choices. Outside, with a hand out in either direction, the younger Hawkins simply opened two paths from Fae Canyon like it was nothing. He wouldn't be joining either of them, it wasn't necessary.

The two men hugged before setting off.

"I'll make sure she's okay," Kenoa promised. "You just look after yourself."

Kai forced a laugh. "Don't worry about me. I am the king, right?"

They parted ways, Kai with one last look over his shoulder and a wave for Brie's family. He didn't really understand how the dimensional passages worked but wasn't surprised that the walk to Hawaii took longer than the trip from Los Angeles. A lot longer, by the feel of it. Several hours passed in relative silence as he plodded forward. Kai started to wonder whether Illion had trapped him in some sort of endless loop. Would he be forced to wander the dark passage until the end of time? Just as he truly considered the possibility, a light shone at the end of the tunnel.

"Oh, thank Gaia. Finally," Kai muttered under his breath.

The passage ended in his very own bedroom at Iolani Palace. *Home,* Kai thought, wanting nothing more in that moment than to crawl into his own bed and sleep. It was light outside, a fact Kai only thought odd because it had been near dusk when he left Fae Canyon. Between the long walk and change in time zones, he supposed it was possible that his sense of night and day was simply off.

Probably better, he reasoned. *I should at least go let Sarah know I'm back.*

Kai started for the door, his mind working up an excuse to give his sister for his sudden and unannounced arrival. He didn't feel he owed her an explanation, but he also didn't want to further the hostility that had developed between them. He wanted Sarah to support him and his decision to pardon Brie. He wanted to her to understand that Brie had nothing to do with their mother's death. The only way he could think to do that was to tell Sarah the truth as he knew it.

"Halt! You're under arrest!"

Stunned, Kai stopped in his tracks. A battalion of shifters cloaked with a silencing spell stared him down in the dark palace hallway. They all had guns, which was even more shocking than their words.

Three soldiers advanced on him.

"Don't be ridiculous," he snapped in the most haughty, royal voice he'd ever used. "Don't you know who I am?"

"You're a caster," said one of the men. He'd drawn within reach of Kai.

"I'm the king," Kai retorted indignantly.

There was a collective intake of breath, and then someone fired at Kai. The dart hit him in the neck before he could react. His vision grew shadowy, and he swayed on his feet. Too late, Kai reached for his magic. Panic flooded through him when he couldn't seem to find it. As he hit the ground with a hard thud that shook his teeth, Kai realized the paralytic must've also contained a binding charm. He didn't lose consciousness right away, though. His eyes flickered open and closed, and a woman bent over his body. She grinned wickedly, revealing several gaps between her teeth. With two fingers, she reached down and closed Kai's eyelids.

"Aren't we lucky, caster king?" She giggled. "Your reign ends today. The Dresdens rule this dome now."

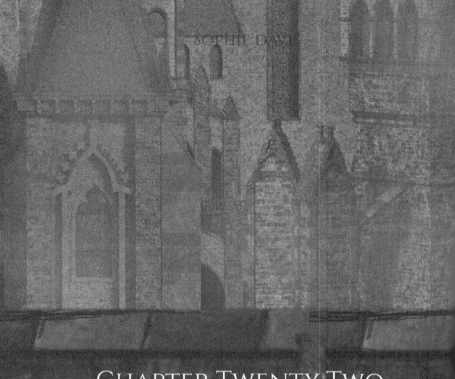

CHAPTER TWENTY-TWO

DOME OF MIDNIGHT

Brie

I DIDN'T SAY his name aloud for fear I was the only person in the room who saw him enter. I thought the poison was making me hallucinate.

"Kenoa! Is that really you?" Botto interrupted something the priestess was saying about the dark practitioner coming to visit me.

Everyone in the room, which now included Delancey Dresden, turned to look at the hulking water fae standing in the doorway.

"How did you get here?" Botto wanted to know.

"Is my son with you?" the priestess demanded, her eyes bright.

Kenoa's gaze bounced around the room before finally landing on Julia. "You must be Brie's mom. My name is Kenoa. I am advisor to King Kai and served as his personal bodyguard for years while he was still the crowned prince," he said in an overly formal tone.

"Impressive resume," the priestess said calmly. "But is Illion with you?"

The name made my heart leap.

"He is not, ma'am," Kenoa replied, casting his eyes down.

"I am Julia Hawkins, which I assume you already know. Why you have come to my home without invitation?"

"His Majesty has requested I come to be with Brie," Kenoa informed her, still speaking in a tone as formal as any he used with the Hawaiian royals. "Illion did help me reach you all, but he did not make the journey with me."

"My brother?" I breathed. "You saw him?"

"I did, Brie. He's a great kid."

"Gaia, I can't believe it. How's Kai? Is he okay?" I interjected.

"He's good," Kenoa promised me.

Tears sprang to my eyes. I had so many questions.

"Kai passed the tests?" I pressed. Julia had told me about my father summoning Kai to Fae Canyon to prove he was worthy of an elder's daughter. To my knowledge, no caster had ever attempted the council's ridiculous tests.

Kenoa grinned. "Did you doubt him?"

More tears fell down my cheeks. "Honestly, yeah." I laughed, though there was nothing funny about any of this. "The tests are an ancient *fae* ritual. They aren't designed for caster magic."

"Many believe fae and casters have common origins in this world," Julia said mildly.

While I'd heard the same thing, I believed the stories linking our races through common ancestors were total fiction.

Kenoa shrugged. "I don't know, but Kai did pass all four of them. The Council of Elders has deemed him worthy of you. So…congrats, I guess."

"Thanks, I guess. Where's Kai now? Did he go back to L.A., or is he still in Fae Canyon?"

Kenoa's gaze panned the drawing room and landed on Delancey. "I think we should speak privately."

Botto's sister scoffed. "Really? You think I care where the caster king is keeping himself?"

"I have no idea who you are," Kenoa replied, his expression blank.

"Delancey Dresden. And I can assure you that I don't care where your king is. Before my father is done, all the caster monarchs will fall."

"It's fine." I sighed loudly. "Just tell us where he is."

Kenoa hesitated. "You trust her? Do you know about the Dresdens?"

"I know enough about the Dresdens to know I don't trust Delancey." That was true, and she wasn't stupid enough to have believed otherwise. "There are only so many places Kai can be if you're here to protect me." My eyes cut to Julia. "And I know Granite Dresden won't storm Fae Canyon, even if Kai is still there."

"He most certainly would not dare," the priestess confirmed.

"Kai returned to Hawaii," Kenoa finally shared. "He thought that was his best chance of bringing you home."

The news was a relief, and I relaxed a little. In Hawaii, in his own kingdom with his own guards, Kai was safe. Much more so than in Los Angeles, since I knew Granite intended to take down all the caster queens and kings. At least on an island in the middle of a frozen ocean, Kai was a difficult target to reach.

"Delancey, what is it?" Botto's voice cut into my thoughts.

I hadn't noticed his sister's reaction to Kenoa's words, but clearly Botto had seen something alarming in her expression. All eyes in the room turned on Delancey Dresden. She took a deep breath, her eyes widening as she took in our group.

"You will all hear soon enough, I guess. Our forces are attacking the Hawaiian Kingdom tonight. Probably about now."

I was on my feet in an instant without any idea where I was going. "Why didn't you say something earlier?" I shouted, throwing my hands up in the air.

Delancey remained calm. "It wouldn't have changed anything. And my father's plans aren't common knowledge. The information was on shared on a need-to-know basis. Honestly, I didn't think it mattered since your boyfriend was supposedly in Los Angeles. Though, since I'm already sharing, I guess I'll tell you that L.A. will fall tonight, too. It may have already."

I looked around at my friends and Julia, silently pleading with someone to offer up a solution. When no one did, I let out a shriek of frustration.

"Kai can't do the citizenship trial! He just can't!"

"Calm down, darling," Julia said.

I swung my ire her way. "Screw you! I will not calm down!" I was acting like a brat and didn't care. Kai wasn't supposed to be in danger. That was why I wouldn't let him accompany me on the run. This couldn't be happening.

"Your caster made it through an ancient fae ritual," the priestess reasoned. "I am sure he is not the first warlock to do so, but I have never heard of a caster surviving it, Maybrie. He will pass the citizenship test. You don't need to worry about that." She tried to take my arm as if to guide me back to the couch.

Snatching my arm back, I was seconds away from shooting fireballs at her. My mother and I locked eyes. "That's what I'm afraid of," I insisted. "I don't want Kai turned into one of you!"

The priestess smiled sadly. "Would that really be so bad?" she asked.

"I don't know," I shot back. "Why don't we ask Dad?"

It was a pretty mean thing to say, even if I thought she deserved it. Though I felt bad about the comment, I didn't regret my words. It was the truth.

"Brie, come on. No reason to be nasty." Of all the people in that room, Sienna was Julia's pseudo defender. She held out her hand to me. "Why don't you rest, before you make yourself sicker?"

I shook my head, venom dripping from my voice as I

turned back to Julia. "Everything that has happened to me is your fault. Your choice to become vampire is the root of all I went through. If you care about me, if you *ever* loved me, you will do something now. You will get Kai out of there now."

My tone surprised even me. I didn't even know how much of what I'd said I believed. Not enough time had passed for me to process all she'd told me. I just needed action. I needed Kai.

"Okay."

"Okay?" I repeated lamely, my shoulders slumping. A part of me had thought, maybe even hoped, she would say no, if only so I could continue yelling at someone to help myself feel better.

"Yes, darling," Julia answered. "I have always loved you. You may not believe me, but every decision I have made has been for you and Illion. If freeing your caster will help you accept that, I will do it."

"How?" I challenged. "I don't want vague promises and assurances. I want to know how you plan to get Kai here. As a *caster*, no turning him."

Julia smiled wryly and gestured to Botto and Delancey. "Well, darling, I do have two of Granite's children. And you, of course. He's desperate to have you under his control."

Botto nudged his sister in the ribs, prompting Delancey to sigh and roll her eyes.

"It's not really Brie he wants," she admitted. "I mean, he does. She's a powerful rebel who killed a caster queen. She makes a great face for the uprising." She shrugged as if bored of the conversation. "So do a lot of people—

people with less complicated attachments to the casters. Not everyone believes the story my father is telling." Delancey turned to me and shrugged. "You're not the reason he jumped through hoops to make sure your little escape party ended up in Revival."

"Which means I am…," Botto said, tone grave.

"Yes, but not for the reason you think," his sister said quickly. "Don't get me wrong, our father would do a lot to meet all his offspring. But we're just research to him. He wants you because you know a lot about the Hawaiian Kingdom. Attacking there early has always been part of his strategy. The more domes we take on the mainland, the quicker the casters will retaliate. Like they did last time. He doesn't want a bunch of bombed out cities to rule. Our father wants a base of operation that is isolated, one the other kingdoms will be unlikely to aid or destroy. A stronghold where he can be cut off from constant threats."

"Probably doesn't hurt that our kingdom has the best and largest royal airship fleet," Kenoa added, crossing his arms over his chest.

"That does have a lot to do with it," Delancey conceded.

"Are you saying that Botto is our greatest bargaining chip?" Julia asked. Her tone suggested she thought Delancey was holding something back or lying so we'd let her go.

"He is," Delancey agreed. "Botto is the one he really wants. It's why he took you up on your terms so readily. He doesn't truly care if Brie returns to Revival, my father just wanted my brother there."

"Why the desire to spill now?" Kenoa wanted to know.

Valid question, I thought.

Delancey shrugged. "Because it doesn't really matter. If the priestess can get Granite to exchange Brie's caster for Botto, my father will just attack to get the royal back at some other point." She looked to Julia. "And if you don't give the caster king up then, Granite will threaten Fae Canyon. You know that."

"I do." Julia nodded. "I will worry about that when the time comes."

Kenoa cleared his throat. "There is another option." He and Julia exchanged glances, which was super weird. "He is very accurate. I've only ever seen one other dimensional fae with so much control of his magic. We could be in and out with Kai and Sarah in a matter of minutes."

I frowned. Sarah wasn't high on my list of concerns in that moment, but I supposed I didn't want her imprisoned either. Even if the reverse wasn't true. Then, something else occurred to me.

"What are talking about? What dimensional fae?"

There were more shared looks between Julia and Kenoa, the two people in the room who knew each other the least.

"How do you think I got here?" Kenoa asked me.

"I don't know, magic? How does anyone do anything?" I shot back, exasperated.

"Illion opened a passage," Kenoa said slowly. "He's the dimensional fae."

Looking back on the conversation, this should have

been obvious.

"Your father has been working with him ever since it became clear Illion possessed dimensional magic," Julia explained. "It was always our intention to send people for you, we just didn't know where you were until recently. Had you never traveled to Los Angeles for the championship, he would have made the trip to save you from Hawaii very soon." She turned to Delancey and Botto. "You two will, of course, remain my guests until we have the caster king in residence."

Botto smiled. "I'm here as long as you'll have me."

Great. He likes living in a vampire hive. Figures.

"Yeah, I don't really care," Delancey added. "A few nights down on Blood Alley are fine with me."

I neither knew nor cared what Blood Alley was.

Julia's gaze returned to me. "First, you need to get better. No arguments. It will take a little time to coordinate everything." She reached for me, placing her hands on my shoulders. This time, I didn't pull away. "We will get to him before he's turned. I promise you that, my child."

Her words didn't soothe me. Though I believed she meant them. I also knew she had no way of keeping that promise. Granite Dresden wanted Hawaii as a base, and he wasn't a stupid man. There was a very real chance he would order Kai and Sarah's executions immediately without the choice to take part in his stupid citizenship trials. I suspected this was why Delancey gave up her father's plans so readily. Like she said, it didn't matter. All the casters monarchs would fall, one way or another.

"We can't wait until I recover from the curse. It took me days to be strong enough to travel," I said with forced calm. "We go as soon as soon as you can get Illion here or whoever we're sending to him." Julia started to interrupt, and I held up my hand to silence her. "No arguments. And yes, I am going. I'm strong enough for now. If we go soon, I will remain strong enough as long as I don't use my magic."

"You don't need to come, Brie," Kenoa spoke up.

"I do. And I will. You said it yourself, we can be in and out in minutes. I know the prison better than you do. I spent time there, you haven't."

"I've been there plenty," Kenoa replied gruffly. "I have been Kai's bodyguard for years."

"Yeah, and I spent some time there, too," Botto added. "I'll go with Kenoa."

I took a deep breath and played my last card. "Do you want Sarah out of there, too? If so, you need me. They won't be together. You need fighters. I don't need my fire magic. My combat skills are the best in this room."

That was a slight exaggeration; Kenoa was probably the best physical fighter in the room. But I had to be a close second, even above Botto. Both men were legendary fighters. I was, too, and I was betting that Kenoa would relent if I brought Sarah into the argument. He loved Kai like a brother and would do anything to help him. But Sarah was young and naïve, and Kenoa had a fierce need to protect her.

"Fine. But as soon as we're back—" Kenoa's terms and conditions were cut short by the barrage of arguments against my participation from both Julia and Botto. Even Sienna seemed too concerned about my health to think this was a good idea. In the end, we reached an agreement everyone in the room could live with. We were all going, except for Delancey. She would remain at the hive under the watchful eye of Julia's people.

Then came the weird part. Well, it was weird to watch. Julia needed to get word to my father to send Illion, which she did via a conversation held entirely in her head. I could only assume there was a lot of argument on Dad's end, since involving my little brother in this meant he would have to learn that our mother was a vampire. I didn't give a lot of thought to my brother's reaction to the news—that was a problem for later. I did spend the time wondering what our reconciliation would be like.

Would Illion look more like a man than a child? Would he be mad at me for disappearing, even if it hadn't been my choice? Did he hate me for falling in love with a caster?

I didn't have to wait long to find out. No sooner did Julia come out of the trance-like state then a portal appeared in the center of the drawing room. I'd seen Tanner open passageways enough times to recognize it for what it was. Moments later, my dad and brother stepped out.

Dad's eyes filled with tears as he looked me up and down, as though unable to believe he was seeing me in the flesh. That made two of us. It had only been five years, but he looked so much older than I remembered. Once the strongest man I knew, Dad looked almost frail.

"Maybrie," he breathed my name and held his arms open.

I ran to him, throwing my arms around his neck. He

stroked my hair and whispered my name over and over again. "My beautiful girl," he said when we pulled apart. "I have missed you so much."

"I've missed you, too," I sobbed, and then turned to Illion. "And you. I…I don't even know what to say."

"Glad you're okay, sis," Illion replied with a smile that didn't quite reach his eyes.

"Thank you for doing this, for helping Kai," I told him.

Illion shrugged. "He's pretty cool. For a caster."

The fact they'd met was more than I could process at the moment. I looked around the room. "We're all here. Let's go."

Unfortunately, it wasn't quite that easy—logistical talk followed. Everyone wanted to make sure we were on the same page, which was fine and all, but I was itching to *do* something. Dad didn't bring up the fact that I'd been poisoned. I wasn't even sure he knew. Either way, at least I didn't have to rehash my arguments for going with the retrieval team. Julia recruited several of her own people, not all vampires, to assist us. I was torn between "the more the merrier" and wondering if fewer people might attract less attention. Ultimately, I decided I didn't care as long as we left sooner rather than later. With every passing moment, Kai's survival was less certain.

Finally, it was time. Our rescue party consisted of ten people. My dad was not one of them. He elected to stay behind, and no one protested. The walk down the passageway Illion created took forever. Julia attempted conversation with my brother, who was having no part in it. I didn't blame him. When I tried to engage him, Illion wasn't much more receptive. I didn't know if I blamed him for that, either.

My brother did, however, buddy up to Kenoa. It seemed the two had developed a fast friendship. Illion even talked to Botto. Apparently, my brother was a big fan of my trainer as well.

"Give him time, Maybrie," Julia said softly when she caught me looking at Illion with my friends. "The past few years have been hard on him, too."

We reached the other end of the passage, which opened directly in the center of the palace dungeons. Unsurprisingly, there were guards there to greet us. Only a few, though, and none were any match for our rescue party. For a second, I let myself believe luck was on our side, that we'd arrived in time. But when I looked up and down the row of cells, Kai was nowhere in sight. I did see a pale blonde curtain of hair in the shadows, though.

"Sarah!" I cried, yanking on the bars as though that alone would force them open.

Kenoa appeared beside me with keys as the princess turned to look at me with a tear-stained face. Her eyes were unfocused, and she looked crazed.

"They took him. Brie, they took him," she sobbed.

My blood ran cold. "Took him where, Sarah?"

She didn't answer.

Kenoa unlocked the door and I ran inside the cell, shaking the princess' shoulders so she would look at me. "Where is he?" I repeated.

She hiccupped. "It's too late. It's too late. He's gone. They took him. And he's gone."

"Sarah! Focus! Where did they take him?" Panic made

my voice crack.

"Easy, Brie." Kenoa placed a warning hand on my shoulder. "She's fragile right now."

"I don't care," I said through gritted teeth, shaking the princess more vigorously.

"Brie!" Kenoa snapped, but I barely heard him.

"Tell me where he went. I know you saw something. Tell me!" I did something I wasn't proud of; I slapped a teenager across the face. Yeah, I'm that asshole.

Kenoa yanked me back, pushing me as far from Sarah as he could manage. "What's wrong with you? Can't you see she's upset?"

"So am I," I shouted back. "She's also hysterical, we need her to snap out of it!"

"Green door," Sarah blurted.

I rounded on her. "What?"

"Green door," the princess repeated. My hand had left a red mark on her pale cheek, but her blue eyes held more life than before my slap. "There's a room with a green door. I heard the guards talking. I think that's where they took Kai."

I barely heard her last words, because I was already out the cell door.

"It's too late, Brie! He's...it's too late," Sarah cried.

Others yelled for me to wait, to think about what I was doing. I ignored them all. Sarah hadn't seen Kai die. She couldn't know for certain he was dead. Or so I kept telling myself.

You would know if he's dead.

I was certain of it. I was certain that if Kai's life was over, a piece of me would've already died along with him.

That was the thought that kept me going as I tore through the dungeons in search of the green door. I had tunnel vision, tunnel hearing. Nothing mattered but finding Kai. Not even my health. The first unfriendly face I saw, I blasted with a stream of fire that I would later pay for dearly. When I encountered locked doors, I blasted them open with waves of magic that I didn't have to spare. By the time I located the green door, I was running on pure adrenaline and willpower. It wasn't an optimal condition for battling the two vampires standing guard outside.

"Who're you?" one asked, more surprised than nervous.

"Move," I growled. Answering him instead of incinerating the guy cost me. It was all his partner needed to attack. Before I could summon a fireball, the vampire's fangs were on my throat.

They never got the chance to pierce the skin. Julia appeared in a blur of motion, snapping the other vampire's neck with zero hesitation. It was enough to save me from the bite, but the sucker would recover. Well, she would've, if I hadn't lit her up like a bonfire. Then, I turned my magic on the one who'd spoken to me.

The sight of Julia was enough to send him running in the opposite direction. Clearly, her reputation proceeded her. She chased the guy down and dispatched of him in quite possibly the bloodiest way I could imagine, literally tearing him limb from limb. Even in my bloodlust, I was shocked at the spectacle.

Not the time to dwell, I told myself, facing off with the last obstacle that stood between me and Kai. I reached for the door handle, suddenly nervous about what I might find on the other side. *You would know if he's dead.*

I turned the handle, only to find it locked. The incantation was on the tip of my tongue, but once again, Julia was faster. She sent a wave of power into the old stone walls that knocked the door right off its hinges.

My heart leapt to my throat. He was there. Kai was on the cold, hard ground. He wasn't moving. My steps faltered. He was so still.

Gaia, please....

"Maybrie, wait!" Julia screamed behind me.

I fell to my knees beside Kai's limp form and rolled him over so I could see his beautiful face.

"Maybrie, get back!" Julia cried.

I went flying backward through the air on a gust of powerful magic. The priestess was between Kai and me in the blink of an eye. Jumping to my feet, I tried to get past her. She was stronger and faster.

"Let me see him," I sobbed, not realizing I was crying until that moment. "You have to let me see him."

"You need to get out of here. Now, Maybrie," Julia snapped, shaking me as I'd done to Sarah.

"I won't leave him. We need to take him with us!"

"We will." She met and held my gaze. "I will get him. But first, I need you to leave. Right now, *go.*"

I shook my head like a child throwing a tantrum. "Not without him. I won't leave"

Julia's eyes held pity I didn't fully understand. "He's dangerous right now, Maybrie."

Dangerous? He's dead! I wanted to shout. My lips refused to form the words.

"Look at his face, Maybrie." Julia moved aside but

kept a firm grip on my arm.

That was when my heart truly broke. Kai's gorgeous face was ashen, his chest still. Then his long lashes twitched over the skin beneath his eyes. My heart leapt, then crashed into the depths of hell. He wasn't dead.

"Brie?' his voice was barely audible. Red irises were visible as his eyes flicked open and closed. When they finally stayed open and looked at me like he couldn't believe I was really there, fangs marred the smile I'd loved with all of my being.

Kai was Eternal.

Throne of blood

DEAR READER,

Thank you for taking the time to read Throne of Blood. Reviews are the lifeblood of all authors. Good, bad, or otherwise, if you could take a minute to review Throne of Blood, we would truly appreciate..

ACKNOWLEDGMENTS

THANK YOU TO everyone at all the local establishments. Without your encouragement and assistance, we'd never make these books happen!

Sophie Davis

For more information on Sophie Davis, visit Sophie's
website, www.sophiedavisbooks.com
To contact Sophie directly, email her at
sophie@sophiedavisbooks.com.
You can also follow Sophie on:
Facebook: @SeeSophieWrite
Twitter: @SeeSophiesWrite
Instagram: @SeeSophieWrite
Tumblr: officialsophiedavis
Pinterest https://www.pinterest.com/sophiedavisbook/

SOPHIE DAVIS

MORE BOOKS FROM THIS AUTHOR

The Fire Fae Series
Throne of Winter
Throne of Fire
Throne of Blood
Throne of Ashes

Eve of Eternals Series
Wolf Rising
Fae Rising

The Talented Saga:
Talented
Caged
Hunted
Created
Exiled

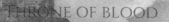
THRONE OF BLOOD

Marked
Privileged
Fated
Delta

Timewaves Series
The Syndicate
Atlic
Legends Untold
Dust Into Gold
Remember Me

Blind Barriers Trilogy
Fragile Façade
Platinum Prey
Vacant Voices

Shadow Fate Series
Pawn
Sacrifice
Checkmate

THRONE OF BLOOD

Made in the USA
Las Vegas, NV
08 November 2023